CW01214258

GOA TRAFFIC

Marissa de Luna

authorHOUSE

AuthorHouse™ UK Ltd.
500 Avebury Boulevard
Central Milton Keynes, MK9 2BE
www.authorhouse.co.uk
Phone: 08001974150

This book is a work of fiction. People, places, events, and situations are the product of the author's imagination. Any resemblance to actual persons, living or dead, or historical events, is purely coincidental.

© 2011. Marissa de Luna. All rights reserved

No part of this book may be reproduced, stored in a retrieval system, or transmitted by any means without the written permission of the author.

First published by AuthorHouse   02/25/2011

ISBN: 978-1-4567-7527-8

Any people depicted in stock imagery provided by Thinkstock are models, and such images are being used for illustrative purposes only.
Certain stock imagery © Thinkstock.

This book is printed on acid-free paper.

Because of the dynamic nature of the Internet, any web addresses or links contained in this book may have changed since publication and may no longer be valid. The views expressed in this work are solely those of the author and do not necessarily reflect the views of the publisher, and the publisher hereby disclaims any responsibility for them.

For Audrey, Henry, and Anna

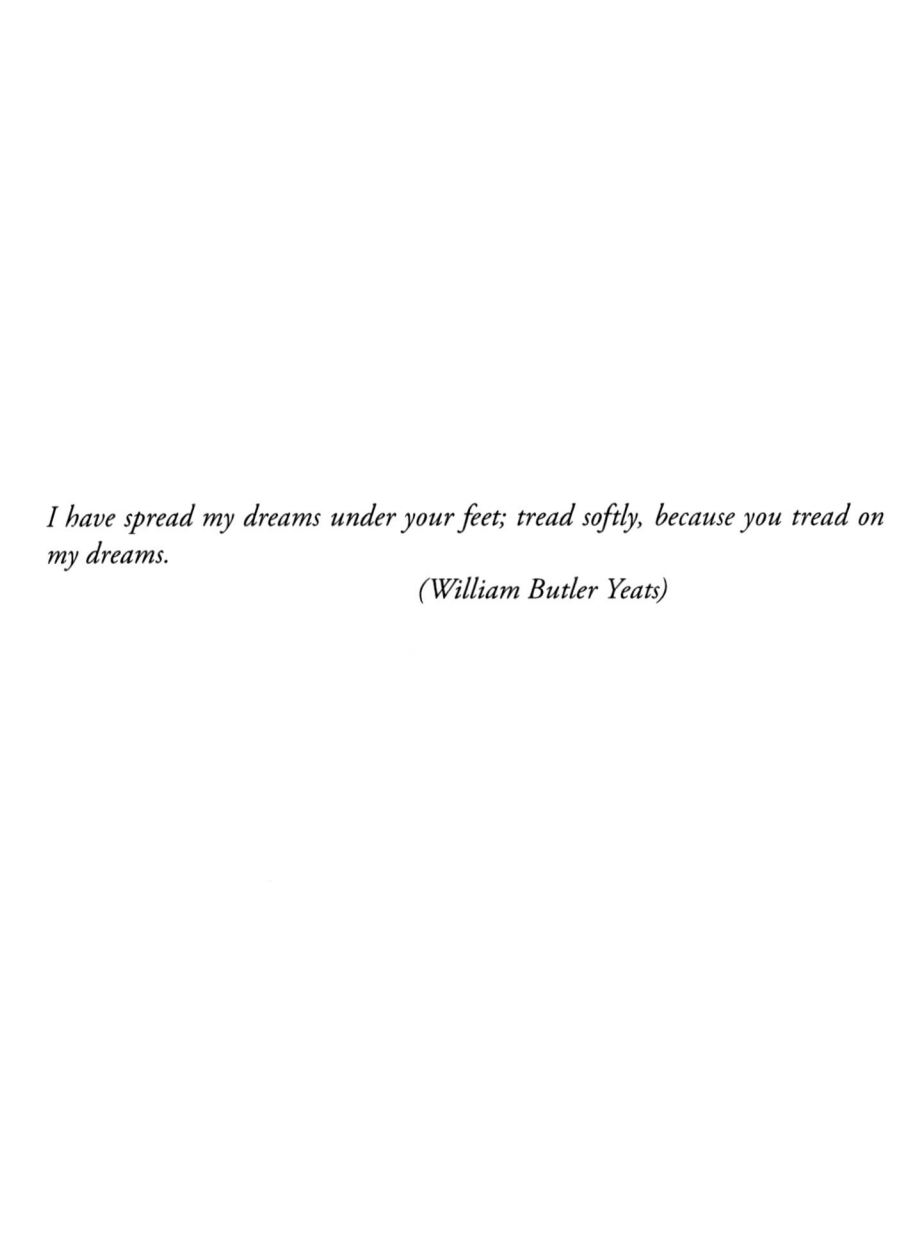

I have spread my dreams under your feet; tread softly, because you tread on my dreams.

(William Butler Yeats)

PART I

*

Lisa felt a hand on her shoulder, bringing her back to reality. She looked up with bleary eyes, somewhat detached. It was as if her soul had left her body months ago. She was an empty shell.

"The verdict is in. We need to go back in there after lunch, for about two." The voice was gentle, but the words pierced Lisa like shards of glass. She rose to her feet and adjusted her suit. At one time, it had been a struggle to fit into. She had last worn it for an open day at her school, and on the way home she had unbuttoned her skirt so that she could breathe again. Her mother had picked it out of her wardrobe this morning, carefully running the lint roller over the dark cloth to remove the tiny fibres from her white mohair cardigan that hung next to it. Margaret had held the skirt open for her, and she had stepped in, holding on to her mother to steady herself. She felt like a toddler, a small and frightened one. The suit was no longer as snug as it had once been; it hung loosely over her gaunt frame. She couldn't believe just how much her life had changed. Just eighteen months ago, she had been on her way back from the holiday of a lifetime.

*

1

Her stomach lurched as the tyres screeched across the runway and ground to a halt at Chhatrapati Shivaji international terminal at Mumbai. Her mouth was dry, and she gripped the armrests. During the descent, her eyes had been fixed on the slum dwellings that had swallowed up most of the land right up to the airport boundary. The shanty town was creeping into her personal space, and the anxious feeling she had managed to sweep away before boarding had returned, but this time with more conviction. *What am I doing?* she thought. If she could have turned back the hands of time to that fateful moment when she had booked this very flight, she would have. Worse than the fear of what awaited her in Goa was the accompanying knowledge that her friends and family were right. She was incapable of making this trip on her own.

"Is something the matter, miss?" asked the air hostess. She didn't look as if she had spent the last eight hours clearing up and looking after the whims of a hundred-odd passengers. Dazed, Lisa turned towards her, "No" her first spoken word in eight hours. It came out barely audible; she cleared her throat and tried again. "No, I'm fine, thanks." The air hostess looked at her expectantly; it was then that Lisa turned around and noticed that all the other passengers had disembarked.

"Oh, sorry – away with the fairies." She tried to sound nonchalant, not wanting to appear rude by saying exactly what she was thinking: *I've made a terrible mistake! Turn this plane around and head back. I'm not as worldly as I thought I could be. I want to go home!*

This was not the kind of thing air hostesses wanted to hear – the personal traumas of their passengers after they had waited on them hand and foot was the last thing on their minds. The flight attendant straightened her navy suit and adjusted her gold neckerchief as she led Lisa towards the door of the aircraft, the same one she had walked in through only hours ago in London. She gave Lisa a plastic smile while silently cursing her for wasting her time.

As she looked down at her sensible black ballerinas, Lisa berated herself for that moment of spontaneity back in October. *Have I completely lost the plot?* she pondered. *Right about now, I should be picking up the turkey or stuffing it, not halfway around the world.*

She swiftly exited, clutching her duty-free vodka; she would clearly need that later. As she stepped off the plane, a gust of hot air almost choked her and left a lump in her throat, which was still with her as she got onto a courtesy coach to the domestic terminal. She had taken the cheaper option of a scheduled flight, which included a stop in Mumbai, and now she had the added stress of catching another flight within the hour. The air was so full of smoke it was smothering her. She was as anxious as on her first day of primary school, and her eyes grew moist.

"Okay, miss?" a short, stocky, dark man shaking his head from left to right smiled at her, revealing a missing front tooth. He had a heavy Indian accent, and he barely looked at her boarding pass as he tore off the bit he needed.

"Yes, fine, thanks," said Lisa, fighting back the tears, as she boarded a smaller plane to Goa. The flight was barely forty-five minutes, but this second landing was somewhat different to the first. Despite not having had a chance for a drink at Mumbai airport, her nerves had steadied. The landing at Dabolim Airport was smooth, and her twitchy knee, which always shook like crazy when she was nervous, was calm. As they descended, she took in the beaches and lush green paddy fields against the vibrant blue pools of water that dotted the landscape, and this time she was ready for the blast of warm air as she left the aircraft. The air here was breathable, though, and not as suffocating as it had been in Mumbai. The lack of slum dwellings was a welcome relief and the atmosphere much more relaxed. The Goan airport was tiny in comparison to any that she had seen before. It was less intimidating. Its white paint glistened against the deep red soil of India.

Lisa slung her black messenger bag across her body and fended off the overly keen porter. She pulled at her luggage trolley that she was almost certain had come from the Dark Ages. It refused to go in a straight line. It took all her might to steer it the way she wanted as she bustled through the taxi drivers, who were desperately vying for her attention. A few strands of hair had come loose from her ponytail and stuck to her face. She pushed them away and felt just how wet her skin was. It was hot; her hair would begin to frizz. The guidebook didn't specify just how humid it would be, and she was rapidly trying to remember whether she had packed any antiperspirant.

She spotted the tour representative from Premier, who was lazily propping himself up on the railings outside the terminal. The lobster-red face and bright pink arms poking out of his standard-issue checked shirt, along with his bleached blond hair, made him stand out like a sore thumb against the sea of brown faces. Judging by his appearance, he was either hung-over or had a bad case of sunstroke. Lisa hoped it was not the latter, for his own sake. She caught his eye, and Rob did his obligatory "Welcome to Goa" speech, after which he placed a beautifully fragrant white Jasmine garland around her neck.

"It's a beautiful country, this one," he said in a Geordie accent. He marked her name off the list on his clipboard and pointed her in the direction of the bus. "Just one more person, and we are out of here." He sounded more relieved than she was.

Lisa was grateful for the coolness of the coach. The twelve-hour journey had exhausted her, and she craved the brochure picture of a cool shower and an air-conditioned room. As the coach moved and Rob started spouting information about the country, the necessary do's and don'ts, Lisa hoped and prayed that she would not be one of those whining Brits abroad who complained at any and every opportunity and refused to sample the local life in favour of egg and chips. Despite the bumpy roads and her increasing fatigue, she was keen to absorb everything the state had to offer. She took in the concrete single-storey houses with roofs made of a mixture of leaves, tin, and tiles. They were painted in vibrant yellows and greens, some noticeably faded in the hot sun. The shopkeepers stood at low windows displaying cold drinks and jars of biscuits, their houses garishly painted with slogans from multinational companies, telling passers-by to "Enjoy Coca-Cola".

Children in shorts and bare feet chased chickens across their gardens, whilst buffaloes and cows grazed in the fields. Billboards studded the route from the airport to the hotel, advertising casinos, restaurants, and shops. Amidst the coconut trees, men wearing lunghis were wielding pickaxes against the strong red laterite stone, and women wearing saris tucked up to their knees were carrying bricks and mortar in *kylies* balanced precariously on their heads. Lisa took in this strange mix of East and West that somehow seemed to work. She eagerly anticipated what the next two weeks would hold in store for her, but before she knew it, she had closed her eyes. Fatigue took over and she fell fast asleep.

2

The next morning, Lisa awoke to the gentle hum of the air conditioner. The hotel was close to perfection, and for once the brochure pictures and her expectations were a close match to the reality. She was lucky enough to get a room overlooking the cool blue of the Arabian Sea and that soft, golden stretch of sand that she wanted to feel between her toes. The abundant coconut trees and the thatched beach shacks completed the scene. Indian ladies in multicoloured dresses carried bags of fresh sweet limes and guavas, selling them to hungry tourists. Teenagers screamed with delight as they tore up the sea on jet skis and banana boats, and para-gliders hung tentatively in the air, pulled along by shiny white speedboats.

Lisa had attended the rep meeting that morning and had learnt a bit about this tropical state in India. She was staying in Calangute, an area promising an eclectic mix of bars and nightlife, authentic Goan restaurants, and miles and miles of sandy beaches. "An ideal spot to explore the rest of Goa", Rob had said. Tourists had cultivated the area, with convenience stores on every corner selling cornflakes, sliced bread, and mineral water. At least a dozen souvenir shops littered the sidewalks, selling large cowrie shells, in which, if you held them up to your ear, you could hear the sea, as well as silver trinkets, joss sticks, and cloth bags in a rainbow of colours.

Rob had used his selling spiel to entice new tourists to purchase organized excursions around Goa. He had planned trips to the flea market, which cost five hundred rupees, even though he knew a taxi there and back between a couple of people would cost less than half that. It was where the commission was to be made, and he needed the money. He knew exactly which type of tourist to target, and Lisa was exactly what he had in mind: single, slightly apprehensive, and keen. Being Lisa, she immediately signed up for some of these trips. Her friend Archana had encouraged her to go it alone, warning her that the tour reps would charge an arm and a leg just for an air conditioned coach and an English speaking guide, something that was freely available in Goa. She had encouraged her to "get lost" in the place, but her cautious side had gotten the better of her. She justified to herself that it was only her first day, so a few trips wouldn't hurt. After all, she did have two weeks.

Her first trip was to see the churches of Old Goa. This was a must on her to-do list, and she was sure it was the reason that she had booked her flight out here in the first place. She followed this trip with a visit to a spice plantation the next day. The coach did not leave till later that afternoon, and with a rough itinerary booked for the next two days, and the potential to meet some fellow travellers, Lisa could switch off and start enjoying her holiday. She happily headed to the pool to sun herself, secretly hoping to try a new courageous side to her personality and meet new people. She didn't really have that bubbliness that came so easily to so many of her friends; she could never strike up a conversation randomly with anyone, anywhere. She had more British reserve than that, but she was hoping that now, being by herself, she would have no choice but to be more outgoing.

*

Lisa applied SPF 30 to her olive complexion which, compared to the others sitting around the pool, seemed a shocking pasty white. Why hadn't she taken Suzanne's advice and visited a tanning salon before her holiday? Everyone else clearly had! She sipped on some tender coconut water served in its shell. A pink cocktail umbrella confirmed that she was on holiday, and she whiled the morning away on a blue-and-white striped sun lounger padded with a towel bearing the Coconut Grove logo. Her novel was open, but her mind was a world away. Even though it was only her first day, she was glad she hadn't turned around and run home with her tail between her legs from Mumbai Airport. She closed her eyes for a minute and felt the solitude. Although a part of her relished this time alone, it was unusual for her. She was so used to having company around her that, for a moment, the silence made her panic. She glanced around the poolside; only half the sun loungers were taken. The Coconut Grove was a small boutique hotel, with only eighteen rooms, and judging by the average age, she presumed an over fifties tour group had taken most of them.

She spotted a tall blond girl to her left who looked to be roughly in her twenties. She was disgustingly good-looking and had the figure of a supermodel. Lisa glanced at the book the woman was reading and cast her judgement. It was a recent Booker Prize winner, and she had enjoyed it. If she approached her and was stuck for conversation, she could at least ask her about the book. An Indian lady in a pale blue sari walked past the blond girl and winked at her. She responded in a Scandinavian accent, the words of which Lisa couldn't quite hear, but the Indian girl smiled and walked on. Her tone was playful, and Lisa couldn't help thinking that she was intruding on something she shouldn't be witness to. She abruptly looked away as the Indian girl disappeared into the lobby. Rob was now attempting to chat up the stunning blond. Maybe, thought Lisa, she would pluck up the courage to talk to the girl, too; she clearly knew people and might be good company.

She managed to pass the entire morning relaxing by the pool, occasionally slipping into the cool water of the infinity pool to beat the heat of the mid-morning sun. She started relaxing in her own company and felt amazingly at peace for the first time in as long as she could remember. The same feeling she'd had as a child, when they'd gone down to Cornwall for the summer holidays, returned to her – the feeling of being carefree and knowing that she could do whatever she liked. This holiday was even better than that, though; being by herself, she did not have to pander to anyone else's needs, only her own. She glanced at her watch as she noticed couples heading towards the restaurant. The pungent aroma of simmering spices lured her over to the coffee shop that looked out onto the ocean. The restaurant was open, and a sea breeze cooled her down as she chose a seat with a sea view. She glanced at the menu and then her attire; she was wearing just a blue bikini covered by a pink silk sarong. Her feet were bare. This was something she had never thought she would do, holiday or not – sit in a packed restaurant in such skimpy clothing. Looking at the other diners, she noticed that they were all in similar dress. A strange feeling of immense freedom washed over her. The last year had obviously been harder for her than she had thought; she had put such pressure on herself to find Mr Right. She was away from all that now; out here nobody knew her or her insecurities. She could be anyone and do anything she wanted.

Comfortable in this knowledge, she put it aside and turned her thoughts to food. Eager to sample true Goan food, she selected as much as she could from the menu. Fifteen minutes later, a polite young waiter brought over her food on a banana-leaf platter. The smell of it was enough to make her mouth water.

Slices of kingfish had been dipped in a rich, spicy red masala and fried in *rawa*, king prawns the size of her fist were served plain with just a drizzle of garlic butter, and thick slices of breadfruit tantalized her taste buds. She started on her main dishes of *caldene*, a Goan coconut-based curry full of okra and prawns, and a spicy *ambotik* of baby shark that had a taste like nothing she had ever tasted before, the tangy sauce dancing on her tongue. The waiter cleared away her plates when she was done and smiled at her, impressed that she had managed to take the spice of the food – and the quantity.

After her meal she felt like a new person, ready to explore everything Goa had to offer. Strangely, she felt as if she were in her native country; she felt understood. She was so lost in her thoughts that it was the young waiter who had to remind her that her coach trip to Old Goa would be departing in ten minutes. Lisa just had time to give him a small tip before slipping on some linen trousers and a kaftan that Suzanne had brought her from Chiang Mai. Then she stepped onto the air-conditioned coach, which bore the name Maganlal Tours emblazoned across the side in the colours of the Indian flag: green, white, and saffron.

Lisa found a place towards the middle of the coach, and as the driver carefully manoeuvred the bus between cyclists and stray dogs, she did what most single travellers do: she scoured the seats for people she might talk to. After disregarding the old-age pensioners, she spotted three possibilities. Instantaneously, she dismissed the first candidate – and felt quite bad in doing so. The man in question looked to be in his thirties, but his blue bum bag and socks-and-sandals combination was just a huge no-no and screamed geek even to a non-fashionista like Lisa. She had heard that *geek chic* was in, but she was almost sure it wasn't to this extent. She justified her decision by the fact that he had already latched on to an unsuspecting American couple, and with his guide book open, he was quizzing them on Indian population statistics. Their forlorn expressions told her she would be better on her own.

There was also an Indian girl – maybe a local, as she didn't seem the least bit interested in what the tour guide had to say – and then there was the blond girl from earlier in the day. Lisa could get a better look at her face this time, as her curly, long, blond hair was scraped back into a ponytail, exposing her high cheekbones and blue eyes that came across as slightly vacant. She looked as if she didn't want to be disturbed. The Indian girl, however disinterested she looked, was more approachable, with shoulder-length black hair and almond-shaped eyes. Little gold studs pierced her ears, and a blue-and-silver pearl-shaped tiny bindi marked the centre of her forehead. She was dressed in a sari, and Lisa wondered how anyone could wear something so cumbersome on such a hot day.

3

Sonya pulled her black hair back into a ponytail and took a large swig of her coffee. It was as she liked it, without milk and cold. Through sleepy eyes she applied thick, black kohl to her lids and rummaged in her make-up bag for her gold name badge. Through her bedroom window, she could see her father on the veranda, the railings of which were painted green to blend in with the trees. Her father was in his favourite outfit of faded khaki shorts and white vest stretched over his protruding stomach; his fine, gold necklace, with a picture of Jesus embossed onto a medallion as small as a thumbnail, was hanging around his neck. He had finished watering the plants and was starting on his breakfast of tea and chapattis. Sonya fastened her gold name badge to her uniform sari, grabbed her new tan purse and car keys, and headed for the door, avoiding her father. She was in no mood for small talk or, worse still, talk of how all her friends were settling down and getting married. Today, Sonya could not cope with that. It seemed hotter than usual, especially for December, but this could be partly attributed to her hangover. This job was seriously starting to impinge on her social life.

She had got back from the club at five this morning and after only an hour's sleep, which had done more harm than good, her alarm had gone off. It was the third part time temp job in the last year and she needed to keep this one. At least it would be an easy day.

As she pulled into the parking lot at the Coconut Grove, she rested her head on the steering wheel. She looked through the window at the hotel reception area, visible between the two palm trees in the driveway. She could see the throngs of faces and hideously garish shorts. It was the busiest time of the year, and she debated whether it was too late to call in sick. It was. Carl was grinning at her from the lobby, whilst he checked in tourists clutching their passports and their Samsonite cases as they patiently waited in line. The Christmas rush was always at the worst time possible for her – the party season had just kicked off. Charter flights were coming into Dabolim Airport thick and fast, and tickets for shows and trips for guests were getting harder to book. Maybe, she thought, if things worked out with Terrance, life wouldn't be so tough. Sonya had never been a fan of equality and women's rights, mainly due to laziness, rather than anything else, but the way Goa was headed at the moment, she felt that she might never be able to realize her dream of being a housewife. Kids were moving out of home, renting their own apartments, getting jobs that didn't involve employment by another family member, and most recently, young couples – heterosexual or not – were living together without the sanction of marriage. Sonya didn't mind this; it was just that with few career prospects and no serious boyfriend, it made her feel as if her life was rapidly veering away from what she had planned. In her mother's words: "This kind of behaviour is fine for other people" – but they wanted a suitable partner for their daughter. Goa was moving on, with or without her.

In the hotel lobby, Sonya gazed at the white marble flecked with specks of pistachio green. She thought about her job and decided there and then that she both loved and loathed tourists. It was true that the tourists had put Goa on the map. They had started this party state. As the last of the monsoons had passed, the charter flights had started, and clubs had opened, drawing in crowds from all over the world. Locals like herself were revelling in it. They were proud to be living in the most modern Indian state, where drinking was a local pastime, and parents didn't impose strict curfews as they did in the rest of India. Sonya herself had befriended tourists and showed them around Goa, glad of new people infiltrating their small group for a week or two.

The hippies had started it all. They had been on the beaches of Goa for as long as she could remember, selling jewellery and tie-dye sarongs at Anjuna flea market, dropping acid, and tripping to Goa Gil for days on end at the infamous Hill Top Rave parties. That was what Goa had been known for back in the day. Now though, there was an influx of non-hippies, a new wave of tourism from Europe that had inflated the value of property so the price of land was comparable to that of some parts of England. The locals were being pushed out. Worse still, the landscape where Sonya lived was truly ruined. Where in the early nineties she had played near a handful of large houses, with the Arabian Sea in full view, now she could no longer even see the sea from the seven-storey high-rises whose permission had been granted with a handful of baksheesh. Yes, it was true: Tourists had created Goa, and now they were slowly destroying it. Either way, there was no question about it: Wherever the white man went, there was money to be made, and Sonya reminded herself of this as she slammed the door of her milky-blue Maruti Suzuki 800 behind her.

"Good morning, Miss De Souza. You are looking bright-eyed and bushy-tailed this morning," Carl said with a knowing smile.

"Ditcher," Sonya quipped back.

"Okay, chill! I'm only teasing, yaar. My mom was not well, but she is okay now. I think it was an illness of convenience." Sonya's face softened. He had never been out with her group in the evenings, but it wasn't his fault. She liked Carl; they made a good team at Coconut Grove. He was only young, and his mother, Priya, was ferociously protective. His father had run off with his secretary two years ago, and now Carl was the only man in the house, so his mother didn't want him to be out till all hours of the morning. This was especially so as the neighbours still hadn't stopped making eyes at her about what had happened with her husband. In their eyes, she was obviously not fit to be a wife, let alone a mother. To top it all off, what Carl's mother was most scared of was his sexual preferences. She knew deep down about her son's homosexuality; she couldn't really ignore Carl and his camp demeanour. To be honest, Priya didn't really mind; she just didn't want it to be said out loud. She felt that the gossip might just kill her, if her son was seen holding hands with another boy by their front gates, and so she tried to stop him going out as much as possible, hoping secretly that he might change his mind.

Carl was good-humoured, and the guests loved him. He was tall, with a slim build, and if Sonya hadn't known he didn't really care for girls, she might have tried her luck with him. He was good-looking, and most of the young female guests at the hotel would flirt with him. Carl, being the guy that he was, would flirt back, while always trying to make his voice slightly more masculine. He loved the attention and hated to let people down. That's what Sonya really admired about Carl: No matter what he had been through with his family and their scandal, he always looked on the brighter side of life, and he always made an effort with people.

He said that good service was one of the reasons that everybody liked India, and the reason why service was so good in India – well, it was that everyone just did their jobs without trying to prove that they were better than the customers themselves. It was this alone that had convinced Carl that service in the West was so shoddy in comparison. He had been to England just once in his life, and he said he would never return. "People just don't have any respect for the customer there. They all think they are better than the person they are serving. What kind of behaviour is that?" he had asked Sonya very innocently one day.

Despite his open views, in some respects he was a typical Goan who would ensure that the *crab effect* remained the status quo. God forbid that people should try to better themselves and crawl above their positions in society. Purveyors of the "crab effect" would do most things in their power to claw these people down and make sure they knew their place. It was a society that ensured everyone was on an even keel in order to avoid bouts of envy and jealousy. The funny thing was that these two traits were common amongst their circle of friends. Considering Goa was so small and designer material objects were so hard to come by, it was surprising that named watches and handbags were the order of the day, and everyone wanted to outdo each other.

"Here, Sonya – this will make you feel better." Carl handed her a green tablet and a mug of steaming coffee.

"What's this?" Sonya turned her nose up at his offering.

"It's spirulina, dar-ling, all natural. You'll feel so much better, yaar – just take it."

"Thanks, but no thanks. Just give me the coffee."

Carl pocketed the spirulina and handed Sonya the mug of coffee, "Was the whole gang there last night?" Carl was propped against the reception desk, his arms crossed. He was leaning to one side and looking towards Sonya, who had now seated herself in the back room. Carl accentuated his effeminate accent, believing it made him appear more naive than he was. He liked that – it always got Sonya's attention.

"Mmm, let's see: Terrance, Ayesha, Teresa, and Sanjay, yaar – they were all there. So boring! It's always the same, just the five of us. Where *are* all the people in Goa?" This was a rhetorical question, which Carl didn't pick up on, and being hungry for conversation, he was keen to answer.

"They are moving away for studies, and then they stay away. Why come back to Goa? For these big shots there is no opportunity here! We are small people, Sonya; we will stay here for the rest of our lives." Carl hesitated. He knew Sonya would pick up on this comment and start her "inferiority complex" lecture. He decided to change the topic quickly to avoid this "So, are you and Terrance an item now? Going steady?"

"Yes. No. I don't know." Sonya looked as if her hangover was getting worse.

"You two, you are the same. You need to make up your minds, and fast. You are not so young any more. A nice Goan Catholic girl like you should be married, no?" Carl mimicked her father.

"Thank you so much for reminding me – like I had forgotten! My mother reminds me every day," she said, half-smiling at Carl. He always knew how to make her laugh. "Anyway, enough of Terrance. Don't eat my brains so early in the morning. The problem is his; he needs to grow up."

Carl changed the subject. "Looking forward to the trip?" he enquired. Although one of his favourite pastimes was a good gossip, Sonya didn't seem to want to dissect the inadequacies of Terrance today. She was being very short, and he didn't want to upset her further as she seemed so troubled lately.

"To Old Goa?"

"Yaar, men, where else?"

"I guess. What choice do I have?"

Carl chuckled. He had offered to go in her place, but the manager had wanted Sonya to go. It was a tourist trip to see the churches of Old Goa to assess the quality of packages they offered at the hotel. It would be a boring and slow afternoon, but nevertheless, it would not require much brain power; it would be a tick-box exercise.

It was after breakfast, when the tour reps had booked up the Old Goa trip, that Sonya realized how busy the trip was going to be. She wouldn't be able to have an afternoon siesta on the coach, in case someone recognized her from the hotel and reported her. It had happened once before and had landed her in a week's worth of filing. The day was growing hotter by the minute, and there were no signs that her hangover was getting better, despite the copious amounts of coffee and water she had swallowed. Carl had picked up a *masala dosa* for her at a local restaurant and nibbling at that had made her feel only slightly better. A hot curry would have been better; it was usually the best way to dissipate a hangover. She popped some mints into her mouth; she had had a spicy lunch, and she still had guests to greet. She lifted up her sari and boarded the coach

*

Sonya was the last to get off the coach at the Basilica of Bom Jesus. She had been busy thinking of last night's events during the coach trip. As her hangover waned, bits of last night were coming back to her slowly and in flashbacks. As usual, she had gotten into an argument with Terrance. He and Sonya had been dating intermittently since they were sixteen, but they were closer now than ever, since this big-shot Mumbai guy had approached them in Joel's and made them a lucrative offer. The deal had made them a lot of money. Sonya still had to work, but with a few more deals she would be able to take some time off. She would be free to do as she pleased. This last project was drawing out a bit, though, and Sonya felt she would have to move things along if she wanted Terrance to oblige and to marry her during the next year, before she turned thirty. Sanjay had warned her that Terrance wanted to have his fun and wasn't really ready to settle down, but Sonya knew him better. Since working together, they had become even closer, despite a few indiscretions that Sonya was willing to turn a blind eye to. All men, in her opinion, had a few indiscretions before they settled down. She herself had had a few one-night stands with hotel guests, which she would never care to admit to within her close circle of friends. Sonya knew in her heart of hearts that it wouldn't be long before Terrance gave in to her.

Sonya's mother was beginning to pressure her, too, and was making her life difficult. She knew that Sonya and Terrance were dating on and off, and she had warned her daughter that she must either get Terrance to commit to her or find someone else. Sonya didn't know what her mother was talking about. Goa was a small place – it wasn't as if she had a choice! Terrance was about the only decent bachelor left. Goa had slim pickings, unless she wanted to marry a foreigner. She had had flings with some tourists who were over for a short space of time, and only with ones she was certain she would not bump into again, but most of them were worlds apart from her. They couldn't provide her with the lifestyle she wanted, and so she was stuck with waiting for Terrance.

"Mamme, please, come this way." A heavy southern Indian accent guided her towards the party, where the other members of the group were making their way into the church. Sonya swatted away the hawker outside selling candles at extortionist tourist prices, and the seller moved on to another in the group.

"*Phipty* rupees, one, sir. This is good price." A young lady hawker in a blue-and-green sari, her hair knotted in a bun, held up a single white candle. It was long and thin and tapered towards the top, where the wick revealed itself. The heels of her feet were cracked, exposing a lifetime of walking barefoot on the red soil.

"But man over there offered me two for fifty," said an elderly English man with a Panama hat and a walking stick. He clearly knew how this game was played. He tried broken English, but his English accent was fierce.

"No sir. His bad, bad quality. They no light when you go inside."

The Englishman smiled at her skill for selling. "They look the same to me," he said, determined not to be swindled out of his rupee.

"Same same, but different." The hawker gave an irresistible smile, exposing her paan-stained teeth. She pulled at her sari and covered her rounded belly with her dupatta, which was stained with oil and wax. The Englishman started to move away. Rickshaws carrying tourists bustled past them, creating clouds of red dust that would cling to their clothes and never come out, no matter how much the *dhobi wallah* pounded them.

"Okay, okay – how much you want?" The seller was beginning to cave in. It was hot, and she wanted to buy a drink from the nearby stand; she could see a tourist receiving a cold bottle of Limca, and it made her mouth feel even more parched. She licked her lips.

The Englishman counted how many prayers he needed to say that morning. "Three for forty rupees."

"Can't do, can't do. I giving you best price," the hawker was determined to get as much from him as possible, but despite his frail white skin, he probably knew India better than most. He started to walk away.

"Okay, okay, sir, three for forty," the hawker said, still eyeing the tourist with the Limca in the distance. The hagglers were both happy. Sonya smiled at them as she walked past. They had made the exchange, and the English gentleman, with his walking stick and Panama hat, no matter how hard he had haggled, had been ripped off.

"So, here we are, the "Rome of the East". This is the Basilica of Bom Jesus, built in 1605, and housing the preserved body of St Francis Xavier, Apostle of India …" Sonya blocked out the thick accented voice of the tour rep. It was information she had heard a thousand times before.

"Hey, excuse me." Along with a woman's voice came a tap on Sonya's shoulder. Half of her didn't want to turn around. Sonya could hear a keenness in the voice. That was never a good sign. *She might want to talk at length*, thought Sonya, *asking me where I live, how to see the real Goa, what foods to try.* Although she was a hospitality officer at the Coconut Grove Hotel, she was not really at her desk right now, and she didn't feel in a very helpful mood today, either. Could this girl not see that she was just observing? There was a perfectly capable tour guide she could address any questions to. But a small part of her knew what it was like to be lonely in a foreign country. She had gone to Bangkok earlier in the year and been grateful to the friendly English-speaking Thai who had pointed her in the right direction. *Well, what goes around comes around*, Sonya thought and turned to face Lisa.

"Hi, how can I help you, madam?" Sonya squinted into the sun; she had forgotten her sunglasses, never good for a hangover. She plastered a fake smile across her face.

"Oh, sorry! I didn't realize you were working." Lisa noticed Sonya's name badge and felt rather foolish. *I knew I would get this wrong the first time I tried.* Sonya was looking at her expectantly.

"Oh, I just thought maybe you were on holiday as well. You see, I'm travelling by myself and just thought …" The blond girl walked past them and shot them a curious look. *This is not going very well. I should have picked her*, thought Lisa.

"That's okay." Sonya was somewhat frustrated by this babbling idiot in front of her, yet there was something endearing in her look. As Lisa said something that Sonya was not quite listening to, she observed her carefully. She had an innocent naivety. She liked her. There was something genuine in her voice, and she carried a little-girl-lost expression. She seemed older, but then Sonya knew she was lucky; brown skin always camouflaged age.

"I'm Sonya. I'm just here assessing the tour for our hotel."

"I'm Lisa, on holiday for a couple of weeks," Lisa stuck her hand out at Sonya, who smiled. *How very British*, she thought.

"Wow, these churches are amazing, don't you think?" Lisa continued.

"Yes, they are," Sonya said looking at them with fresh eyes. "They are, aren't they?" she said, taking in the beauty of the Basilica. "I've just seen them so many times, I fail to look up at them any more. They are just part of the landscape to me."

"You can kind of grow immune to beauty if you look at it long enough. You stop appreciating it," Lisa said, glad to have someone to talk to.

"Yes, I guess you do." Sonya looked back up at the Basilica. It was beautiful, and she was warming towards Lisa. Maybe she would make a friend of her. She had been growing tired of Ayesha and Teresa lately, and they needed some new life in the group. The girl seemed simple enough not to cause a stir amongst their existing friendships. Sonya had noticed her choice of dress for the occasion and labelled her as sensible, not one of these tarty types you saw hanging out in Baga beach wanting something for nothing. Besides, she would only be around for a few weeks. She might be just the thing.

4

Lisa checked her watch again. She was sitting anxiously in the spacious lobby, her large brown eyes examining the green-and-white marble floors and the huge pillars that framed the entrance. Guests bustled in and out, some stopping in the coffee shop for a bite to eat, others lingering around the Christmas tree. She was nervous; if her mother had known what she was doing, she would have given her a talking-to. She could almost hear her.

Lisa Claire Higgins, has the sun gone to your head? You know what they say about mad dogs and Englishmen? Well, this is a silly idea. Going out with complete strangers – to where? A nightclub in the sky? Well, don't come running to us if you get raped and murdered in one ignorant act of yours. Do you know how many people are abducted when doing stupid things abroad? You are too old to be going through adolescence now!

Yep, thought Lisa, *that's what "the Beast" would say.* Lisa herself was beginning to have doubts. She played with the flyer for the nightclub in the sky. The picture of a vixen vampire suspended in a cloud of darkness looked out at her. Maybe this wasn't such a good idea after all, going to a club with people she hardly knew. She had only met Sonya yesterday and had spent time with her at the spice plantation today. Yet they had seemed to hit it off, and when she had invited her out that evening, without thinking, Lisa had accepted. Lisa was growing tired of her own company, and last night she had been persuaded to play cards with a couple old enough to be her grandparents. This wasn't the kind of "getting to know you" holiday she had in mind. An evening out with a few people of her age – how bad could it be?

Lisa scolded herself for being such a worrier. She had seen Sonya at the hospitality desk with the staff uniform on, and from what Lisa could see, she seemed to have a good rapport with the other members of staff. If she didn't like the group Sonya was with, she could always leave after the meal. She knew that the restaurant was local, so she could get a cab back. Lisa quickly checked that she had her mobile phone with her, pressing the menu button. The green glow of the display told her it was alive. She was moving out of her comfort zone – maybe now she would start realizing what she wanted from life; maybe, as Suzanne would put it, she would "find herself". Nothing bad would happen – that was, if Sonya showed up. She was already half an hour late, and it was pushing nine o'clock. Lisa considered going back to her room and admitting that the first friend she had made had stood her up.

"You must be Lisa, right?" A tall man with dark skin approached her; he had a friendly face.

"Yes, I am," she said, wondering just how he knew her name. She then noticed his T-shirt with the Coconut Grove logo, two silhouettes of palm trees with an orange sun setting behind them, emblazoned on the breast pocket.

"Hi, I'm Carl. I work here too. Sonya told me about you. You are going out with them tonight." He sensed her nervousness. He prided himself on his perception of other people's feelings. He smiled, putting her at ease. He had heard of people disappearing whilst on holiday, but this had never happened in Goa. Things like that didn't happen in this part of the world. If people were going to kidnap tourists, they could have their pick of strays in Anjuna, where most tourists were stoned out of their minds on acid.

"Yes, she was supposed to be here at eight thirty," Lisa spoke, breaking his train of thought.

"Oh, this is Go-a, yaar." Lisa liked the way that he pronounced Goa, stressing on the "a". He pointed out, "Nobody here is ever on time. She will be here – eight thirty normally means around nine thirty–ten; don't worry. Anyway, I just thought I would introduce myself and let you know that people here are never on time; you were looking anxious."

"Thanks for the tip." She was grateful he had taken the time to speak to her and surprised at how friendly everyone was. She was beginning to see why so many Brits moved out here, although she could never imagine doing that herself – a holiday, yes, but not for longer than two weeks. It was rather too quiet for that.

"I'll see you around. Don't look so worried. Sonya will take good care of you." Then, hopping onto a black bike and clutching onto the man in front, he was gone.

She was somewhat embarrassed that her nerves were so obvious. That was the last thing she wanted to show her new friends. Lisa looked towards the back of the lobby and noticed the blond Scandinavian girl again. She was seated in the coffee shop and was dressed in a long black dress that contrasted with her pale skin. A bright fuchsia shawl caressed her shoulders. Lisa wondered if she should go over and talk to her, but maybe the girl had wanted some time alone. Today she didn't look so aloof and distant. She was reading her book, and she looked lonely. Just then, the girl looked up and caught her eye. She gave her a warm smile. Lisa reciprocated and then quickly looked away.

She was about to go over and speak to her when she saw Sonya walking towards her. At first she didn't recognize her; she had gotten used to seeing her in her usual traditional Indian dress, and now she looked so different. She wore faded tight blue jeans and a red camisole with beading on the edges. She'd left her hair down, and the glasses that she'd worn at reception were gone. She was holding what appeared to be a Louis Vuitton bag, and bright red heels that added at least three inches to her height. She looked amazing, and Lisa felt that she should have made a bit more of an effort. She had chosen a purple halter-neck dress and black silk flip-flops, and she now felt a little underdressed. The two of them exchanged hellos.

"Come on Lisa, we'll be late," Sonya said, linking her arm in Lisa's as casually as if they had been friends for years. She smelled of cocoa butter and jasmine.

"Oh, I was just going to ask if I had time to run back and put some shoes on. I had thought you said casual." Sonya's new height and shiny accessories made her feel self-conscious and she started playing with her hair.

"You look fine, Lisa, and I did say casual. Anything goes in Goa; there are no dress codes here. Come on," Sonya reassured her as they walked towards the car waiting at the entrance.

"Jump in," Sonya instructed, opening the back door of the white saloon car. "Ayesha, sit on Sanjay's lap, no? Sorry, Lisa, it is a bit of a squeeze back there." Sonya got into the front and Lisa in the back as a petite girl clambered on top of Sanjay, her long, black hair flying carelessly out of the open window as the car started moving. She was dressed in red and black. Her clothes looked as if they'd been made for her. Sonya made the introductions.

"Lisa, these are my friends I was telling you about. Teresa, Ayesha, and Sanjay – and this is Terrance, in front." Sonya turned towards the back seat and rested her hand lightly on Terrance's shoulder. They all said hello in unison, and Lisa tried hard to remember all their names.

"*Aye-yah,* you are so heavy, yaar," Sanjay said to Ayesha.

"Shut up, man. So mean you are," Ayesha replied, and pushing her long black hair behind her ears, she turned to kiss him lightly on his nose.

"So, your first time to Go-a?" Teresa said with the lilting sing-song Goan accent that Lisa was growing accustomed to. Teresa was petite, a size six at the most, and sitting next to her with her size-twelve frame, Lisa felt cumbersome and bulky. She looked very similar to Ayesha, with her silky, long, black hair. She wore a black choker around her neck, a pair of boyfriend jeans, and a strapless top. A small mole just above her lip differentiated her from Ayesha.

"Yes, I've only been here for three days, and I love it already."

"So, what do you do?" Sanjay asked. He shifted under Ayesha's weight, pulling up the collar of his orange-and-white striped shirt. The air conditioning was not working, and it was stiflingly hot. Beads of sweat were beginning to gather on Sanjay's forehead.

"I'm an English teacher in Oxford, back in England. Here I just lie on a pool lounger and work on my tan!" Lisa said. It had sounded witty in her head before it actually came out.

"Oh, that's nice," Sanjay smiled. He didn't really want to know; he was just being polite. She could tell that he was more interested in Ayesha. There was a long, uncomfortable silence until Sonya broke it.

"So, we are going for a bite to eat on the Strip. There are lots of bars and restaurants there. Chinese or conti?"

"Conti, yaar. I really feel like Chi Chi's Italian place with the chicken pizza and that ham, oohh!" Ayesha was quick to reply. She pronounced pizza phonetically, and Lisa smiled to herself. It was like going out in England, pizza and beer, only it was warmer.

"Yes, Ayesha needs to feed her food baby," Sanjay said, not taking his eyes off Ayesha, while lightly rubbing her belly.

"Shut up; I just feel like pizza," she replied.

They soon arrived at a packed open-air restaurant with fairy lights dotting the shrubs between the wooden tables. The night air was warm and the restaurant was atmospheric. The owner of the restaurant sauntered over to them. Chi Chi looked almost eccentric in a bright blue-and-gold floor-length kaftan that clashed terribly with her vibrant red hair. She was a hippie from the sixties, who had settled in Calangute and believed in free love and ganja but somewhere along the way had found a touch of glamour and a passion for home cooking.

"Darlings, welcome, welcome," she said with a deep Italian accent, kissing Sonya and Terrance on each cheek. It was the traditional way of greeting each other in Goa. "You will try my new pizza, no? The Sofia Lauren. You will love it." She led them to a table and ordered the waiters to find another table to accommodate the group. Within seconds, starters and drinks had arrived, and Chi Chi pulled up a chair next to Sonya. She lit a cigarette and inhaled deeply on it, displaying red nails that were almost the same colour as her hair. She chatted with the group for at least ten minutes, until suddenly she stood up abruptly and said goodbye. She hurried over to the entrance, where a tall, elderly Indian gentleman with a white beard, accompanied by a young mistress, had entered.

Lisa was glad of the cool vodka that loosened her tongue and relaxed her slightly. She was surprised at how large the measure was and made a mental note not to exceed three that evening. The last thing she wanted was to embarrass herself in front of her new acquaintances or be unable to get back to the hotel safely.

The vodka worked its magic and the conversation flowed. She was soon talking to the rest of the group as if they were long-lost friends, glad that they were all so easy to talk to and so accepting. She couldn't imagine this happening back home; making friends there was hard. She noticed that Sonya was different to her usual self and that it was Terrance's presence that seemed to make her tense. She could not work out whether or not they were a couple. Sonya was quite attentive to him, but he did not seem the least bit interested. Instead, he seemed to be giving Lisa a lot of attention and was currently very engrossed in hearing what Oxford was like. Sonya was quick to distract him.

"So, Terrance, what is the plan for New Year's?"

"I don't know, but we will have to leave early this time. I'm not going to be stranded in the car for the countdown, like last year," Sanjay piped in.

"Yaar, not like last year, men. The traffic is getting too much," Teresa added. The conversation turned to Christmas.

"I can't believe that we are missing midnight Mass today, for the first time in so long."

"Soon you will be a Hindu, love; you won't need to go to midnight Mass," Sanjay quipped.

"When we marry, Sanjay, I shall be Catholic *and* Hindu. I am a woman – unlike you, I can multitask."

Sanjay shot Ayesha a knowing grin that Lisa couldn't help but smile at. They were so at ease with different religions in India. She remembered the problems Suzanne had had being accepted into Arjun's family. They were Hindu, and Suzanne, well, she was atheist if anything; her religion changed like the wind, and Lisa could never keep up with her. At first, they had wanted Arjun to marry a girl from the same religion and caste as him. It seemed rather antiquated to Lisa, but she had kept quiet and not said much when Suzanne asked her for her opinion. She was never comfortable giving advice on things she did not really know about, and the only thing she knew about Indian culture was that they did a mean rogan josh at her local balti house. It hardly gave her the necessary voice on the subject.

Arjun's parents had threatened to disinherit him, and his mother had even said that she would die of the shame he would bring on the family if he was to marry this girl – this girl being Suzanne.

Suzanne was devastated. She had finally found a man that she wanted to spend the rest of her life with, and his mother expressly hated her. Arjun had held his ground, though; he had had to put an impending engagement between them on hold. He needed time for his family to adjust and get to know Suzanne, but he needed Suzanne to understand where they were coming from, as well.

"They are so scared of diluting their culture and traditions. Think about it, Suze, from their perspective, for just one minute," he said as he was trying to comfort her. "They are Hindus, right? They have a set of traditions, and if you marry away from those traditions, you and the children that you have are not going to carry them on. If I marry someone who knows nothing about my religion and culture, and does not want to know, there will be no hope for my children. They will grow up not knowing who their gods are. They will marry whomever they choose, and their kids, my grandkids, would not even know that they were Hindu. They would have names like Noah and Rebecca – do you get it?"

She couldn't help but laugh at Arjun's last remark. A part of her did understand where his parents were coming from, but mostly she thought it was wrong. Who were they to tell their children whom they could or could not marry? Was it not hard enough to find someone to fall in love with in the first place? Add the religion and caste requirements, and surely their kids would be single for a long time! Since they were living in England, had it not occurred to them that their child might actually meet someone who was English? It was not sensible in Suzanne's eyes, and it hurt her on a deeper level than she could care to admit.

"You eat beef, and the cow is sacred, and I don't see you wearing a turban. You are a fraud," she threw back at him. "To me it seems you have a very convenient religion, picking and choosing the bits you want to believe in." But her response had somewhat discredited her.

"Exactly *their* point," he said. "Sheikhs wear turbans – not Hindus."

"And beef?" she questioned, determined to expose him and his family as hypocrites.

"Right, you've got me there," he said, holding his hands up, "but my parents don't touch the stuff, and I, well, I love *you*, and I don't believe in the dilution of culture theory. I know that our kids will be brought up knowing about all religions." He kissed her lightly on the forehead. "Look, this is just the way my parents are, but I will speak to them, I promise."

True to his word, he had spoken to them, and they were slowly coming around. It had taken months, but eventually they had accepted it. They were civil with Suzanne, and she, in turn, had really tried with them. She had even dragged Lisa to Melton Road in Leicester to a couple of Indian dress shops, where she had selected two pairs of salwar kameez. They were much more expensive than she could ever have imagined, but their vibrancy appealed to her alternative side.

She had selected a peacock-blue outfit with gold filigree work along the edges, which really looked stunning on her, as well as a more subdued terracotta one. The expense was worth it when she was next invited around to their house and his mother had opened the door with a genuine smile for once. She even showed her how to make chapattis later on in the kitchen, where Arjun's sister-in-law and the mothers had gathered to drink masala tea after dinner.

When Suzanne set her mind on something, she usually accomplished it, and soon, armed with a *Hinduism for Beginners* book, she was learning about Ganesh and Krishna. She wanted to impress and win over his family and one day be able to teach their kids about it, too. Lisa didn't doubt her – she knew that at the end of it Suzanne would know more about the Hindu culture than Arjun's whole family. Yes, there was room in her life to embrace a new culture and pass it on to the next generation.

Lisa had marvelled at Suzanne's acceptance of this new religion and her gung-ho approach. She was winning over his parents day by day, and they would soon accept her despite her atheist background and white skin. But Lisa noticed that they had dug their claws in deeper with Archana. She was now regularly being forced to attend "chai" parties, as she put it. When a prospective husband and his family came to visit, she and her family, in Indian get-up, she would serve the whole family tea. She had met dozens of men this way, all of whom she had rejected or been rejected by. It was a cruel and disheartening process, arranged marriage.

Arjun and Suzanne's relationship had piled on the pressure for Archana. There was not a chance now that her parents would let her marry outside their religion, just in case Suzanne had her own way with their grandchildren. More than that, his parents believed that girls were easily influenced, and that Arjun could sway Suzanne if he chose to. They did not believe for one second that Archana would be able to get her own way in a marriage, but then, they didn't know just how strong-willed their daughter could be.

Archana was used to pleasing her parents, and so, when Arjun had mentioned just how serious he and Suzanne were, she had taken it in her stride and known it would be her duty to carry on serving tea until one day a respectable young Hindu would catch her eye.

"Lisa, are you okay?" Teresa asked. "It is rude, no, talking of religion over dinner? Someone from the UK once told me that. She said that you should never talk about religion, sex, or money at the dinner table, no?"

"Well, I don't know about that," Lisa said, not wanting to seem a prude.

"Well, if you take out those three subjects, we would have nothing much to talk about in Goa," Terrance said.

Lisa decided to change the subject "Wow, it's Christmas Eve today, so it's Christmas day tomorrow," she said. With all the sunshine, she had completely lost track of time – in fact, on one level her mind was convinced it was August. Terrance grinned at her; he found her ignorance very amusing.

"Did you not notice the Christmas Father in the lobby of the hotel?" Sonya asked.

Lisa laughed, recalling the tanned Father Christmas dressed in shorts, clutching a surfboard, and surrounded by balls of cotton wool. It was bizarre but quite appropriate. She missed the Christmas lights in England and the cold evenings made unique by crackling log fires and a hot toddy in a well-used English pub, the smell of Christmas filling the air, freshly cut pines, cloves, and mulled wine. She had taken the festivities in England for granted. There was nowhere she had ever been at this time of year that could be compared to an English Christmas.

"Look at the stars," Terrance said, fixing his gaze to hers. Lisa blushed as she looked up. The night was so clear, and the stars shone brightly. She had never seen so many constellations before – Orion's Belt beaming down at her with such vivid clarity – the light pollution at home had seen to that, but here, despite the cloudless sky, the night air was warm still. "No, not those stars," he said. Lisa shot him a questioning look. "Look – hanging outside all the other restaurants and shops."

She noticed the different-coloured stars with tiny cut-outs that acted as lampshades for the single bulbs hanging outside each premises. It was almost ten o'clock, but the shops remained open. From where she was seated, she could see tourists and locals making last-minute Christmas purchases. In her line of vision was a little pastry shop. It was doing a roaring trade selling *bibincas* and *san rivals*, local favourites for Christmas. The customers spilled out onto the street carrying blue-and-red boxes in white carrier bags. Above the entrance hung a single white star.

"The star is a symbol of hope and happiness," Terrance said. He winked at her, making her blush again; she could feel the heat in her cheeks. "Sorry to break your rule again, but the star of Bethlehem led the three wise men to the birth of Jesus. There is such a strong Catholic tradition here and hardly any friction between the other religions. You see that *pastaleria* you are looking at? It is owned by a Muslim couple, but you see, they still hang up a star."

Lisa smiled. He was proud of his country, and rightly so, where different religions could live side by side. She knew it was rare these days, although she couldn't help but think the star's origins had been diluted in the commercialism of Christmas. Now it was just a decoration to adorn houses and shop fronts. She bit her lip, not wishing to contradict her hospitable company. The stars did look beautiful. She would buy a few to take back; they would make inexpensive, but novel, belated Christmas gifts.

"So, now that you know it is Christmas tomorrow, what will you be doing?" Terrance asked, his eyes fixed on her, much to Sonya's annoyance.

"Well, I guess, I'll do exactly what I did today: laze by the beach and eat seafood until my sides split."

"Oh, Ayesha is on a seafood diet, too." Sanjay added, "Whatever she sees, she eats." He laughed at his own joke, whilst the others ignored him. They were obviously very used to his comments about Ayesha's weight. Ayesha did not bat an eyelid this time, tucking into a slice of pizza. Given that her frame was as small as Teresa's, she seemed comfortable with her figure, but you could tell that she relished the attention Sanjay gave her. The conversation continued.

"And in the evening, you will come out with us. That's settled – you can't spend Christmas day all by yourself," Terrance smiled at her. She noticed his dark eyes and his floppy black hair against his tanned skin. He looked to be in his late twenties. She smiled to herself. He was about five foot nine; he had broad shoulders and looked as if he worked out, and his biceps were snug in the arms of his white T-shirt. He could just wrap her up in his arms. She blushed, catching herself daydreaming about his masculinity. The alcohol must have hit her fast. She was on her second one, but why was she having these thoughts? She had only just met him, and this was very unlike her. She put it down to all the sun and the extremely large vodka.

Back in the white saloon car, they made their way towards the club. They drove along mud roads, passing paddy fields and sleepy villages. Soon the car was making its way through a tree-lined dirt road. The car swerved to avoid a pink-and-black pig that darted across their path. There were no street lights, and if Lisa had not had that second drink, her paranoid side would have been on high alert, but she was calm, her body jostling in the back seat, moving with the rhythm of the car and the music that was playing so loudly she had to struggle to hear what Teresa was saying. "Look, there it is," Teresa said, pointing out a distant light high above them like a star. Lisa strained to see it, leaning over Teresa to get a better look – her British reserve had disappeared. The light was, in fact, in the sky. Teresa continued "It's high up on a hill – good job you wore flats! It is a steep climb to the top from the car park."

As they approached the hill, she could see a large whitewashed building. Bright lights illuminated it, and she could hear the thud of music. There was a faint background noise of laughter and glasses clinking. Several flights of stairs later, they reached the club. The heady mix of incense and the alcohol she had consumed was making her feel light-headed. She held on to Terrance to steady herself. As she held his forearm, she could feel the strength in it. His skin was warm to touch. A bolt of electricity shot through her as he placed his hand on hers, and she could smell the bergamot and olive wood in his aftershave. He smelt masculine, and standing close to him, she could see the contours of his chest under his T-shirt. Her heart skipped a beat.

Sonya, sensing the chemistry between them, immediately grabbed Lisa's hand, leading her towards the entrance of the club.

"Girls are free," she said. "Let the guys queue for their tickets; we'll see them in there." Lisa allowed herself to be led by Sonya, feeling rather guilty that she had developed a crush on the man Sonya so clearly had her sights set on.

Once inside, Lisa was awestruck. It looked like something out of a music video. A large open-plan house on one side and a large pool on the other took up the hilltop. Euphoric House music was playing from the DJ booth in the central core of the house. Girls in bikinis danced in cages around the hot tub, and champagne was flowing freely. Scantily dressed girls lounged by the pool, obviously drunk. A large spa was carved into the edge of the hill, and a slender brunette in a gold bikini danced precariously close to the rim.

It was quite possibly the most glamorous and hedonistic club Lisa had ever been to. Men and women were being massaged by the side of the pool. A chef, standing by a hot tandoor, was putting tiger prawns and chicken onto skewers as long as his arm and then dipping them deep into the traditional oven. Hungry clubbers handed over fifty-rupee notes in exchange for fresh, hot naan breads and spicy meats. The entire club was set amidst trees. It was stunning. Standing close to a flimsy wire rail that circled the hilltop, Lisa could look out over what seemed like the whole of Goa.

They made their way over to one of the club's several bars, where Terrance purchased a round of drinks. They found a large four-poster bed, several of which were propped against the terrace of the house. Clubbers in short skirts and harem pants lounged on them with their brightly coloured cocktails.

Terrance sat close to Lisa, and she could feel the hairs on her arms stand on end as he brushed his arm against her skin. Teresa pulled Ayesha and Sonya towards the dance floor, declaring that it was her favourite track and that she just had to dance. Sanjay was deep in conversation with a tall Indian man dressed entirely in black.

"I have never been to a club like this before; it is so different!" Lisa said, trying to keep her distance from Terrance; she could see Sonya looking at them from the dance floor. She felt like she was a teenager again, unsure of how to behave or what to say.

Terrance ignored her comment. "So, how long are you down for?" he asked.

"Just two weeks" she replied. Terrance slipped his arm around her and pulled her closer. Lisa felt her stomach flutter. She looked towards the dance floor for Sonya, who was busy now, her gaze averted elsewhere. Ayesha and Sanjay had disappeared. Lisa didn't want to tread on any toes, especially after how welcoming Sonya had been.

"So, what do you do?" she asked. Her head was fuzzy; the measure at the club seemed even larger than at the restaurant. The alcohol had hit her fast. She would get the next round and get herself a soda. She needed to be able to think straight.

"I work for my dad. He runs an auto shop in Panaji."

"Oh, I think I passed through there the other day; it's a pretty little town."

"It's okay." He was looking intently at her lips. She could feel his eyes all over her, and more than anything she wanted to feel his lips on hers.

"So, do you have a boyfriend?" Terrance asked. He was playing with a strand of Lisa's hair and clearly flirting with her. The vodka took over, and she couldn't help but flirt back.

"No, do you?"

"And how come an attractive girl like you is single?" It was clichéd and Lisa knew it, but he mesmerized her.

"You didn't answer my question," she said, having another sip of her drink.

"No, I don't have a serious girlfriend."

"Just lots of flings with unsuspecting tourists," she quipped, impressed with herself. She was normally no good at flirting, but she was managing it tonight. It made her feel good. It was the first time, after a string of failed relationships, that she actually felt wanted. Even Chris, before she had known of his sexual preferences, had never made her tingle as Terrance did now. He was looking at her with desire.

Terrance laughed. "No, not lots of flings." He tilted his head to one side and looked straight into her eyes. She looked away, his look was so intense, and her desire for him was growing stronger. She had not felt like this for years. The feeling enthralled her, especially as she had just met him – it was the unknown that gave her that slight thrill.

Just as they were drawing close together, his hand on her thigh, Teresa and Ayesha sat down at the end of the lounger. Lisa was somewhat relieved and somewhat annoyed. Sonya joined them and gave them a curious look. She had hardly spoken to Lisa all night, and the last thing Lisa wanted to do was intentionally hurt her. Somehow, though, she felt that this was not in her control; she needed to sober up. She had not come to Goa to get involved with a new man; she was there to get over the last and to find out what she wanted from life. When Teresa suggested that they go to refresh their "wodkas", she felt relieved. She quickly ordered herself a soda, which took away the edge that the alcohol had given her and and helped her head stop spinning. They joined the others, who were now on the dance floor, and she kept her distance from Terrance this time. Before long, it was four in the morning, and they were heading back down the hill towards the Coconut Grove.

Lisa opened the door to her cool, air-conditioned room, and as she did so, she smiled. It had been a bit of a journey getting to this place in her life – the fruitless dates; the incessant whining from her mother, who seemed to think she would never settle down; and the countless evenings spent with Suzanne, looking for Mr Right. She thought back over the last couple of months. She remembered just three days ago sitting at Heathrow Terminal Three, swinging her legs beneath the mossy-green seat.

*

She had made the right choice, she thought, on the matter of what shoes to wear for her flight: flat ballet pumps. That pretty much summed up Lisa: stylish but practical – maybe too practical. She was a sensible sort of woman. She always arrived at the airport in good time, good time meaning four hours before her flight. Well, she would reason, she was either going to be sitting at home or sitting at the airport; she always chose the latter. Lisa Higgins didn't believe that you could be too careful.

The sushi bar at the terminal was in Lisa's direct view. A hungry audience sat around the conveyor belt carrying its little plates of food. Lisa watched as they greedily devoured vibrant red and pink pieces of sashimi with their wooden chopsticks, and this bothered her slightly. A little bit of her envied them, a little bit of her knew it was her own hang-ups once again preventing her from living a little. *Sushi before a flight – raw fish – you're bound to get sick.* That's not to say that Lisa Higgins was a boring character who never took risks; she just didn't like change. For years she had driven the same route to work, despite knowing several others she could have taken to avoid having to sit in traffic. It was a "quirk of her character",

she often said when defending her own rigidity. *But look* ͼ
thought. She had shocked all and sundry and was taking a wı..
a holiday for one, at the age of twenty-five!

Lisa was of average build; a size twelve, with poker-straight brown hair and big brown eyes that complemented her olive complexion. She had a penchant for designer accessories and bought the rest of her clothes from Primark. She loved fine food but would occasionally devour a Pot Noodle. She had been basically an average twenty-something, cruising through life, until one particularly bad dating experience gave her rather itchy feet.

She had never been a particularly adventurous dater, but at twenty-four, when the last of her single friends had coupled up, she'd known it was time to put herself out there, before she really was "left on the shelf". She had started the year desperately on the lookout for a man in her life to fill those increasingly lonely evenings and make her feel complete. She'd never had commitment issues; through school and university she had had a steady string of boyfriends, but she'd just never found Mr Right. She pondered over her dating mishaps and realized that her last proper relationship had ended when she was twenty-two. From then on she had concentrated on her career. Was it true what Suzanne had said – that you can't have love, health, and wealth all at the same time?

The first half of her twenty-fourth year had been a complete disaster. Lisa had attempted every type of dating experience possible, from speed dating to lock-and-key parties, all of which had spectacularly failed and made her feel even worse than when she'd started. She was almost certain that there were no sane single men left in England. She had even tried an online matchmaking site, which just proved to her that the only men left out there were certified no-hopers – and made her wonder if she was in that category, too. However, she plodded on, and it wasn't until a speed-dating llama-trekking event, which proved to be the final straw for Lisa, that she succumbed to Suzanne's plan to look closer to home for a possible date.

Suzanne was Lisa's best friend in the world, her flatmate and partner in crime for all things ludicrous. They had met on the first day of high school, and since that day they'd been attached at the hip. They say that too much familiarity can sometimes cause people to take on each other's attributes, and it was not long before most people began to mistake Lisa and Suzanne for sisters. They looked similar, with matching eye and hair colour, high cheekbones, and pretty decent complexions for young adolescents. But where Lisa's brown hair was without so much as a kink, Suzanne's was a mass of tangled curls, giving her the nickname *mop top* in those early school years.

Suzanne didn't manage to tame her hair until the lower sixth, when she started looking more like Carrie Bradshaw than Crystal Tips. After this transformation, and the loss of their hideous green-checked uniforms, Suzanne used the newly found confidence she'd gained from her sleek mass of curls to gain ultimate popularity. Lisa, the quiet one of the two, benefited from the party invites and the male attention that soon followed, even if some of her dates were Suzanne's rejects. The two had then gone their separate ways for university. Lisa had moved to Oxford, securing a place at Brookes and preferring country life, while Suzanne had braved London. They had studied Literature and Business Administration respectively, and after they'd been apart three years, fate had brought them back together, by which time they had come to know themselves individually. They relied on each other, as friends should, but each was her own person. They had finally grown into their own skins.

They were currently living together in a two-bedroom duplex apartment in the up-and-coming area of St Clements in Oxford, instantly attracted to the buzzing restaurants and pubs, and more so because it had a student vibe – a part of them that they were keen to hang on to. They spent most of their evenings out at restaurants or drinking cocktails and wine in lounge bars in the nearby alternative Cowley Road, and they enjoyed the fact that they were earning real money for the first time in their lives.

That was when they had first moved in together and were in the so-called honeymoon phase. Suzanne had met Arjun just six months into their new twenty-something lifestyle, and their relationship seemed to be growing stronger and stronger. Arjun did something in economics, which Lisa knew was quite important but never really understood – she understood only that it was making him lots of money. They had met him after several cocktails in Leon's, and he had instantly turned on the charm with Suzanne. Coincidently, he happened to be the brother of Archana, one of Lisa's colleagues, and this had given him the green light to spend most of the evening with them. By the end of their first two months together,

Suzanne had been smitten and eager for Lisa to find someone so that they could do "couply" things together. "Don't be so childish," Lisa would mock when Suzanne hinted at this, but secretly, she was hoping she would find someone, too. She had always wanted to go on a double date.

So they had spent an entire Saturday, amidst hot chocolate and almond croissants, listing all possible single men, from their days in primary school until the present time. And that's how the second half of Lisa's twenty-fourth year went. The dates were considerably better, and with the aid of social networking sites, they were able to weed out the potential hapless losers. At first these sites completely devastated Lisa. She had thought she wasn't doing too badly in her chosen career and in her social life until she saw what her peers from about ten years ago were doing.

She had left high school rather proud that she was never picked on and she was generally liked. She had finished a tough teaching qualification and presumed she was doing what most of her friends would be doing round about this age. She wasn't. How did all her ex-schoolmates manage to go on trips around the world and fit in getting married and having kids alongside fabulous careers?

Lisa felt rather cheated. Her mouth hung open as she stared at an image of spotty Sandra from Year Nine, who had clearly lost the spots, along with two dress sizes, and was currently on her honeymoon in the Bahamas.

"She can't be having that good a time if she has time to update her status," Suzanne was quick to point out. "On these sites, Lise, people just make their lives look better than they are. Here, look at my page – we all look good on paper!"

Suzanne pushed a brown curl of hair behind her ear, nudged Lisa out of the way, and clicked on her profile. Admittedly, Suzanne's profile picture did make her look more like a size eight than a twelve, and the recent holiday photos that she had uploaded, with Arjun, a six-foot-something, on one arm and a Louis Vuitton on the other, made her look as if she were doing pretty well – as if she were smart, sophisticated, and stylish. If she hadn't been aware that Suzanne was a smart, bumbling hippie who didn't know Louis Vuitton from Next and who currently favoured garish fisherman pants in hues of blue and yellow, then yes, Lisa probably would have had an ounce of envy for her life, too.

So the dates with the old acquaintances started, and it wasn't until late autumn that she finally met up with Chris Peters. Chris was an old crush from her A-Level days who used to go out with the likes of Kym Stevens – one of those girls that you just had to envy because she had beauty, brains, and a kind personality. Everyone either wanted to *be* her or be *with* her. Lisa and Suzanne had never fitted into her circle of friends, yet you couldn't help but like the girl.

"Oh, look" Suzanne chimed, "our Mr Peters lives in Oxford and is newly single. Now, isn't that convenient? Nothing mends a broken heart like a new relationship." Suzanne shot Lisa a knowing smile.

"I know Suzanne – he could be the one!" Lisa pretended to look lovesick and held her hand to her forehead. "Oh, Suze, you are my saviour! How did I manage all this time without you?"

Suzanne smirked "You didn't, my dear friend, but I'm here now." Lisa picked up a blue-and-white cushion near her feet and hurled it at her.

So Christopher Peters's position in the list of potential dates had just moved up to the top of the pack. Lisa had been sceptical when he picked her up on their first date. She had had a feeling that something wasn't right, but she couldn't quite put her finger on it. Suzanne had once said that relationships that started out like that turned out to be the worst. By the time you actually realized what that tiny, insignificant thing was that had initially made you turn your nose, it had grown into something big and ugly and was always there to remind you that you should have trusted your instincts. Relationships like that always ended badly, mostly with resentment at yourself for not trusting your "inner self", as Suzanne would have said. She was into some kind of spiritual fixation these days. *Relationship breakups are always bad, especially when they make you feel bad about yourself,* Suzanne's words echoed in Lisa's head.

These feelings had flooded Lisa's mind as she stepped into Chris's car earlier that evening. She could see herself in a month's time saying, *Next time listen to your instincts*! But by the end of a three-course meal, a liqueur, coffee, and petits fours, Lisa had seen a glimmer of light, and she pursued it with rose-tinted glasses. Finally, she was getting somewhere with a guy, and she wasn't going to ruin it for herself now.

Within a month they were dating on a regular basis. He had much improved over the last six years, and he had grown into a gentleman, even taking her shopping without so much as a complaint. This made her content, and for once in her life, she stopped waiting for something to go wrong.

She had questioned why this amazing idea of stalking old school friends hadn't come to her earlier. She was verging on being deliriously happy, and as far as she could see, everything was running smoothly. She was so drunk on love that she thought she could even risk tempting fate and calling her mother to tell her the good news. Lisa's mother had become increasingly paranoid, after her retirement, that Lisa had an aversion to men. She could never see the day that her daughter would marry, and worse still, she feared that she was a closet lesbian and that she would never give her grandchildren. But Margaret was a funny being, and at the same time, she congratulated herself for knowing that she had been right about Lisa being the selfish one of her two children.

Lisa could never forget this, as she was reminded of it every time they spoke. However, she never did make that call to her mother – the thought of twenty-one questions so soon that she probably wouldn't know the answers to prevented her from doing so. Lisa could almost hear the *tut tut* across the telephone line. On one occasion, she began to dial her mother's number but then swiftly replaced the receiver. It was a good thing that she had held off, as it was not long after she had professed to Suzanne that she and Chris were officially exclusive that Lisa found herself single once again.

*

The painful Friday night in question had started off quite innocently, with a girl's flirt-free night inspired by happy coupledom, a bottle of cheap Supermarket Own Brand rosé, and an episode of *Sex in the City*. Lisa and Suzanne had decided to go to Rainbows, a local gay bar in town. The evening had started off well, and three cosmopolitans later, they had hit the dance floor, pretending they were back in the eighties with the queen of pop herself, Madonna. Just then, a drag queen, who looked more queen than drag in a wedding dress and a blond wig, jumped onstage, bellowing out "Like a Virgin". The whole club seemed to go into slow motion. Lisa was reminiscing with Suzanne about their days in high school, when all of a sudden she felt awfully queasy. At first, she thought she had just had one too many. She could feel the remnants of their make-do pasta dinner wanting to make a comeback, along with that last shot of Apple Sourz, which she had known at the time was a mistake. But then Suzanne had clawed at her arm, and she heard a muffled voice saying the words *bastard* and *home,* as she felt the tugging at her arm. But Lisa was glued to the spot.

Right before her eyes was her very own Chris and what appeared to be a leather-clad bodybuilder, and yes, they were devouring each other right in front of her. The scene was somewhat odd, and Lisa's brain was in a state of confusion. Chris, too engrossed in what he was doing, failed to notice her. Lisa stood there, dejected, humiliated, and instantly sober. She could see the fantasy life involving a veil, a house with a white picket fence, and two kids (a boy and a girl, of course, for whom she had just about settled on names) come crashing down around her. It wasn't like Lisa to start confrontations, especially in a public place. But at that point, Chris had seemed to be her last shot at a relationship. She did what she would never have thought possible and flew at him in rage.

Suzanne, who in ten years had never seen Lisa behave like this, was both mortified and proud. The quiet, timid Lisa was finally standing up for herself. Lisa had always had it under control but had often gotten trampled on by men. Suzanne recalled a particularly bad boyfriend she'd been smitten about in high school while he was having it off with Sally Jones. It had been insulting, not only because she was in a lower year, but also because she had a very bad case of muffin top as well. To add insult to injury, he hadn't given two hoots when Lisa confronted him. She had risen above it, though, and casually walked away from him.

"Didn't you want to slap him?" Suzanne had asked.

"I would have," she put on a brave face, "but I'm better than that." Suzanne could see her holding back the tears. "I'm not going to stoop to his level."

Suzanne had been impressed at the time; they were so young, but clearly she was right.

Now, as the effects of the cheap rosé wine, cosmopolitans, and Apple Sourz rapidly wore off, Suzanne thought this was surely a good thing for Lisa, if a little embarrassing. She quickly scanned around for familiar faces; there were none, so she thought, *Why not? Let her scream and shout a little – get it out of her system.* Maybe this was what she needed. She had bottled up all those feelings for years. It would be cathartic, Suzanne mused. It was usually Suzanne who made the scene; she'd never really had to pick up the pieces. As Lisa leapt on Chris, Suzanne gave her a couple of minutes to let out her grief before she eyed the rather large doorman heading towards them and sprang into action.

"You lying scumbag! Why would you do this to me?" Lisa screamed, punching his torso. Despite being hysterical, she was aware there were people around and thought it best not to swear – not that the clientele would have minded or even noticed – but the teacher within her held her back. Chris turned around, along with a dozen other partygoers, who looked like they were used to this kind of behaviour from crazy heterosexuals and secretly enjoyed the drama despite it interrupting them from the best Madonna performance of their lives.

Chris looked genuinely scared. "I'm sorry … I was going to tell you," came his feeble reply.

"When? After we had kids?" She was surprised that this secret fantasy she had sworn to keep hidden in the recesses of her mind had exposed itself to make her look like a bunny boiler. Had she been sober, she would have shut up at this point, but she wasn't, and so all the hatred she had had for all the men who had broken her heart came out at once. Chris stood there staring at Lisa but unable to placate her. He apologized again, this time focusing on Suzanne, hoping that she would drag Lisa off before leather-clad Joe decided to take off as well, and to his relief, she did just that. Eyeliner and mascara ran down Lisa's cheeks as Suzanne helped her into a black cab. Aptly, the DJ played "I Want to Break Free", and Suzanne heard a roar of laughter from the club as the door slammed shut behind them.

5

Almost a week had passed, and Lisa could just about see the funny side to yet another failed relationship, but it had left a bitter taste. She wondered just why she could not seem to meet the right man. Armed with a very creamy korma from the local balti house and well into her fourth glass of Chardonnay, Lisa was playing Sad Love Songs Volume 2 on repeat. Suzanne, fuelled by alcohol and knowing that she had a captive audience, was spouting advice on love.

"I love you, Lise, I really do, but you need to shake it up a little," she said. Happy in her long-term relationship with Arjun, she felt that this qualified her to have the upper hand in this instance.

"Why would he date me if he was gay? Huh? How could I have been that stupid? I should have known when he agreed to go shopping without even one complaint. I mean, what boyfriend does that? *Aargh!* I am so stupid – thank the Lord I didn't tell my mother." Lisa stared into the pale liquid in her glass; the smell of the fermented grapes consumed her.

"At least he gave you some good clothing advice," Suzanne quipped, but she was not smiling. Maybe it was too soon for jokes.

"He may have been gay, Suzanne, but that's not to say he had good taste," Lisa said, thinking about the vibrant pink skirt he had made her buy. Suzanne was right; he had given her some good style tips. That pink skirt had opened the door of colour for her, and over the last few weeks, her cupboard had been transformed. Instead of blending in with the crowd, she now stood out, and compliments were abundant. Chris might have given her a helping hand in the clothing department, but she was not ready to accept that out loud, just yet.

Nevertheless, Suzanne, who was quite inebriated, still had some words of advice: "Maybe, Lise, you need to complete yourself before you meet someone – know what you want from life." Suzanne, a bit of a hippy at heart, had had these feelings compounded after a three-week trip of detox and yoga in Chiang Mai last year. Chiang Mai had changed her. She had cropped her hair to a more manageable length and had stopped dyeing it black. Now it was naturally brown and luscious, and it suited her more. She also looked happy. Although she had always been the more confident of the two, she was now making decisions more carefully and thinking about how they would really affect her life in the long term. At the retreat, her life coach, Chandra, had pointed her in the right direction. She had changed a lot of things in her life since then, and she was much happier for it.

Lisa had heard this spiel before, and quite frankly, it generally skipped her by. She had seen Suzanne's phase of Deepak Chopra pass, then the Buddhism phase, and the Feng Shui – the list was endless – but the most recent was this life-coach propaganda. It was the drunken stupor and the fact that the traditional methods of sorting her life out didn't seem to be working that made Lisa want to pay closer attention to what Suzanne had to say. However, she had some reservations; she had not completely accepted the notion that her life was slowly making it down the drain. Her pride took over, and she was desperate to prove to Suzanne that it was all okay and her life wasn't in complete disarray.

"I kind of know what I want, Suze. My life is pretty complete and on track. I am happy with my job – well, it's okay. No, I enjoy it. I love where I live – well, England is so cold; that annoys me, but the summer makes up for it … but sometimes … I feel like my life is work, home, sleep, work, home, sleep. Well, okay, the lifestyle may not be great – but I haven't had any traumas growing up, so I'm not a sociopath, and I don't think I'm an emotional retard. I have had relationships, and it's not like I have had a serious problem forming friendships."

The reality of her breakup hit her again with sudden force, accelerated by the third bottle of Chardonnay. "Maybe I am just not a likeable person," Lisa whispered. She started curling a section of her hair around the first two fingers of her right hand. It was a childhood habit that she had not quite grown out of; she did this when she knew that things were not going her way. "Maybe it is just too late. Maybe I am going to be single forever. Maybe it's just me. Maybe I turn men gay. Oh no, you're right, maybe it is just me! Pass me the bottle." Lisa swung her arm out for the Chardonnay.

There was a look of dawning awareness on her face. In trying to disprove Suzanne, she had realized that her best friend was right. Her life was in tatters!

Suzanne handed over the bottle and went to the freezer for the Cherry Garcia. There was nothing like ice cream to cheer someone up. She wondered whether she had pushed her friend too far and whether the negative energy that Lisa now exuded was going to impinge on her life further. She had many a time practised it in the shower when she envisioned leaving the world of Human Resource Management and becoming a life coach herself. Sucking on her ice cream spoon, she realized that the response from Lisa gave her the green light to carry on with her mantra.

"No, Lise, it's not you. You are *so* not the problem here! Maybe you just need more life experience, so you can make better decisions. Remember, we define our lives by the choices we make!" Suzanne smiled at the intelligence of her own last remark. It sounded good. She was determined to put a positive spin on things. "Tell me, Lisa, are you happy with your job? I reckon you don't challenge yourself enough. I know you want to be Head of Year, and I know you are more than capable. But will you ever try? Is it fear of rejection? Or is it because you would be out of your comfort zone?" Suzanne was surprised that she had said all this. She wasn't really sure where it had all come from; maybe she was saying what she felt about her own life, but she was too drunk to think about it now, and whilst Lisa was hanging on every word, well then, she would carry on. She liked the sound of her own voice.

"Maybe you are happy cruising through life, but maybe you are settling for less than you should. You need to achieve something for *you*! Do something different! You are only in your early twenties."

"Twenty-five to be exact, that's mid-twenties, and there ain't no going back – and you watch far too much *Oprah*," said Lisa, knowing her friend's penchant for daytime television and growing somewhat bored of being attacked like this, although she did detect an element of truth in Suzanne's words.

Suzanne sensed the tension building. "*Loose Women*, actually," she said, trying to dispel Lisa's frustrations. They both fell about laughing; they had both watched the show whenever they had time off together, generally on a sick day caused by too much alcohol on a weeknight. They had always said that it would be a perfect job, where they could put the world right, with a cup of tea, and get paid for it.

"I've always wanted to be a travel writer, I guess," Lisa said, still twirling her hair. "I do love seeing new places, but I can't really write well – you know the saying, 'Those who can't, teach'." Lisa lifted her hands to make air quotes as she said this, and then she reprimanded herself; she hated when people did that. "Oh, Suze, you are confusing me."

"I think that's the alcohol," Suzanne said in a knowing way. She continued, "Why not travel? You are a teacher; you have loads of holiday," she said slurring her words. It was true that Lisa had many holidays, but she did get annoyed that everyone thought teachers had it easy. There was always marking and lesson plans to do, plus dealing with children all the time. She was mostly drained by the time the term was over. She needed the holidays to recharge her batteries. But Suzanne was determined to inspire her friend.

"Go to a spa, then, if you don't want to leave the comfort of good old Blighty. Get away from it all; spend some time with yourself. Think. Most importantly, forget about men! One will come along when you least expect it. You have been acting a little desperate since you have been on the search, and you are only twenty-five. Quite frankly, I don't want a Lady Havisham as a friend."

It was okay for Suzanne, Lisa thought; *she* was in a relationship. Lisa's loneliness was getting worse, though, ever since she had realized what was missing. Her friends were increasingly moving in with partners and settling down, and socially, she felt, it was unacceptable to be single. At her age, it was like wearing a sign on your head, saying: "There is something wrong with this one."

"All right, Suze. I'm not that bad," Lisa said, but her heart had sunk a little deeper, and the thought of her dreary existence almost sobered her up.

"As yet," Suze added.

"Sod off!" Lisa threw a cushion at her, narrowly missing the overly creamy korma, before they stumbled into bed.

6

Saturday morning hit Lisa with a bang. *Bang bang bang* she heard at her bedroom door. She was in the midst of thinking that her head was exploding, when she heard Suzanne's high-pitched voice.

"It's me, Lisa – I'm off out for the day." Lisa tried movement to see if her hangover could get any worse. She was not too bad. She padded over to the door and opened it to a bright-eyed and fresh-faced Suzanne, who was dressed in a vibrant orange that almost blinded her.

"Hi – how are you so chirpy this morning? We totally drank the same amount. And you are dressed! What is it, like nine o'clock? " Lisa squinted at Suzanne. The light from the corridor was too powerful to take in and a whiff of Suzanne's Clinique Happy was enough to make her gag. Lisa was never impressed when she was the only one with a hangover. It made her feel cheated, coupled with the feeling of uselessness which currently surrounded her; she was now sure that she had an inadequate liver.

"Eleven, you lazy cow! Arjun is picking me up, and we are off to London for the day. Do you need anything? I can always nip by Selfridges for that to–die-for bacon chocolate."

"The thought of chocolate is not very appealing right now; I'll take a rain check. I need to go back to bed."

"Here, take this; you'll feel a whole lot better." Suze handed her a purple and white sachet.

Lisa squinted as she held it up. "Dioralyte! I don't have the—"

"No, Lisa, it's to replenish your lost salts and sugars. A hangover is basically dehydration."

"Am I still drunk? You actually sound like you know what you are talking about."

"I'll pretend I didn't hear that! But take it; you will feel a lot better. If you took it before you went to bed, you would have been as fresh as a daisy."

"Oh, and I'm supposed to be the sensible one. How did I miss that trick?"

Lisa crept back to bed and buried herself under her duvet for at least another hour before she attempted the flight of stairs down to the kitchen. She fixed herself a mug of sugary tea, a bacon sandwich, and the rehydration sachet, although she was not confident that this would sort her out.

It was three in the afternoon when Lisa could finally shift herself from the sofa and discard the remnants of last night's curry. Clearly, Suzanne had failed to see the mess. Suzanne Chapman had been her best friend through school and university, and when the fun of living in shared houses with at least three other people's mess wore thin, they'd decided to move in together. Suzanne was messy, but she made a mean lasagne that even rivalled her mother's. Apart from the mess and Lisa's borderline Obsessive-Compulsive Disorder with checking that doors were locked, they rarely got on each other's nerves.

But there was a nagging feeling at the back of Lisa's mind. She had an increasing worry that Suzanne would be settling down soon with Arjun. They had been together for three years, and although they had met in a cocktail bar, Oxford was one of those places where everyone seemed interlinked. Lisa had been to university with his sister, Archana, and now they worked together. Rumour had it that his parents were pushing for an engagement now that they had come to accept that Arjun was really in love and not interested in marrying a Hindu girl, although they had hoped and prayed for that. Suzanne and Arjun's relationship had become increasingly intense over the last couple of months, and Suzanne was spending less time at their flat and more time at Arjun's plush new apartment in Jericho. It was obvious to anyone who knew him that he was the settling-down type, and with the added pressures from his family, Lisa knew it would not be long before Suzanne would be moving in. Maybe a change was needed.

She certainly wouldn't stop her friend from leaving, although the idea of Suzanne not living at the flat unsettled her.

At four in the afternoon, with nothing to do and her hangover slowly disappearing, Lisa started channel-surfing. It had been a terrible habit since childhood; she could spend a good half hour changing channels before deciding what to watch, by which time a new set of programmes would have started. Lisa, much to Suzanne's annoyance, would never use the programme guide.

*

It was in that brief moment of nostalgically flicking through the channels that Lisa saw something that would lead her to a hotel room in Goa.

Whilst she was changing channels, a stretch of perfectly manicured, lush, golden sand had flashed before her eyes. She started flicking back to find the channel again. Now there was a burst of colour on the screen. People were hurtling handfuls of coloured powder at each other. *Bizarre*, she thought, and was about to change channels, when a beautiful old church appeared on the screen. There was something about it that drew her in. She had always loved old-world things and absolutely loved the character of old buildings. This was one of the main reasons she had decided to stay in Oxford after finishing her degree. The beauty of Christ Church and the old colleges in the sandy Cotswold stone could captivate just about anyone.

"And you could be here. Yes, escape the winter blues, and head to the sun this Christmas." A smug television presenter, looking very orange, with perfectly straight white teeth, appeared on screen. The easiest job in the world, after being a presenter on *Loose Women,* thought Lisa. His complexion and cheesy grin had already begun to fray her nerves, but she was keen to find out where he was. The presenter appeared to be staring at her.

"You – yes you – could be here, and this is where you could be staying, at the four-star Coconut Grove resort!" An infinity pool looking out towards the sea invited her, along with the golden beach that looked as if it went on for miles and miles. A poolside bar imitating a beach shack, and a view of mouthwatering lobsters, crabs, prawns, and spicy curries in vibrant reds and yellows rendered her incapable now of changing channels. For a split second, her hangover had disappeared. More than anything in the world, she wanted at that moment to escape from her own thoughts of the last couple of weeks and be there in that hotel, in that pool, on her own.

"Over to you, Craig and Sally," the annoying presenter had interrupted her ogling, and now there were a further two annoyingly orange presenters on her screen.

"Call Premier today, and book your bit of winter sun, your little bit of luxury. Go on – you've earned it!" It was like the QVC shopping site, but for holidays. A counter on the left-hand corner of the screen was counting the number of callers to the show. Lisa had never seen this channel before.

"You know, Craig, I went there last winter, by myself, and the spa was fabulous! It's such a great place, and with no single-person supplements, it's cheap, as well." Had this Sally person been spying on them last night? wondered Lisa. She was annoyed that they had her where they wanted her. She was now actually contemplating going away by herself – something she had thought she could never do. *But I have earned it*, she reflected on the presenters' words. They had had a curry last night – maybe it was a sign! What had that Chardonnay done to her? She didn't usually think such immature thoughts. Maybe she was spending too much time with Suzanne.

Sensible Lisa was mentally making a note of all the reasons why she could go away by herself. Suzanne's rantings last night had hit home more than she had thought at the time. She needed to do something for herself, by herself. That was reason enough, and of course, the fact that she didn't really have anyone to go with. *Why do friends get so busy as you get older? When we were students we had oodles of time for one another*, she mused. Nowadays, nobody had time to do anything, with boyfriends, family, kids, and work taking up the majority of their waking hours.

"A trip, a journey of self discovery …" Sally was still preaching in her daytime selling voice.

Marissa de Luna

In a rare moment of spontaneity, which she would later berate herself for, Lisa Higgins had picked up the phone and booked a non-refundable (not at that price, they had said) trip to Goa.

It took roughly an hour before she started having serious doubts about her sanity. Not only had she booked a holiday for one, she would be missing Christmas at home. She would now have to sit through hours of painful lecturing from her mother, at the same time wondering what exactly she was going to do by herself in a foreign country for two weeks. Her hangover instantaneously returned, but this time accompanied by dread in the pit of her stomach at having to face her mother's reaction.

7

"Lisa Claire Higgins, what on earth has gotten into you? Why would you do this? Have you been drinking?" Margaret paused. She was waiting for a response, and Lisa's heart sank a little deeper. Not only was she regretting her foolish actions of the day before, but now she had to hear all those reasons that were already in her head out loud from her mother. But she couldn't give her mother the satisfaction of agreeing with her. That would not do her any favours for any future decisions she might want to take on her own. At twenty-five, Lisa wondered how her mother was still able to control her so much.

"No, mother," Lisa said defensively, although she did consider whether it was the effects of the alcohol the night before that had caused such rash behaviour.

"Then why would you do this? You're missing Christmas! Your father will be so disappointed, and your brother is coming down with the little one especially; oh, he will be sorry." It sounded as if her mother was about to burst into tears. *Why me*? Lisa thought, deliberating on whether her mother honestly thought she had booked a holiday solely to spite the rest of the family.

That's it, Mother, lay on the guilt trip. Stupid, stupid holiday channel!

"This is quite selfish of you, Lisa."

Selfish! I am forever doing what you want me to do, trying to live up to your expectations of me. You are the selfish one! I should have gone through Paul or Dad – they are better at handling you than I am!

"I know why this has happened," Margaret said in an authoritative tone. "You are lonely, aren't you? I keep saying to you: find a man, Lisa. Settle down, have some children. Don't leave it too late. You don't want to have adolescents running around whilst you're going through menopause."

Where did that spring from? Why am I still listening to my mother droning on about her inadequacies? Don't you think I would like to settle down, Mother? It's just that nobody wants to settle down with me. I turn men gay!

"You could bring Suzanne, if she is free and you want your own company." She paused before adding, "Oh no, she will be spending it with her lovely boyfriend."

That's it, Mother, rub it in. Lisa was seriously considering cancelling at this point, if only to stop her mother's incessant whining over the next two months.

"I don't want children yet, Mother. Gosh, I haven't even got a boyfriend yet!" Why couldn't she have one of those friendly mothers who laughed with you rather than at you?

But when was the last time I did something selfish, just for me, thought Lisa, excluding the very extravagant recent purchase of the new Mulberry Milton clutch in mint green. Just the thought of the bag calmed her nerves. It was a two-week holiday to the most westernized place in India – what could go wrong? Suzanne had said she needed to shake it up a little, and that was what she was doing.

"Oh Lisa, it's a third-world country. You don't speak the language."

"Look Mum, I just need some *me* time. I want to know what I really want from life. At least I am not donning a backpack and travelling around the world for six months, like Paul."

Lisa knew this was a cheap thing to do – make her brother look bad, so she wouldn't – but given the circumstances, she felt he wouldn't mind.

It did not create the desired effect, however. Her mother instantly dismissed it. "That's different, dear. He was so mature at twenty-four, and he is a boy. There is not as much danger for boys travelling on their own. Now, for girls, local people will take advantage of them."

How naive – and sexist, at that.

"And you could have gone to Dublin and stayed with your brother if you needed some time away."

She felt as if she were slowly being suffocated. She decided in that instant that she did, in fact, need the time away without any interruptions, so she could truly understand what she really wanted from life.

"It's two weeks, Mum. It's the first Christmas I'll miss in my twenty-five years. Look, that's my phone. It may be important; I'll call you back," she lied, but the conversation had been going nowhere, and she had made up her mind she was not going to cancel the trip on her mother's say-so. She was twenty-five, and it was time she let go of those apron strings.

*

"Hey, Suze – how was London?" Lisa asked, peering into the oven; she was roasting a shoulder of lamb. They usually took it in turns to cook a Sunday roast and have a good catch-up before another Monday came around, but with Suzanne being away with Arjun so much, Lisa had taken on most of the Sunday cooking. The sweet smell of lamb and rosemary filled the room as Lisa opened the oven door.

"Really good. We mooched round the shops and then had an early dinner at the Grill."

"The steak place?"

"Yeah, that's the one. Très chic inside."

"Ohhh, fancy!" A sliver of jealousy ran through Lisa; she wished someone would take her for fancy meals. But now she was going to do something herself that she was sure Suzanne would feel a hint of envy for.

"Oh, and tomorrow night, I'm cooking at Arjun's new flat. You are invited, of course. Just the usual suspects."

"Oh, that sounds nice," Lisa tried to contain her excitement whilst Suzanne muttered mundane ideas of how her party should go. She was going though her menu, deciding between a Moroccan or Thai theme for the evening. Suzanne had a passion for all things social, and she had clearly been planning the dinner all weekend. Arjun's new flat would be ideal, and Lisa could envision them ending the night at Leon's for cucumber and apple martinis. Suzanne was busy talking, but Lisa had switched off and was waiting for her to finish, so she could tell her about her trip. After her mother's outburst, she knew that Suzanne would be fully supportive – after all, she had taken her advice. She would be having some "me" time.

Lisa couldn't wait any longer, and she came out with her plan. Suzanne's reaction, however, was not quite what she had hoped for. There was an uncomfortable silence, and Lisa started playing with her hair again.

"Well, what do you think?" she blurted, unable to read Suzanne's blank expression.

Suzanne looked a little stunned, and Lisa reassured her it was no joke. "I think you are very brave," Suzanne said cautiously.

"But you said—"

"I was drunk, and I remember saying *a spa*. You don't even like getting on a train yourself!" Her true feelings exposed themselves. She could never quite keep them hidden.

"They never tell you which train is which – that's why! Nobody checks your ticket till you are on the train, by which time you are halfway to Doncaster instead of Gloucester. You can't do that for aeroplanes. They check and double-check," Lisa said out loud – to reassure herself more than Suzanne.

"Anyway, when do you ever listen to me?" Suzanne was hoping this wasn't her fault entirely. She didn't want Lisa to be in some foreign land feeling even more alone because of some frivolous comment she had made in a drunken moment. She knew what Lisa's experiences abroad were like. "It may be a bit uncivilized for you, and it's pretty far if you don't like it."

This aggravated Lisa. She clearly knew why Suzanne was saying this, and it all boiled down to a school trip they'd taken when they were doing their GCSEs. They had gone to Greece to learn a bit more about the Greek gods, as part of their Classical Civilization Module. Four days into the trip, Lisa had become moody and depressed. She had been fussy about the food, which was hardly that exotic, and she'd not been happy about having to dispose of the loo paper in the bin as opposed to the toilet. In fact, she had ignored the inadequate plumbing of the century before, only to see their bathroom flooded on the last day. At the time, Lisa herself didn't know why she had felt so much like a fish out of water, but deep down, she had a sneaky suspicion that she'd just been missing home. She had never admitted it, though, and from then on she'd never ventured far, excusing herself as a simple homebody. The fact that she was only fourteen at the time and that it was the first time she had been away from home did not occur to her as the reason why she felt so awful.

It was true that she'd never been a big fan of travelling, though. She liked the idea – she just never did it. When her brother, Paul, had announced his round-the-world trip three years ago, she'd been glad it wasn't her. The thought of multicoloured hostel bed sheets and shared bathrooms gave her the creeps. Since Greece, she had only ever ventured on city breaks, where the flights were less than four hours and the duration was less than four days, allowing her the luxury of at least three-star hotels with crisp, white sheets. How was it that these fears had not materialized when she had booked the trip? Now her palms were sweaty and cold.

"That was a long time ago. Thanks for the support," Lisa said again. She was trying to convince the part of herself that was having such huge doubts, but her look was clearly desperate.

Like a true friend, Suzanne recognized this look instantaneously and immediately understood. "Oh, silly me. I didn't mean it like that. You are going to have the time of your life! I am just completely jealous. Come here and give Suze a big ol' hug!"

"It's only two weeks," Lisa said, recognising that deep, southern drawl that Suzanne often mimicked when she was trying to diffuse a situation, but she was glad of it and released some of her anxiety in Susanne's embrace.

"Don't add any more doubt to my mind. I've already tackled 'the Beast' today."

"Wow, that was quick! I would have waited at least till a week before I left before I broke the news to her." Suzanne was well aware of Lisa's mum's know-it-all attitude, and she knew that "the Beast" recognized exactly what buttons to push to make Lisa feel guilty about her own existence, thus slowly destroying her confidence. Her heart gave way slightly for Lisa. She was her best friend in the world, and who knew? This trip might be just the ticket to give her that little bit of confidence.

"I don't know why everyone is so freaked out about it. It's a two-week holiday. Millions of people do it every day," Lisa said, releasing herself from Suzanne's grip.

"I know, Lisa. I guess we are just being a little protective of you," she said, pushing a strand of brown hair away from Lisa's eyes. She really did want to wrap her up in cotton wool and protect her.

"Overprotective!" Lisa quipped. She had allowed everyone in her life to mother her, and it was time to break free.

She knew if her parents and friends hadn't been so careful of her she might have had more confidence to get what she wanted from life. Suzanne flashed her one of those smiles that she just couldn't refuse and invited her to sit with a cup of chamomile tea and discuss the trip.

"It's just that you're not normally so rash with making decisions. You normally take about a decade to decide before you even buy a pair of shoes," said Suzanne as she put the kettle on.

"Well, Suze, you are looking at the all-new Lisa Higgins. I am now taking control of my life. Doing just a little bit of what I want to do." Lisa swallowed down her fear with a big gulp of tea.

"Well done! Now, bring the bikkies and we can discuss this in more detail. The important things, like, which bikinis are you going to take?"

8

It was two days before Lisa's trip, and she had started packing. Soon she would be basking in the sunshine with not a care in the world. Archana had given her the low-down on Goa, having spent a couple of weeks there with relatives the previous Easter. She had told her what to see and do, and she had also given her her uncle's number just to calm her nerves, although Lisa, who was never keen to impose, did not intend to use it.

She stared out of her bedroom window and looked at the bleakness of England in December. It was raining, and there was a cold blast of air coming in from her window. Her room overlooked the Angel and Greyhound pub on St Clements, and she could see groups of office workers gathering for their post-work drinks. She could hear talking and fragments of conversation involving home-cooked Christmas lunches, plump butterball turkey with golden skin and fragrant meat, sage and onion stuffing, lashings of gravy and cranberry sauce, and bacon rolls. She would miss that this Christmas, and despite her mother's faults, Lisa knew that nobody cooked a Christmas turkey, trimmings and all, as well as her mother did.

A sharp knock on the front door brought Lisa back to reality. She had lost herself in the gourmet delicacies of Christmas, and her mouth was beginning to water from the thought of all the food she was going to miss out on this year, not to mention the present opening, the EastEnders Christmas special, and the Boxing Day leftovers.

She pushed a strand of her brown hair away from her face, tucked it behind her ear, and pulled her white cashmere cardigan around her. She opened the door to see a box and a small face with fluffy white hair peering out from above it. It was Gladys, her neighbour.

"You look well, love. You've padded out a bit since I last saw you," Gladys reported.

Great! Lisa said to herself. She'd been hoping she'd lost enough weight to get into the skimpy green bikini Suzanne had made her buy only last week.

"This is for you, love. You were at work, so I took it in from the postie."

"Thanks," Lisa said, recognizing her mother's handwriting and the postmark of Leicester, her home town. A warm sensation washed over her. This would be her mother's way of saying: *We still love you. I'm sorry for being difficult, and have a good time.* She was eager to rip open the thick, brown paper and obtain that approval. She held on to it protectively; she could feel Gladys's intense desire to open the packaging and see what was inside.

"I hear you are off somewhere foreign this year. That will be nice for you, dear. Going with anyone special – Chris, perchance?" Lisa had known this was coming. Gladys, despite her innocent appearance, loved a bit of gossip, especially as far as Lisa's love life was concerned. Chris had always been pleasant to her. Lisa had not dared to share her embarrassment with her entire building, so she'd simply said that things had not worked out between them. Gladys stood there, looking at Lisa with a slightly pitying expression. Her look said: "What do you do that scares men off?" It was the same kind of look her aunts used to give her at family parties when she said she was still single. Being single was a reality occurrent at some point in most people's lives – it wasn't as if she had contracted an incurable tropical disease.

Lisa was tired of that look, so she thought she would just hit her with the truth. "I'm going alone, Gladys," she said with an air of nonchalance.

The shock was apparent, despite Gladys's best efforts not to show it. "One of those singles holidays, dear?" she asked, clearing her throat.

"No, just myself. Just a little resort, all by myself." Lisa didn't owe nosey Gladys a justification for this. Besides, she had done nothing but justify her single holiday to all and sundry ever since she had booked it. This time it wasn't a look of pity that Lisa caught in Gladys's eyes but one of envy. Lisa smiled to herself and shuffled back into her apartment, taking with her the large brown box.

Gladys retreated into her own apartment – and no doubt straight on to the phone to talk to Alice in number twenty-six, Lisa thought, as she took a knife to the parcel and started attacking it. Her mother always double-wrapped presents after she had watched a documentary on thieving postmen. She was surprised her mother hadn't put an exploding ink device on it as well, just to disturb anyone with postal criminal intent. It was a nightmare to open, but Lisa was excited; it was her first Christmas present. She herself hadn't bought any, but she wanted to get something from Goa for them, something exotic.

By the time she got into the parcel, her anticipation was at peak level, and then, as if someone had hit her with a brick, it shattered. Accompanied with a handwritten note was a book, *Seven Steps to a Happier You*, and a box of Imodium instants. Was her mother serious? Whom did she think was going to steal these choice items? More likely, she was protecting the employees at the local post office from mass hysteria at her humiliation. Lisa considered not reading the note attached, but she thought, *Could it get any worse? Probably*, she answered herself.

> Dear Lisa,
> I hope you receive this parcel in one piece and without any tampering. I found this book on the shopping channel, and after our conversation the other month, I thought it might clear a few things up for you, and then maybe you could stay for Christmas, after all.
> If not, I bought you the Imodium instant tablets, which I hear from the chemist are very good and come highly recommended by your cousin, Neil, who went to India last year <u>with his wife</u>. Anyway, Lisa, I have a casserole in the oven, so must go. Take good care of yourself; I will call you before you go. You know we care about you; it's just that it's so unlike you. A bit of a shock to us, that's all. Your father sends his love.
> Love,
> Mum

9

The shrill sound of her room telephone woke Lisa up. It took her a moment to register that she was on holiday in Goa.

"Hello dear. Happy Christmas," a distant, familiar voice echoed down the phone line.

"Hi, Dad!" She was surprised at first, but then she realized she had texted them with the hotel number and her room details when she had first arrived. "Merry Christmas. What time is it?"

"It's eight o'clock; your mother said you would be up by now."

Lisa looked at her watch by the bed. It was one thirty in the afternoon. How had she slept in for so long? Come to think of it, she couldn't exactly remember how she had gotten home. The dread of not knowing how the evening had ended began to seep in. Then it registered. After they had danced the night away at the nightclub in the sky, Terrance had dropped her back at the Coconut Grove, with a kiss that had left her speechless. *It must have been the alcohol,* she thought, touching her fingers to her lips. How could she do that to Sonya! She remembered the others being dropped of in villages around Calangute, and then she and Terrance had been alone in the car. She had watched him intently as he drove, concentrating on the road ahead of him. He'd looked so confident and in control. There had been a pleasant silence between them until they reached the drive of the hotel. He'd pulled in a few meters away from the entrance, beyond the watchful eyes of the bellboy and the chauffeurs who were huddled in the corner waiting for their employers to return. Terrance had taken her hand in his and had kissed it tenderly. As he'd leaned into Lisa, she couldn't help but let him kiss her. She knew she had wanted that very thing all evening. Her whole body had tingled with excitement; she could feel the little hairs on the back of her arms stand on end. He had kissed her with such passion and intensity that she had found it difficult to break away. But she had,

Goa Traffic

and then she'd quickly stepped out of the car, hoping that Carl was not watching from the reception desk.

"Happy Christmas, Dad," she said, realizing she was still on the line.

"Well, I'll quickly pass you to your mother and brother. They want a quick word." Lisa could here them bustling about in the background and the sound of one of the children crying.

"Hey, sis! Look at you on holiday all by yourself."

"Hi, Paul, and a merry Christmas to you, as well."

"Is it warm? It's freezing here. I am very jealous."

"Say merry Christmas to Sandra and little David, will you?"

"Yeah, I will. Take care, sis, and have a blast. Will pass you over to Mum; Dad is getting a bit jittery about the cost of this call." She could her father muttering in the background, "She sounds half asleep".

"Hiya, love; it's your mother."

"Hi, Mum. Merry Christmas." Lisa held her breath, waiting for an ear-bashing about something.

"Merry Christmas, love. Having a good time, are you, dear?"

"Yes, thanks. The weather is sweet, as is the food." Lisa thought she would leave out the new friends she had made. She didn't want her mother worrying any more than she would be already.

"Well, dear, have a good time. You deserve it. We'll see you when you are back in England."

Lisa spoke with her mother for some time. She was grateful that she hadn't said a single negative word about her or this trip, but she was very surprised! She wasn't used to her mother being this nice, and she wondered if she had she hit the eggnog at six in the morning.

As she placed the receiver back in its cradle, she blinked back the tears that were beginning to form. She did not want to start feeling homesick now. It was a bad idea speaking to them on the fourth day of the holiday, usually the day she crumbled on. This was the closest she was going to get to her family this Christmas.

Yesterday Terrance had invited her out with the others, but no firm plans had been made, and she didn't have a phone number for any of them. She no longer wanted her own company. Left alone with her thoughts of how her life was going nowhere, she wanted to be in the company of others, especially as it was Christmas day.

Just as she was thanking the big guy upstairs for not cursing her with too much of a hangover, the phone rang again.

"Hello," Lisa put the receiver to her ear.

"Hey, Lisa." It took her a minute to register the familiar voice on the other end of the phone – the accent with the slight Goan lilt.

"Hey," Lisa said, her voice softening; she couldn't help but smile. It was Terrance. Her thoughts drifted back to the kiss from last night. "How did you get this number?"

"Sonya. I hope you don't mind." There was a cheeky tone in his voice, and she breathed a sigh of relief. If Sonya had spoken to him and given him her number, they were sure to have sorted out any lingering issues between them.

"No, I don't mind," she said, glad that there were obviously no data protection laws that were being adhered to here. The only thing that had put a dampener on that incredible kiss last night was the burden of guilt that came with it, guilt that she might have betrayed Sonya.

"Okay, so I'll be there for about two. You have twenty minutes – because I mean two, not Goa time two which, in case you were wondering, is actually about four."

"For what? It's Christmas! Don't you have Christmas lunch at home with your parents?"

"Yes, I do, and I told my mum that you are all alone for Christmas, and she said I just had to bring you over. She is a bit soft like that."

"Mmm, I don't think …"

"Well, then don't think! I'll see you in twenty." Terrance had disconnected.

Lisa reflected on what had just happened. She couldn't just intrude on some family's Christmas lunch. She had only met him last night. Surely things didn't move so fast in this part of the world. Not even a first date, and she was already meeting the parents. Lisa thought about her options. She opened the curtains and took in the sea view; then she grabbed her towel and headed for the shower.

*

As Terrance introduced Lisa to his family, she felt a slight pang of regret. What would his family think of her? She was sure that this was not appropriate behaviour. She knew how strict Archana and Arjun's parents were, and they had been born and brought up in England. Terrance's family, however, seemed to feel this was completely fine, run-of-the-mill stuff. She hoped that he didn't do this every year with another unsuspecting girl on holiday. Maybe Christmas was not strictly family as it was in England.

When Lisa arrived, she was happy to see that it was a traditional Christmas lunch, minus the cranberry sauce and with a couple of Goan specialities added to the mix, like *soropatel,* a spicy pork curry accompanied by *sannas,* fluffy, white rice pancakes. The food was mouthwateringly tasty, and she couldn't help but take seconds.

She spent most of the time talking to Terrance before the meal was served. He had talked fondly of his aunts and uncles as he pointed them out to her and described their likes and dislikes. Lisa was touched by how family-oriented he was. It seemed to be the way of life in Goa. Kids did not grow up wanting to leave home as soon as they could, and they knew who their uncles and aunts were, no matter how many they had, it seemed.

"Those two kids," he pointed in the distance to two children playing with a litter of pure white kittens on the verandah, "they are Aunty Reshma's kids; they moved to England just a couple of months ago. They are flying back by themselves in a week or so. They are my favourite cousins. They have come a long way in the last couple of months. I am just so proud of them."

"Why did they move?" Lisa asked, curious as to why anyone would want to leave this beautiful country.

"You know what it is like here?" he said pushing a strand of her brown hair behind her hair. "No, actually, I suppose you don't. It is pretty hard to earn enough here to travel or give your kids opportunities. Reshma is good like that; she wants to give her kids the best opportunities she can. In England, they will have a better chance to make something of themselves than here."

Lisa could see his point, of course. Goa was beautiful, but she presumed opportunities were limited, as they were in most places where tourism was the main line of work. It would have been tough for the kids; she knew how difficult it was for children adjusting to a new school, let alone a new country. She could see why Terrance was so proud of them.

His family was so genuine and welcoming. There must have been at least ten of them, uncles and aunts and at least three or four children chasing each other around the garden. She couldn't tell them apart. Reshma had done a splendid job of painting their faces: the boys were tigers and the girls butterflies.

Terrance's house was fairly large and was a pale yellow. The main part of the house had large archways leading to spacious family rooms filled with dark teak wood cabinets and having stone floors. Most of the rooms had verandahs, with attractive railings painted white. The window shutters were lined with translucent shells, which let a glimmer of light through from the midday sun. She felt privileged to see the inside of such a beautiful home. She couldn't quite place in which part of Goa she was. Their journey from the hotel had taken a good half hour, up hills and through winding roads. Terrance had mentioned the name of the village, but it now escaped her, the name being too unfamiliar to her. It was something the old Lisa would have scribbled down, making sure she did not forget it, but the new Lisa was far too carefree. She felt better for this change in her personality. How impressed would Suzanne be with her now? She congratulated herself on this little triumph.

"It's an old Portuguese house," Terrance's mother said, handing Lisa a coffee on the verandah after their lunch. She had seated herself on a wooden rocking chair, the seat of which looked as if it had moulded to her shape. Terrance was her only child, and she doted on him. She was a short, stout lady with thick black hair and round glasses. She wore a satin lilac dress that emphasized her round figure.

"It's beautiful," Lisa said. She had been drawn into his family, and they had made her feel so welcome, as if she belonged. She couldn't quite believe that she had only met him yesterday.

"Dear, it was nice meeting you. Now, I don't mean to be rude, but you must excuse me. I have to head for my afternoon siesta, or I will never make it to the dance tonight. Please make yourself at home."

Lisa perched herself on an old grandfather chair and sipped her hot, black coffee. The chair was a peculiar shape, with extremely long arms and a low back. She had seen one once before in a magazine; you were supposed to rest your legs on the long arms, making it quite comfortable, she assumed.

"Hey, when you finish that, let's go for a drive. Let me show you a few places off the tourist track that I think you may be interested in." Terrance had re-emerged from inside the house.

"Thank you – that would be nice," she said, calling him over to her with her eyes.

He perched on one of the long arms of the chair. "Good; we won't be going out till late tonight. Some people will have family over for dinner, so we

Marissa de Luna

will not all meet up till later when the families have dispersed, but I would like to take you out. Just us two."
"Wow, after all that food at lunch, and this heat. I don't think I could manage another whole meal."

Terrance laughed "You eat so little. A light bite? Surely you can manage that. I guarantee the company will be good." He slipped his arm around her waist and pulled her close to him.

"Okay, you've convinced me," she said, enjoying this attention he was paying her. "I'll need to go back to the hotel and change, though." She pulled away, worried that a member of his family would see her and think she was being disrespectful in their house. She didn't quite know what the protocol was here.

"Yeah, I can take you back to change," he said, scanning her body with his eyes. He winked at her.

There was something about Terrance that drew her towards him. He was kind, and he was more of a gentleman than anyone she had ever been out with before. If she had not been burnt so many times, she would have said he was perfect, but her bruised heart had made her wary of men. Although she had instantly found a fault – they would never be able to have a relationship, as they would never be in the same country.

Terrance drove her around different parts of Goa, stopping at various beaches and at several beautiful viewpoints. He took her to the Fort Aguada, where the sun was about to set. They snuggled together on the beach and watched the orange yolk of the sun disappear into the sea before Terrance dropped her back to her hotel.

"I'll pick you up in an hour," he said as he leaned over to kiss her. It wasn't just because she was drunk that the kiss was so amazing. This was real.

Lisa skipped back to her room; for the first time in a long while, she was elated. She felt as if she'd fallen in love in less than forty-eight hours. She waved hello to Carl at the hospitality desk and padded over to enquire about Sonya. She knew that she would have to face her sooner or later, and she had hoped it would be sooner.

"Hi Carl; where is Sonya?"

"Hi, Lisa." His voice had lost the friendly tone it had had before. "Sonya is off until first January." He was short, but he had a caring look in his eye, Lisa noticed. The guilty feelings returned to her. Carl and Sonya were clearly good friends, and he must have seen Terrance kiss her as she got out of the car. Lisa did not know what to say.

"Well, say hi to her for me. Will she be coming out with us tonight?"

"I guess. I'll tell her you said hi."

"Thanks." Lisa turned to walk away, and as she did so, she was sure she heard Carl mumble under his breath to be careful. She didn't want to hear it. Lisa carried on walking towards her room.

10

Mia dug her spoon into the soft, white flesh of the custard apple. She tasted the sweetness of the fruit, being careful not to swallow any of its jet-black seeds. She had grown addicted to this fruit since she had moved here six months ago. The bumpy green-and-black exterior, so fragile and so easily broken, encased something most delicious.

She knew that she had been lucky to get this assignment, but of course, it was not just luck. It was determination on her part and hard work, and then, of course, there was Simon. She had known that he was married and that he had a child only a few months old. But he had pursued her for months. She had not even wanted him at first, but his broad masculine shoulders, his soft-spoken manner, and most importantly, his persistence, had eventually won her over. It had been a brief affair. As quickly as he had fallen for her, he soon grew tired of her. Mia did not mind. He was not even her type, but it passed the time in a world where she felt she did not belong. When he'd broken up with her, she'd been more than happy to walk away and not look back – but now this had cropped up, and blackmail was her only ticket out.

It was not that she was not qualified. In fact, she was more than qualified for the position. She had the added bonus of being fluent in Hindi. She spoke it like a native, although you would never guess by looking at her. Her stepfather had been from Calcutta, and as a child, she had been obsessed with India. By the time she was in high school, she knew more about the country than most Indians. College and boys had taken over after that, and her passion had subdued, instead taken over by cheap marijuana and vodka.

She had played her role very well, and did not flinch even when she heard the comments from groups of teenage boys who sat outside Dempo college or Miramar beach, where they gathered in break times and in the evenings. They would talk about her loudly in Hindi, about her smooth skin and her long legs, her clothes and her hair. She enjoyed knowing that she could understand what they were saying and that they would never expect her to. This talent had its disadvantages, but it most certainly had made her life easier, too.

So far, she had accomplished what she had set out to do. She had infiltrated the group, and like most groups she had worked with, she knew that behind the perfect exterior lay a labyrinth of complexities. She had started, as her training had taught her, with the weakest link. Simon might not have been the best lover, but he had taught her how to do her job with such skill and perfection that she was rarely uncovered.

She had been providing Simon with weekly updates. These had been a requirement of her position, and she always had new information to tell him. Lately, however, these weekly updates had turned into monthly updates, with less and less information to pass on. She knew she would have to provide some answers soon.

She had recently taken a lover, someone who she thought would prove useful. Instead, this had just created a further problem to her situation. The initial weeks had been full of lust and passion, a great tool by which to gather information, but the relationship had affected her more than she expected. The feelings she had were much stronger than she had ever had with anyone before, and as the weeks went by, a stronger bond was forming. This scared her. She was afraid she was losing control, afraid she was falling in love. She was not ready for a relationship like this – and not with the enemy! But that was love – it was never expected. It just happened, and then, like most beautiful things, it changed the way you felt and the things you did.

Mia discarded the casing of the eaten custard apple and took another from the six that were on the hotel dresser. She gently broke into it, her red fingernails piercing its skin. She had enjoyed the last six months, settling in Goa, and the lifestyle that accompanied it: the afternoon siestas, the richly spiced, fragrant food, and the friendly people. She did not have many friends, but then she needed to keep a low profile, which was difficult given that her looks instantly set her apart. Goa was a small place, and gossip spread like wildfire. She was better off not involving herself in a friendship group in a country where *Desperate Housewives* was more reality than fiction.

She had however, found solace and comfort in the arms of her lover. She had located a two-storey house with a small courtyard in Povorim, near the Mandovi River, away from the hustle of Panjim. The property had a cheap rent, and the landlord was keen to let it out quickly due to an incident that had happened with the previous tenant. The house was most beautiful at dawn, when the sun was breaking through the cloud and a thin mist of fog hovered above the river. She felt serene as she watched the fishermen in their trawlers heading out to sea. The location was perfect, and the property housed a curious mix of mismatched wooden furniture. Old green, black, and white Portuguese tiles lined the floors. Mirrors hung everywhere, some with cracks, some without, mixed in with an old stove and a well in the middle of the courtyard, amidst the pink bougainvillea.

Mia would go to the fish market every other day, ensuring that she always had fresh food. Both her mother and stepfather had taught her how to buy fish when she was a child; she could judge just how fresh a fish was by looking at how red its gills were and ensuring the eyes were not glassy. The fisherwomen had tried to overcharge her when she first started visiting the market, her white skin obviously flagging her naivety of the country. She had given them a wry smile and haggled fluently in Hindi. How startled they had been when she'd spoken with such grace in their native tongue; what respect she'd commanded! They'd wanted to know her roots, where she had been in India, and what she had seen. Most importantly, they'd shared their cooking tips and secret recipes with her, so that now her cooking rivalled that of some of the best chefs in Goa.

From the minute Mia had stepped off that plane at Dabolim, she knew that she had come home. Whilst she was growing up, she'd never quite known where she belonged. They had moved around so much, first with her father and then with her stepfather. She had the blood of four cultures running through her veins, and she had never before been at ease as she was in Goa. Finally she had found her home.

She was now determined to carve out a life for herself here, even if it did mean making some cutbacks on the lavish lifestyle she was used to living on her current wage. She would no longer be able to treat her lover to weekends away at the Taj or the Leela.

Mia discarded her second custard apple and lay back on the cool, white sheets of a freshly made bed. Her lover would be here soon, and she would need to decide. She had been given a year as a maximum timescale to accomplish what she needed to do here. It was not a generous time frame, but results were expected from her. And, for the first time in her career, she had begun to lie, being creative to disguise her relationship with one of the group members. She needed more time, and she needed to stall, but she knew she could not continue this way. Her lover's proposal had come at just the right time. She needed to make a decision, and quickly, before she had to go back.

11

Sonya was livid. She couldn't believe his audacity! Terrance had called her for Lisa's number, and worse still, she couldn't quite believe she had given it to him. But then, it was not a difficult number to obtain, and she didn't want to seem so possessive, considering they were not currently dating. Things had been a bit rocky over the last year, and after last night, they were definitely more off than on.

At least this little indiscretion of Terrance's would disappear after two weeks, Sonya thought as she lowered herself into the steaming hot bath. Something by Whitney Houston was playing on the radio. After all, it was her own fault; *she had* made the introductions. She just never would have guessed that Terrance would take a liking to Lisa, but he had.

She had noticed the way that he looked at her last night over dinner, with his big puppy-dog eyes. He was irresistible when he was like that. She could hardly blame Lisa, so confused and desperate to be loved. She would have fallen for anything. Sonya should have predicted it happening. Terrance had said that he wanted her number to arrange tonight with her, but Sonya was no fool. She had asked him what his real intentions were.

"She is only here for two weeks. As you said, she may be useful," he replied to her barrage of questions. "Do you have a problem with that?"

How silly she was to feel jealous. Of course Terrance would use Lisa, just as she had suggested. It would be very lucrative, but sometimes playing with fire meant that you could get burned. It had been done before, a couple of times, and it was risky but worth it. She just hoped Terrance wasn't trying to dupe her in the process. Sonya relaxed. He would never do that, and if he did, she would just have to come up with another plan. This thought calmed her. Lifting herself out of the bath, she wrapped herself in a soft, white towel and padded over to her bedroom to get ready for the night.

*

Sonya was fixing her gold studs in her ears just as Sanjay and Ayesha pulled up outside her house. She could see the car through her bedroom window. She heard the horn of Sanjay's car blaring outside as she kissed her parents goodbye and headed out.

"So, Sonya, what is the deal, yaar, with that Lisa girl and Terrance? Are you annoyed? I thought she was your friend, *no*?" Ayesha was always good at making Sonya feel bad about her lack of control over Terrance. Sonya looked over at Sanjay; he was quiet, but if Terrance had told him anything, it would have gotten back to her through Ayesha; she was certain of that. Nevertheless, she didn't want Ayesha to make her feel any worse about the budding relationship between Terrance and Lisa. Regardless of Terrance's true intentions, whatever he did, it hurt.

"Terrance and me are over; you know that, Ayesha," Sonya said. Saving face was a regular necessity in Goa. Sanjay glanced at her through the rear-view mirror, giving her a knowing look. This had happened before, and the conversation was merely a formality.

"Oh, really; I thought you two were still an item. You are always making and breaking up. I bet you can't even remember why you broke up the last time, *no*?"

"You are right, but maybe this time it is over for good."

"Yaar, you are better off without him – no, Sanjay?"

"Maybe we can find you some traveller tonight, eh, Sonya?" Sanjay replied, smirking slightly.

"Thank you, Sanjay," Sonya's reply was laced with sarcasm. She was not in the mood for such comments from her so-called friends. They arrived at the beach shack just as Terrance and Lisa pulled up. Sanjay got a round of beers.
"Hey, guys," Sanjay said.

"So, the two lovebirds have arrived together," Teresa whispered into Sonya's ear. Sonya ignored her. She didn't want to fan the flames. Her friends were clearly enjoying her downfall, and this relationship Terrance was starting would be the talk of the town. Sonya decided to quash her humiliation as soon as possible. She would make a show of friendship with Lisa.

"Hi, Lisa," she said brightly.

"Hi, Sonya. Carl said that you wouldn't be back at the hotel till January. The Grove will be dull; who will I talk to now?" Lisa tried to sound upbeat. She could see that Sonya was not being herself, although she had made a big effort tonight and looked stunning in all black with an oversized gold clutch to match her earrings. Lisa felt a little sad that they would not be friends, but as bad as she felt, the intimate dinner she had just had with Terrance compensated her for the loss of friendship.

"Yes, I'll miss our little chats, Lisa, but you are here till what date?"

"Till the third of January."

"Oh, not long. Have you done your souvenir shopping?"

"No, not yet."

Sonya swallowed her pride and spoke. "Well, don't. Not until Terrance takes you to the Saturday night bazaar. There is so much to buy there. Maybe we can make an evening of it before you leave, no, Terrance?" Sonya put her arm on his shoulder. She forced the words out. She wanted him, and most importantly, the others to see that she was fine with this, although deep down she was seething.

The six of them sat on brightly coloured cushions that littered the floor of the beach shack, watching the lights glimmer in the dark of the night. Sanjay, Ayesha, and Teresa soon dispersed along the beach, joining the crowd that had created a makeshift dance floor on the seafront, leaving Sonya with Terrance and Lisa.

*

"How are you going to tell her? You *are* going to tell her, Terrance?" Sonya said in a hushed voice.

"Why are you so worried?" He was growing agitated. "I will convince her. Don't take so much tension, Sonya, you will—"

"Convince whom of what?" Lisa interrupted their conversation. She noticed Sonya was holding Terrance's hand and felt a pang of jealousy. It had only been a few days, but her feelings were so strong. She had never felt this way before, and in that instant, she felt determined to hang on to him. Anger for Sonya suddenly began to seep inside her; it was a feeling she had never felt before. She finally understood the saying that some things are worth fighting for. She was certain that Terrance felt the same way about her; she could feel the intensity in his eyes when he looked at her.

Terrance swiftly moved his hand away from Sonya and smiled at Lisa. She immediately softened, being unable to resist him. She reminded herself that she was in India, after all, where people were much more physically expressive than in England. She recalled seeing local men strolling along the beach holding hands like lovers, but clearly just friends, and she quickly excused their behaviour, her anger dissolving as quickly as it had risen.

"I was just telling Sonya that I am going to try to convince you to stay for a while longer," he said, his tone brightening. Lisa's heart skipped a beat. Her head told her not to believe him, but her heart desperately wanted to. It had only been a few days. Staying in Goa a little bit longer hadn't even crossed her mind. Lisa thought she would play it cool, although she was dying of excitement inside.

Reality of her life in England took over. "Sorry to disappoint; I have classes to get back to on the fourth," she said nonchalantly. An uncomfortable silence ensued, and Sonya looked uneasy. Lisa tried to break the tension that was rapidly forming between this threesome. "Listen, I was thinking I would have an early night, so I can do some sunbathing tomorrow," she said. It was an uncomfortable scenario to have a conversation like this with Terrance in front of Sonya, who was sitting between them like a chaperone, quite plausibly with ulterior motives.
"I'll drop you," Terrance said, rising to his feet rather swiftly. "Let me go and tell the others." He squeezed her arm and then left her alone with

Sonya. In that moment, Lisa found courage, with the help of the beer she had consumed earlier in the evening, and decided to broach the subject about Terrance. She couldn't shake from her mind the sour expression Sonya had had on her face when she had interrupted her conversation just a few minutes ago.

Lisa braced herself – she hated confrontation. She briefly tried to talk herself out of what she was about to say, but then she knew that this holiday was about making her own decisions and sticking to them. "Are you okay with me? I mean, did you and Terrance have a thing? I should have said something earlier. I just presumed that if you gave Terrance my number everything was okay between you. It just seems that there was something, and I get a slight feeling that I have unintentionally stepped on your toes." Lisa stopped herself from saying everything that she wanted to. She was babbling, nervous of what Sonya would say. She had asked some legitimate questions, and if Sonya told her to back off from Terrance, she would have to, *wouldn't she?* It would ruin what she had with Terrance, and the thought of that sent a shiver down her spine.

Sonya bit her lip as she contemplated her next words. She had a message to convey, but she needed to be nice. Her dark eyes shone in the moonlight, masking her jealousy. She spoke. "It's kind of you to ask; not many girls would," she said, looking at Lisa directly. "Earlier this year, Terrance and I had a bit of a thing. We were very serious a long time ago, but that's over now, and despite the occasional lapses, we are still good friends. It's just that I don't want to see him get hurt, that's all." Sonya took a swig of beer. Her voice was firm. "Be careful with him. You have been here for a short time, and you will be leaving soon. This is a holiday fling; don't make it more than it is."

Her last comment exposed her venom, and it stung. Sonya noted Lisa's reaction and inwardly smiled. She needed to correct herself, play her part. "I mean, where will it end up? You will leave soon to go back home, and it will leave him heartbroken. I know what it can be like. Tourists come and go all the time, and the people who live in holiday destinations, like Goa, are the ones who always get left behind. Sonya placed her hand on Lisa's back to reassure her. She knew her work here was done; she had executed her part of the plan perfectly. She was just annoyed that Terrance was being so stubborn and at the last minute had decided to keep their deal from Lisa rather than letting her in on it. That had always been part of the plan; it had worked before that way – why was he changing the goalposts now? This way, she knew, it would be much more of a risk, it was her responsibility to make sure it all ran smoothly and she was quietly confident that it would. She could never trust a man entirely, and he had proved it by pulling this little stunt on her just now. With a man, there was always a danger of mistakes being made. From now on, she would have to ensure she had more control.

Sonya's words had struck a chord with Lisa, because she had not thought about what would happen when she left. Maybe Sonya was right. Maybe it was only a holiday fling, but the thought of this upset her, which made her realize that she was in deeper than she knew. She took a moment to think about this relationship, if that's what she could call it. To Lisa it didn't feel like a holiday fling, but then again, she had never had a holiday fling to compare it to. Her conversation with Sonya had made her look into the future. She had avoided the topic in the car with Terrance, when he'd dropped her back to the hotel, but now, alone with her thoughts, she asked herself if she would be able to live in Goa or if Terrance would move to England. Would Terrance even want to take it that far? Or was it just a two-week romance and she the unsuspecting holidaymaker that he had wanted – someone who was guaranteed to disappear shortly? Suzanne would say that she was analysing it too much and thinking way too far ahead of herself, but she was scared that she would never see Terrance again. She had to find a way to make sure she did.

12

Lisa knew that part of her infatuation with Terrance was due to her rebounding from Chris. She would never have admitted this to anyone, but she was scared of being alone, worried that soon she would end up just settling for anyone, someone she didn't really love. An image of Terrance formed in her mind. No matter how hard she pushed her feelings away, there was something about him that held her captive.

She sat on the edge of her bed, absent-mindedly rubbing suntan lotion onto her arms. She only had a week left in Goa, and if she carried on the way she had been– up all night and asleep all day – then she would never get an enviable sun-kissed tan. She wanted physical evidence that she been on holiday, a glow that her colleagues in the staff room, desperate for a bit of escapism themselves, would notice, leading them to ask her if she had been somewhere exotic. Sitting there as the lotion absorbed into her skin, she was caught in a daydream. *How did Terrance make her feel so special?* He had treated her as no other man had done before – buying her flowers, showering her with affection – and even his family had welcomed her with open arms. More than anything, he made her feel safe and protected. She knew when she was with him that no harm would come to her. Lisa stood up, waking herself from this daze. She must try to be more sensible.

She had only managed one day of exploring Goa. She had wanted to discover some more. She wanted to lose herself in the Indian culture and make the most of being alone, doing things that only she wanted to do, with no one else's needs and wants to accommodate. It was, after all, her first holiday alone, and she wanted to take advantage of it. She decided to take Archana's advice: "Get lost," she had said. "Lose yourself in Goa. It is easy enough to do that there, and if you really get lost, ask the nearest person to you. Over there, nobody has that stiff upper lip that we are so famous for here. You ask someone in Oxford how to get to the Ashmolean, and they look at you as if you've asked them for blood!" she had exclaimed, and she'd been right. The British were far too busy going somewhere or doing something to concern themselves with directions for mere tourists.

She slung her messenger over her shoulder and shoved a bottle of Himalayan water and her guidebook into it. She walked down the drive from the lobby, away from the protection of the hotel, and into the street outside that housed coconut leaf thatched houses, stray dogs, and hawkers. She hailed a rickshaw and unsuccessfully tried to haggle for a cheaper fare to Panjim, the capital of Goa. It was a hot day, and she was grateful that she had worn shorts, but now her thighs were sticking to the red pleather seats of the autorickshaw. The driver averted collision with high-speed buses that were dangerously full and leaning to one side; he skirted past cattle and dogs who believed that they were the sole owners of the Indian roads. She noticed a picture of the elephant-headed god, Ganesh, stuck to the steering wheel and another picture that looked like a Bollywood star hanging in the cockpit of the rickshaw. In his rear-view mirror, the driver saw her look at the picture, and he pulled himself up so that she could see his face in the mirror. He smiled at her.

"Shah Rukh Khan," he said with a south Indian drawl. "Everybody's favourite, number-one Bollywood star." The driver looked up at the picture and touched it with his hand, taking his eyes off the road – in the process almost killing a squealing pig running through the traffic.

"Yes," she agreed without thinking, trying to be polite, although she could see some charisma in the Bollywood actor's eyes.

"Here you are, madam" he said fifteen minutes later. The hotel said that the journey would take about half an hour, and as she got out of the rickshaw, she was grateful to be alive. When she stepped out into the dusty promenade in Panjim, she could see the bluey-green hue of the Mandovi River.

"Over there, madam." The rickshaw driver pointed across the road to a bustling market. She had asked the driver to take her to the food market in Panjim, where her guidebook suggested would be a good place to start exploring the capital. She thanked him as he twisted the handles on the autorickshaw, revved the engine, and hurtled towards the tourists who were standing in their visors, ten metres down the street, waving him down.

From where Lisa was standing, she could see the activity of the market already. It was a busy place, with the vibrancy of juicy red tomatoes, yellow sweet limes, and green watermelons stacked high into pyramids and balancing precariously on little carts. Ladies sat protectively cross-legged behind their produce, with their saris hitched up and damp tea towels laid flat on their heads, trying to keep cool in the mid-morning sun. They shooed away the cats and swatted at the flies that were scavenging for pieces of unattended food, whilst they shouted out their offers at passers-by as market traders do across the world.

She wandered through the entrance, passing a man with an unusual looking contraption. He was selling juices in various colours. He offered her a glass of a bright pink liquid, which she could only assume was watermelon. She politely declined. She was parched, and a juice would have been a welcome relief, but her bottled water would have to do for now. The vendor wore a patch over one eye and a very grubby looking shirt with large horizontal stripes. She knew she was being foolish, and her stomach would be able to take it, but she also knew that her mind definitely couldn't, and she would end up making herself sick. She smiled politely and walked past him into the thick of the market.

Whole assortments of goods were for sale in the market. Several children were there with their fathers, picking out fluffy yellow chicks, which fit neatly into the palms of their hands, to take home as pets. There were shellfish – she saw mounds of prawns so fresh they were jumping out of the woven baskets that displayed them. There were piles of glimmering silver fish in all shapes and sizes: mackerel and pomfret and kingfish were just a few names she heard the fisherwomen shouting. She was amazed at how they scooped up handfuls of fish, wrapping them neatly in newspaper and tying them with string before they placed them in the bags of their customers. Everyone seemed to be an expert in haggling; even a few white faces that Lisa could see seemed to have mastered it from the locals themselves. *Better than a buy-one-get-one-free offer from Sainsbury's*, she thought as she strolled through.

"You are staying at the Coconut Grove," a voice behind her said.

Lisa turned; despite her sunglasses, the sun was so bright she was still squinting. "Yes," she said hesitantly, not knowing how the man in front of her knew this and what exactly he was going to do with this information. A young man stood before her, smiling, in a blue-and-red striped T-shirt and brown trousers. It took her a second, but she then recognized the face that was beaming at her as that of Carl, who worked at the hotel.

"Hi, Carl." she said, taking off her sunglasses to greet him and tilting her head ever so slightly to avoid the glare from the sun.

"You taking in some Goan sights?" he asked as they walked through the market, past the fragrant flower stalls, towards the other side of the vendors.

"Yes, I've been so busy lately. You know, with Terrance," she added cautiously remembering the hostility in his voice the last time he he spoke with her "I've hardly managed to see anything at all, and I go back in a week. I want to see and do as much as I can now."

"Yes, you have been busy," he said. She could sense that he was being protective over Sonya and understandably so. In fact, if it had been her and Suzanne, she would have completely blanked the other woman. Lisa though it best to steer clear of talking about her new relationship.

Carl, however, had something to say. "You should be careful, you know, Lisa. A holiday fling is one thing, but anything more could be disastrous. I have seen it happen time and time again, and trust me, some people are meant to be together; some are not." She wasn't sure what he was trying to say, but assumed that he meant that Sonya and Terrance would be together and that she was an outsider who would never fit in. It was the second time in twenty-four hours that her new relationship had been defined as a holiday romance. She felt uncomfortable, and she wished that he would leave. She was just about to show the new side of her personality and tell him to do so, when he suddenly smiled. His voice brightened, and he said, "That's all I wanted to say, just so you know. If everything goes sour, don't say I didn't warn you. I like you, Lisa, and Sonya is my friend. You have to understand that. You are innocent, even if you think you are not, and trust me, you will get trampled on in this game. I am rarely wrong."

Marissa de Luna

Lisa stopped and took a step back, unsure what to say next, but Carl didn't stop; he leaned forward and pinched her cheek.

"Now, enough about that, sweetie. I'll tell you what. I have the morning off – let me show you what this little gem of a state has to offer." He winked at her. Carl glanced at his watch. Sensing her apprehension, he said, "Look, I just wanted to make sure you had your eyes open, that's all." Lisa briefly considered his offer. She wasn't quite sure why he would want to show her around, especially as he was Sonya's friend. She wondered how somebody could be so dark one minute and then so cheery all of a sudden. But he seemed so genuine and harmless enough. Taking risks was a new thing for Lisa, and so far she had met Terrance this way, so she decided to take Carl up on his offer. Learn from a local – you couldn't get better than that, surely.

As they resumed their walk through the market, Carl spoke. "Firstly, this is a *chikoo*," he said, picking up a round, brown piece of fruit from a vendor at the edge of the market. He handed five rupees to the uncomfortable-looking woman, who sat unsmiling as a Buddha behind her fruit. She had not even mentioned a price, but when she saw the five-rupee note, she greedily grabbed it, her expression unchanged, and shoved it into her bra to keep it safe.

"Here," he said, handing the *chikoo* to Lisa. "Put it in your bag, and try it later. It's sweet; it tastes sweet, like a …" he stopped walking and looked deep in thought. "No," he said, "I cannot describe it. It tastes like a *chikoo*."

Carl walked with her along the river to the sea, towards Miramar beach. They stopped at a bright blue *gado* that had a large sign hanging on it, saying "Bombay Bhel." He insisted that she try a pani puri. He held up a bite-size puri, which was a crispy dome-shaped shell filled with a mixture of water, masala, tamarind, chilli, chickpeas, and onions. It had a beautiful aroma, and Lisa was tempted, but her old demons held her back. Carl noticed her hesitation, as she quickly assessed the hygiene.
"It won't kill you, yaar. If you want to experience the true identity of Goa, you have to try the food, the street food. It is what Goans live for. They live to eat – never, ever eat to live. Soropatel, sannas, sausage pilau, fish curry, cutlets, bhelpuri, pani puri. This is what Goa is about, the food,"

he said, devouring the little puri he had held up for her. The vendor stood quietly behind his bright blue cart; he had a pile of puris behind a glass wall that showed his wares. The hawker smiled at her, and she knew he had understood what Carl had said. She was aware that most people in Goa understood some English; all the tourism had made sure of that. She felt embarrassed. She was in another country, and she needed to experience it all. Carl picked up another puri from the plate and held it up to her face.

"Here, take it. Look, I have brought you to the best and most hygienic pani puri wallah in the whole of Miramar Beach." The vendor smiled, displaying his surprisingly white teeth.

Lisa looked around. There were at least twenty other vendors standing behind similar carts with different names. There were also other hawkers selling balloons and battery-operated monkeys with long brown bodies and arms and bright-red lips, which looked as if they would fall apart if you touched them.

Women in saris chased after their children along the beachfront, laughing into the sea breeze. It was beautiful, and Carl was right – she needed to throw caution to the wind and live a little. She took the pani puri from him, careful not to spill any of its contents, and carefully placed it on her tongue. As she bit into the crispy shell, she experienced an explosion of flavour on her taste buds. The heat of the chilli, the sour tamarind, and the calm of the chickpeas – it worked beautifully, and she couldn't help but have another. Together she and Carl finished the plate.

"Delicious," she said. "It is like an amuse-bouche."

"Yaar, yaar, whatever that is. It is delicious, *na*? Wait and see what I am thinking for lunch," he said. With a huge smirk across his face, he hailed an autorickshaw and gave the driver directions where to go.

They stepped out of the rickshaw outside the Hotel Mandovi.

"This hotel has been here for years. It's like an institution, but it is not where we will take lunch," Carl said, pointing up to the big sign on top of the hotel that read "Hotel Mandovi." A doorman stood anticipating their entrance. As they walked past, Lisa looked up; she could see diners on the shaded balcony sipping cool lime-juice sodas, and she felt her dry throat. She was thirsty.

They looked in the shops, and Lisa was impressed with the vast selection of stores. She picked up some Levi's jeans for herself at a fraction of the cost in England and some Lacoste T-shirts for her brother.

"My mother should come to Goa" she said flippantly to Carl as she examined a pair of Nike trainers. "She still thinks it's an undeveloped country, India."

Carl took the trainer from her, turning it over and poking at the sole. "Sometimes I wish it was still undeveloped, untouched. We are overrun with tourists. Most of them live here now. We are losing our identity, slowly, but it is happening. Soon there will be more Maggi Noodle wallahs than bhelpuri wallahs, and then where would we be?" He sighed deeply, and Lisa could see Carl's disappointment with this influx of tourism in his homeland. It was sad, but it was happening everywhere. Even in England people were getting fed up with new influxes from other nations. It's human nature, she concluded. She tried to put a positive spin on it.

"I am sure tourists have boosted the economy, though. Job creation and all that malarkey," she said cheerily. She was growing a soft spot for Carl. He was so genuine, and his feelings were so raw. He spoke from the heart, like a child suddenly finding out that the world is not what it seems. She wanted to protect him. She put the trainer back on its shelf as Carl opened the glass door, letting the heat from the outside penetrate the coolness of the air-conditioned shop.

"I'm sure," he said. "I'm sure."

Later that morning, Carl took her through the winding hills of Althino, where he pointed out the Portuguese architecture displayed in the houses that lined the streets. The Portuguese had ruled over India for over four hundred years, and their influence was everywhere: in the food, in the architecture; some Goans even spoke fluent Portuguese and conversed freely in this language with one another. She was in awe of the huge houses, with their spacious rooms and verandahs, where three generations sat on rocking chairs watching the world go by and discussing the neighbourhood gossip. *It is what makes Goa,* she thought, *the rich mix of the east and west.*

It was mid afternoon, and they had still not stopped for lunch. She could hear her stomach rumbling. The combination of the heat and the walking had tired her, and she needed to sit down with a cooling drink. Carl had been an excellent guide. He had told her so many interesting facts about the smallest state in India.

By the time they had reached the restaurant, Lisa was famished and nearing dehydration. She was glad that Carl had not even waited to see a menu. He had taken the liberty to order for them both.

"This place, it does the best *Chicken Cafreal* in Goa, for sure, yaar." He had ordered them both a cold, sweet lassi, which arrived in a couple of minutes. Lisa took a large gulp without even thinking of any bacteria that it could be harbouring.

"Mmm, this is good," she exclaimed. It was slipping down easily, and it cooled her, increasing her already ravenous appetite.

"It is made from yogurt, guaranteed to replace your sugars and salts after walking in the hot sun. Your body must not be used to that, and I don't want you to get a sunstroke." He ordered a jug of water. "Just in case," he said. "This chicken dish is hot."

By the time the food arrived, her mouth was watering. The bhaji puri arrived in a metal bowl and tasted delicious. It was a delectable mix of lightly spiced potatoes and large puris, which were made from dough and ghee. It was so tasty that Lisa had seconds, ignoring the double helping of carbohydrates she was consuming, knowing it was working its way straight to her hips. After all, she was on holiday.

The *Chicken Cafreal* followed, in a large earthenware pot, accompanied by a large bowl of fluffy white basmati rice. Lisa helped herself to a couple of pieces, as she was still hungry. Everybody in the restaurant seemed to have ordered the same. She smiled as she took her first bite of the pungent chicken.

The flavors danced on her tongue, awakening all her taste buds. It was slightly similar to a Portuguese piri-piri style chicken she had eaten years ago when she'd gone to Faro for a week one summer. But this had a violent kick to it – it was so full of flavor.

The first piece had burned her tongue, but she could not help but take another.

"Well done! Most tourists stop at the first," Carl said, looking towards a large man in the corner of the room who wore socks with his sandals and a bum bag around his waist. He was dabbing his face furiously as sweat poured down from his bald head. He looked defeated.

"What's in it?" she asked Carl, who was taking another piece of chicken onto his plate as he ordered another jug of water. "I know it has chillies, lots of chillies," she said, taking a large sip of her second lassi.

"Red chillies, green chillies," Carl said

"And garlic," she added.

"Try, at least fifty cloves of garlic, Lisa, minimum!"

Lisa raised her eyebrows. "Wow! No one will want to come near us today, Carl, eh?"

Carl ignored her last remark and continued, "Ginger, lemon, salt, pepper, some masala, I suppose. If my mother knew I was eating here, she would kill me, yaar. It would be like I had betrayed her. She makes a good *Cafreal*, but not as good as this one." As he said this, he made the sign of the cross. They laughed in unison.

After their meal, Carl left. She was surprised when she felt slightly disappointed that he had to go. She had had such an enjoyable day with him. He was so endearing, and she had really enjoyed his company. She was beginning to realize that it was in Goans' nature to be friendly. No one was ever in a rush; everyone always had time or made time for other people. They were happy to take people under their wings, no matter who they were, and make them feel welcome in their country.

As Lisa sat in the back seat of a taxi heading back to the Coconut Grove, she envied the Goan people their carefree ways and laid-back lifestyle. She almost wished she lived here.

*

Lisa returned to her room later that afternoon exhausted from the walking in the hot sun. Her mind drifted back to Sonya and Terrance and what Carl had said to her earlier that day. She had not seen Sonya since Christmas day, and it was a welcome relief after their last conversation. There was something in Sonya's tone that had made her feel uneasy and set her on edge. Today, after wandering around the streets of Goa with Carl, she had looked at her relationship with Terrance with fresh eyes. She rolled around the brown fruit that Carl had given her earlier that day, and she decided there and then to treat her relationship with Terrance as a holiday romance, which right now seemed exactly what it was. Carl had said it as well, and she decided to accept what Sonya had said that evening on the beach. Deep down, no matter how much she tried to quash it, she had a nagging feeling that there was something more to their relationship, especially after the way Terrance had held Sonya's hand that night. He had had a look in his eye that Lisa could not place. Although she tried to deny her true feelings, life would not let her lie to herself for very long. Even though her head said she would forget him, the minute she heard his voice her heart refused to believe it.

Not long after Lisa had made her decision, Terrance had called her to tell her that they were all planning to go to the Saturday night bazaar, and he would pick her up at seven. Almost instantaneously her heart gave way, and despite berating herself for being so foolish in love, she secretly enjoyed the feeling that accompanied those initial days of being in a new relationship: the butterflies in her stomach, her racing heart, the smile that reached her lips every time the phone rang. She had heard good reports about the night bazaar. Her guidebook confirmed what Teresa had said, that it was a must-visit shopping attraction. Over the last few days, as Sonya had not been around, Lisa had grown quite close to Teresa, who had shed her initial indifference and realized they had quite a bit in common. At first Teresa had found Lisa difficult to understand, her accent being too strong for her to grasp all she was saying, but she was glad of the company, someone new to talk to other than Ayesha and Sonya.

It was a short drive to Arpora, and Terrance dropped them off outside the market while he went in search of a space in the makeshift car park in a nearby field. As soon as Lisa stepped out of the car, she felt the electric atmosphere. She could hear the monotonous thud of acid music coming from deep within the market. The air was sweet, a heady mix of jasmine, incense, and marijuana. Hippies with bleached dreadlocks and wearing low-slung harem pants showed off their slender, tanned figures and new tattoos. They arrived on bikes, churning up clouds of red dust that Lisa was growing quite familiar with. It had stained the bottoms of her jeans and trousers. She knew the stains would never come out. Local Goan families arrived, precariously balanced on scooters. Lisa marvelled at how four people fit onto something that was designed for two. They made it look effortless. A lady with a peach-coloured sari gracefully stepped off the two-wheeler, with a baby in one hand and a seven-year-old on the other and waited whilst her husband parked the scooter. Young groups of girls and boys in jeans and slogan T-shirts gathered at the entrance, talking and laughing.

"Leesha, if you like something, ask me, na? I know how to bargain with these people. They will see your face and hear your accent, and the price will shoot up." Ayesha, who had at first tried to pronounce Lisa's name correctly, had given up trying and had reverted to calling her "Leesha" again.

"Thanks, Ayesha. Wow – an elephant!" Lisa said, in awe of the massive creature that filled a space near the entrance to the market. It was a dusty grey, with pink marks on its ears. She had never before seen an elephant so close and out of the environment of a zoo. How graceful and elegant it looked. Its sheer size commanded attention; it was completely at home outside the market.

"Go on, Leesha, stand next to it, and give me your camera. I will click a snap for you," Ayesha said.
Lisa shuffled herself towards the elephant, slightly unsure of whether she was allowed to do this, but Ayesha's encouragement confirmed that it was. She wished Terrance would hurry up so that he could be in the picture with her; it would make a lovely memento. After Ayesha took the photo, Lisa tipped the keeper of the elephant. He thanked her profusely, placing the

money between his palms and raising them above his head in the *namaste* position as he bowed. It made her wonder if she had overtipped him. It was a routine she was still getting used to, and with the exchange rate, she never knew if she was giving too much or too little. She noticed Terrance heading towards them, in polo shirt and jeans, with Sonya at his side.

"Guess who I bumped into in the car park?" Terrance said mischievously.

"Sonya, hi!" Lisa responded almost too enthusiastically, exposing her false excitement. She would not let Sonya get to her now. Both Sonya and Terrance had assured her that there was nothing going on with them, and she had been with Terrance every day over the past week, so she was sure there could be nothing to worry about. The tight skirt that Sonya was wearing made her legs look twice as long as the last time she had seen her, and her close proximity to Terrance unsettled Lisa. She reminded herself that she was just having fun, nothing serious.

Ayesha and Sanjay entered the market and started walking through the rows of market traders. The hippies and locals were sitting cross-legged on straw mats amongst their brightly coloured sarongs, handbags, and shiny silver jewellery set against the dull mud beneath them. The colours and sounds were incredible; the acid music had now turned to live jazz, mingled with chatting and clinking of glasses. Fresh bhajis were being fried, and the appetizing smell of onions and chillies surrounded them.

"This is magnificent!" Lisa said as she stood by the entrance to the market, the dry red mud packed tightly under her feet from hundreds of tourists trampling the ground. She could see people dancing in the market, multicoloured fabrics tied to the dancer's wrists. The smell of marijuana mixed with incense was taking over her senses. She let Terrance take her hand and lead her into the throng of people. She felt a surge of excitement inside – this was how she wanted her life to be, and it was finally happening! She had finally found herself in this hedonistic and exotic land with a man that she loved. There was no going back; nothing could stop her now. She felt invincible.

Sonya rolled her eyes and headed towards Teresa, who was bartering for a silver necklace. Lisa could not understand a word of what she was saying; she was shouting animatedly, her arms flailing about. From what Lisa could understand, she was talking in Konkani. She could identify occasional English words: *local*, *Panaji*, and *cheaper*, and Lisa caught the gist of her argument. Terrance gave Lisa's hand a slight squeeze. He admired her enthusiasm for all the different little quirks she was being exposed to.

"Where are you from, miss?" A little shoeless girl in a torn yellow dress approached Lisa as they waited for Teresa to make a purchase.

"England," Lisa responded as she dropped a pinkish fifty-rupee note into the wooden bowl of a beggar. He wore a patch on his right eye and was missing an arm and a leg. He beamed at her as the note fell into the bowl, covering a few one-rupee coins.

"England?" The child mimicked a perfect cockney accent. "Which part, miss?" She sounded as if she were right off the sets of *Oliver*. "Manchester, Birmingham, Liverpool?" The child swiftly changed her accent to match the regional differences. Lisa looked at Terrance and back at the child. It was surreal.

"Come on, miss, I can show you some pretty skirts; they'll suit you just fine. Indian hand-stitched, with mirrors." The girl encouraged Lisa to follow her. She looked under ten years old, and Lisa felt sorry that such a girl was being made to help her parents in the market. The girl had done a good job. She had made an impression on the foreigner, and Lisa was now following her. The little girl thought that this foreigner would be sure to buy something now; the women she targeted mostly did, out of pity, if nothing else. Her mother would be pleased.

"Lisa, you are so easily drawn in. Now, if you like something, let me haggle for you," Terrance scolded her gently.

"But how is her accent so perfected?" Lisa enquired. "She probably speaks better English than some of the kids I teach, and I bet she doesn't even go to school."

"This is Anjuna, baby. She must have been hanging out with tourists and hippies since she was born."

Lisa bought two skirts, in blue and green, for Archana and Suzanne. They were ankle length, with intricate stitching in silver, red, and gold holding tiny mirrors in place. She doubted if either of them would ever wear them, but she didn't mind. For a few pounds, she had seen the little girl's face light up. The mother of the young girl was laughing with the vendor at the next stall. She was plump and jovial, and she expertly folded the skirts into a thin orange plastic bag. She pocketed the three hundred rupees with her sausage-like fingers and continued her conversation with her neighbour.

Lisa rested her bags full of shopping next to her chair as she joined the others seated at a table next to the jazz band. There were plates of half-eaten food on the table. Terrance returned with two cold beers and a plate of steaming *momos* stuffed with chicken and chillies.

The atmosphere of the market, coupled with the beers and the heat of the evening, made Lisa feel happy. She pushed her earlier thoughts of *just having fun* out of her mind. She wanted this to last. She'd felt so carefree since meeting Terrance and his friends; she wondered if she wanted to ever return home. A tarot booth was in her direct line of sight, and her slight intoxication made her want to try it. She looked up to the sky and decided that if the tarot gave her an inkling that this would last, she would put all her energy into making this work. The way she felt right now, she did not want to let Terrance go.

"I'm going to try the tarot," she announced. "Does anyone want to join me?" The group looked hesitant and excited at once.

"It's a load of rubbish," Terrance proclaimed. "She'll just con you out of your rupees."

"I know," Lisa said, "but I've always wanted to try something like this, and it will be a laugh. I *am* on holiday." The beer spurred her on. Lisa headed in the direction of the makeshift orange-and-blue tent, with the others following close behind. The area was much smaller inside than it looked, and so only Lisa, Terrance, and Sonya managed to squeeze in. The others decided to get some more food and drink.

The lady sat behind a small wooden makeshift desk. There were multicoloured lanterns everywhere, giving the tent a yellow hue. When

Lisa whispered to Terrance, "This is a fire hazard waiting to happen," the tarot lady heard and gave a small laugh. She didn't look like the stereotypical gypsy that Lisa had imagined did this sort of thing. She was young, in her thirties, and she wore black fisherman pants, with a green vest and matching green scarf around her neck. Her hair was blond and thick; it looked like it could do with a wash and some Frizz-Ease, Lisa thought. The lady had several silver and gold chains around her neck.

"'Ello, please sit down. My Name is Camille. It is you that wants a reading, no?" the lady said in a French accent, looking directly at Lisa. Her voice was hoarse, evidently from smoking too many roll-ups. Her fingertips were stained yellow, and a tin of tobacco lay open on the table. Lisa hesitated slightly as she seated herself on the threadbare stool.

"Yes. My name is Lisa," she said, now a little bit apprehensive at her decision.

"For five hundred rupees, I can do a twelve-card reading for you. For two hundred and fifty rupees, a three-card spread, telling you about your past, your present, and your future." Camille smiled at Lisa as if she knew her answer already.

"That is too much, yaar." Terrance said. Lisa could sense he was about to haggle for a cheaper price, and she cringed. There was a reserve in her that made her not want to barter for anything. Camille saved Lisa further embarrassment as she shot Terrance a cold glance.

"That is the price. There is no bargaining for these services," she said coldly. Terrance looked at Lisa, who signalled with her eyes that this was fine. He reluctantly took a step back, joining Sonya in the dark recesses of the tent.

Lisa, as Camille had known she would, decided on the three-card option. She looked carefully at the deck of cards. They looked well used and had an intricate red design backing each one. She was nervous, but with her change of luck over the past week, she was anticipating good things in the cards.

Lisa paid Camille, who carefully counted out the fifty-rupee notes. She asked her to pick three cards from a selection she had laid out on the table. Lisa did so, her hand shaking ever so slightly as she placed them on the table exactly as she had been told. The lanterns had made the tent warm, uncomfortably so.

"The past," Camille said, silencing them. "The Magician — but *'ee* is reversed. In your past, Lisa, you have had an inability to make judgements, an inability to use your talents to your best advantage. You were, how do you say … mmm … uninspired, and you, you gave up easily. Worse still, you 'ad a poor image of yourself. It was not good."

Lisa gave a reluctant smile. It was true, she thought. She hated her flat hair and her muffin top that spilled ever so slightly from her jeans, and she had felt increasingly uninspired at work. She was about to voice her agreement, but Camille, who did not need affirmation, did not give Lisa time to reflect on this. She declared, "That was in the past, and you can learn from that. It is not good to be like that. Now, what is more important is your present." She turned over the next card, saying, "The Fool." Lisa held her breath; it was going to predict that she was a fool in love, that her actions were foolish this holiday. She knew it, and she didn't want to hear it. She rubbed her sweaty palms together under the table; the beer was still having an effect on her. She looked at Camille in anticipation.

Camille continued, "The Fool. I like this card when *'ee* is upright. It is new beginnings, Lisa. Don't look so nervous. Maybe the beginning of a new life, a new energy, and new force." Camille looked up from the cards, first straight ahead at Lisa and then to Terrance.

"Remember, Lisa, a new beginning is a good, useful card to get in a reading. Whether or not you believe it." Lisa blushed, looking down at her hands, and Camille shot a cold look into the darkness where Terrance and Sonya stood. She added a warning, "It is something to be aware of – and use this knowledge to your advantage. But listen carefully. Do not think that any passing opportunity is a new beginning. You have to be selective and eliminate the demons of your past first, before you can move on." Lisa grinned. Surely that was a sign that they were starting something new, that there was a possibility that they would be together in the future.

"And now, Lisa, what you really want to know. Le future, no?" Camille flipped over the card and looked confused. It was the Justice card reversed. "The Daughter of the Lords of Truth," Camille said hesitantly; she looked up at Lisa apprehensively, searching for something in her eyes. "This is strange," she said, staring at the card as if she was willing it to change in her hand. "Your future holds an injustice to you, an unfair judgment." Camille glanced at Sonya, who had stepped into the light, and a chill ran down her spine.

Camille looked at Lisa with a new seriousness. "Your reading 'as finished," she said. Lisa was momentarily mystified. A judgment? It then occurred to her that maybe it would be her mother. "The Beast," of course, would have something to say about her relationship with Terrance, and she was not looking forward to that in the slightest. But the look Camille had given her seemed to convey more than a mother's disapproval. Lisa rose to her feet, not wanting to know any more about the last card, and she followed the others out.

"Be careful." Camille said as Lisa was leaving the tent. The words resonated with Lisa as the effects of the beer had worn off. She turned around to Camille, hoping for more of an explanation, but she was busying herself with her cards, her eyes focused on the deck.

"Don't worry about the reading," Terrance said as he dropped Lisa back to her hotel. He had perceived her anxiety. "These things are all made up; she has to have some kind of job to fund her drug habit. The whole tent stank of ganja." He squeezed her knee and kissed her gently on the cheek. She did not have to deter him from coming back to her room with her; he already knew she would not want his company tonight.

"I'm not worried. I mean, at least I didn't get the card of death or something," Lisa said, shrugging off any untoward thoughts. By the time she had slipped into bed that evening, she had forgotten about the tarot reading. It was Sonya who couldn't sleep that night.

13

Sonya withdrew into the back office as she saw Lisa and Terrance approaching the lobby. They were holding hands and fawning over each other; they looked in love. Sonya didn't know what to think. She leaned on Carl for support. She was not supposed to be working today, but the general manager had called her last night and asked her if she would cover for Melanie, who was conveniently sick. With New year's Eve looming, there was a lot to do.

"Look at him, Carl, and right in front of my face. He knows I work here! Why can't they take their public displays of affection elsewhere?"

"Ignore him, yaar, Sonya. You can do much better than him."

"And tell me, Carl, who else is there left in this godforsaken place?"

"There are others out there," he said, giving her a knowing glance.

"But we are supposed to be together. Everybody knows that. I can see Ayesha and Sanjay and Teresa laughing at me behind my back."

"Look, Sonya, relax. You and I both know that he is using her." Carl looked at his watch. "By this time in a couple of days, she will be out of here. The same evening, Terrance will be phoning you to go to Club Cubana, no?"

"Why do I have to suffer? So publicly, at that?" Sonya was close to tears.

"This is Goa, yaar. Tomorrow it will be yesterday's news. There will be other stories to talk about. You can put this behind you and get on with your life." But Carl knew that in Goa it was what was visible that mattered, and he knew that this was why Sonya was so upset. It was not that she loved Terrance completely; it was because his affairs made her look bad. Carl had even heard a rumour about Sonya, and that is why he had come to this conclusion. He decided to broach the subject with her; she was clearly not going to bring it up herself.

"So, I've heard the story about you and you-know-who." Carl nodded in the direction of the queue of tourists at the breakfast buffet. Sonya looked up from her computer screen and put her glasses on her head. She looked over at the hungry crowd ladling fruit salad into little bowls and drizzling their portions with yogurt and honey. Her eyes were fixed on her true object of affection. She felt a warmth rise to her cheeks and hoped that he had not noticed.

"I can't believe you didn't tell me," Carl said, waving his hand in front of her eyes. Sonya turned to face him. He was genuinely upset that she had not said anything. She scolded herself for being so careless in love. She had let someone see them, and if she was not careful, it would soon be public knowledge. It would ruin everything.

"Who told you?" She probed him with her eyes, slightly disappointed in herself for not confiding in the only person she knew who would never sully her name.

"Lilly in Finance. Finding out from someone like that was not a pleasant experience. You are lucky I like you and I saved your skin. I said it was all lies and that she'd better shut up about it."

Sonya's expression soured. "Lilly is always sticking her nose in where it doesn't belong. I can't wait till she goes back to Bangalore." She took a sip of her cold coffee and slipped her glasses back on. She started entering the New Year's vouchers on the system. "Thanks, Carl," she said. She was genuinely happy that he had attempted to quash the rumour before it spread. She hoped he would drop the subject.

"'Thanks Carl' – is that all you have to say! I save your ass, and that's it? Employees and guests, rule number one: No hanky panky! It does not bode well. You could have got yourself fired!"

Sonya and Carl were both well aware of this policy, and both had broken it on several occasions. This policy was a general one, no matter which hotel you worked in, but it was really only a piece of paper that no one ever adhered to. Waiters' chatting up lonely singletons was part of the package holiday. Everyone wanted to be a Shirley Valentine.

Carl continued, "So, tell me – what is it all about?"

"It's complicated," Sonya responded. "We have a thing, you know, one of *those* things that will fizzle out and will last all of the two-week holiday," Sonya tried to deflect him. He took her hand, and he noticed how frail it was. She had lost so much weight in the last couple of months. But he had noticed the look she had had in her eye earlier; it had been a glint of happiness, and she deserved it. It made him smile. It was not as if Terrance was not at it himself. He had seen him leaving Lisa's room the last few nights as dawn was breaking, sheepishly nodding, acknowledging Carl as he crept through the lobby.

Carl had never liked Terrance that much and could not see what Sonya found attractive in him, but he knew that Sonya and Terrance would ultimately marry each other. That was a given, an unspoken notion between them since they'd started their on/off relationship at sixteen. He knew that in a couple of years they would be married with kids, but they would always have their own infidelities. The marriage would be a façade to show the gossiping Goan public that they were respectable adults who fit into a box that society wanted to see them in.

There was something going on with Terrance that Carl could not put his finger on. He knew he worked for his father in an auto shop in Panaji. Fixing cars in Goa was a big business these days, and he was always willing to pick up the tab; he was a generous guy. But now he was buying designer watches and Louis Vuitton bags for Sonya – not one, but two. Carl didn't want to say it, but maybe that was his attraction. He wondered just how good his business was. He had googled the handbags after seeing a show about "It" bags on *Star World* and seen that just one would cost at least six months of his salary. He was glad that he had warned Lisa; she was so naive. He had done his bit, even if she took no notice of what he had said.

He pulled a seat up next to Sonya and switched his computer on. The sooner the vouchers were completed, the quicker they could get back home.

*

Mia was sitting in a chai shop in the middle of Mapusa market sipping a sweet milky tea from a small glass. A tin plate of steaming bhaji puri was placed in front of her. It was past one o'clock, and she was starving. She no longer stood out like a sore thumb in this establishment. She was now one of the regulars, and her order of tea and bhaji puri normally arrived without her having to order. After she'd eaten, she jumped into a yellow-and-black autorickshaw to make the long journey back to Calangute. She would soon be able to buy a car, if everything went according to plan. She had the urge to be at the beach this afternoon. Her work was now taking care of itself, and she no longer had to bother with details.

She had found the perfect, secluded spot on Calangute beach whilst swimming there one morning. It was a little cove tucked behind a mass of rocks at the north end of the beach, cut off from tourists and only accessible when the tide was out. She had grown accustomed to the tides and knew them now by instinct, so that she could get to her little bit of solitude. Armed with her large canvas tote and oversized sunglasses, she clambered over the rocks away from the throng of fishermen and sunbathers. Once in her sheltered space, she dug her feet into the soft, silky sand, her red toenails disappearing under a mound of white powder.

She thought about the last twenty-four hours and the decision she had made. Her lover had been right – it was the only way she could stay in Goa permanently. This way, she knew that she would receive a healthy income. A small part of her knew that it was wrong. She was taking a huge risk and getting involved in something very questionable. But the money was good, and looking after herself was a number-one priority.

She thought about the night of passion that they had shared just yesterday. It brought a smile to her lips. How fortunate she was to have met such a wonderful person. Even if she would have to just be a mistress, he was someone she could work with. Together they would be unstoppable.

This plan would come into fruition soon, but until then, she knew that she would have to stay on with Simon. The thought of having to report back to him repulsed her, but soon she would be her own boss, and she could stay on in Goa on her own time. Comforted by thoughts of the lifestyle that awaited her, she drifted into a deep sleep.

14

On the eve of New Year's, as Lisa was lazing by the pool, she realized that she had never spoken to the Scandinavian girl whom she had seen at the beginning of her trip. How long ago it seemed that she had stepped onto that coach to Old Goa, nervous about being a single traveller. How things had changed since then!

She whiled away the morning hours, daydreaming about taking Terrance back to England with her, introducing him to her friends, and showing him all the sights. She knew he had never been to England before, and she wanted to show him around, take him to the theatre, and introduce him to fish and chips and mushy peas or a full English breakfast in the local greasy café at the corner of her road. With his height and exotic looks, she would be the envy of all her friends. Her mind turned to the evening ahead, of what she could wear. Now that she was hanging out with locals, she felt a bit foolish in her bright, flowery holiday dresses. She wished there were a few decent shops at the resort where she could buy something special for tonight. There were none, and so she was obliged to pick something from her suitcase. Terrance had planned a whole evening for them before they met the others in the early hours of the New Year's morning, and Lisa wanted it to be perfect. Her Nan always used to say a good New Year's Eve would mean a good year ahead – and this year she had a good shot at getting it right!

Her last New year's Eve had been spent with her friends back in Oxford. They had paid an extortionist amount to get into a new bar, which they then had to queue for in the freezing December weather. The bar then ran out of vodka, which was criminal and they ended up at home at one in the morning completely sober and out of pocket. It was a disaster and worse still Lisa was dateless that night so when midnight hit, and her friends were embracing their partners, Lisa stood there alone. It was a harsh reminder that she was single and probably would be for the forthcoming year. It would be a very different scenario for her this year, she grinned to herself glancing at her watch it was nearly time for her appointment at the Spa. She stood up wrapping her towel around her and headed towards the lobby.

*

Terrance arrived at the hotel earlier than she had expected; she was not even close to ready. In fact, when he knocked on her door, she was still in her bikini, lying on the sun lounger on her balcony and allowing the oils from her massage to soak into her skin. As she opened the door, he winked at her, drawing her close. She was glad she was wearing her more flattering brown bikini – unlike the green one Suzanne had made her buy – it actually fit her and did not look like she had borrowed it from a skinny friend.

"Mmm, you smell good," he said, kissing her neck.

Lisa kissed him back as he wrapped his arms around her. It was a lovely feeling having a boyfriend; she blocked any thoughts about what would happen when she left in a few days' time. "You're early, about four hours too early," she said, pulling him towards her bed.

"I know. I couldn't bear to be away from you," he said, playing with her hair.

"You are such a tease," she said, secretly enjoying this attention. They were sitting close to each other on the crisp white sheets of her king-size bed, the sexual tension pulling them together. Terrance slid his hand over her hip and started kissing her. She inched closer towards him, knowing exactly how this impromptu visit would end.

Instead, he broke free. "Come on, get ready," he said, drawing himself away. He glanced at his watch. "I have to be somewhere in half an hour, and you are coming with me. Just slip something on."

"But what about tonight? I can't get ready now," Lisa said, trying to shake off her need for him.

"No, you gorgeous thing. You will be back in time to change for this evening." He kissed her neck again, and Lisa hoped it would be more, but she had sensed the urgency in his voice. He released her and she went to select a pale-pink pair of linens and white racer-back vest from her wardrobe.

On the way to their destination, she was curious as to where they were headed. He had picked her up on a white scooter that looked similar to a Vespa. She initially worried that they did not have any helmets on, but this feeling soon passed. That was the old Lisa – her new persona threw caution to the wind. She enjoyed the feeling of the hot sun burning her back and the cool breeze that engulfed her as they sped through the countryside.

"Where are we going, Terrance?" she asked. She had been to so many different places over the last two weeks, but she never quite knew where she was in Goa. The paddy fields and lack of road signs made it impossible for Lisa to know where she was, and her sense of direction had never been that good. Even in Oxford she'd needed a satellite navigation system to get to most places. She held on tightly to him as they rode through winding mud roads. She felt so safe with Terrance that it did not bother her that she didn't know where anything was.

"You'll see. It's somewhere that is very special to me, and I want to share it with you." Her smile widened with the thought that he was sharing something with her that perhaps he had not shared with Sonya.

Fifteen minutes later, they arrived at a pale yellow-and-white building, with a faded blue sign above the door that read "Sweet Haven." Terrance squeezed Lisa's arm, and as he led her through the dusty brown door, he looked anxious.

"It is an amazing place, the work that they do here. There are so many orphans in Goa, like you wouldn't believe." Lisa cast her mind back to a documentary she had seen back in England. It had taken place in Pakistan, where a group of young children had been abused and murdered. She remembered seeing their mothers wailing into their saris as they were shown the remnants of their children's clothing. The children had been missing for years from poverty-stricken families. They were mainly runaways, and their parents hadn't been able to afford to keep going into the town to make missing-person complaints. They were too poor for the officials to take notice. Worse still, the perpetrators, finally desperate to be caught, ended up having to hand themselves in to the authorities through a journalist. Nobody had ever even looked for the lost children. The documentary had sickened Lisa, and she had vowed to do more. At twenty, she'd believed that she could make a difference in the world. Five years later, she had long forgotten that ideal – until now.

As Terrance led Lisa through the corridors of Sweet Haven, she noticed that the sallow yellow walls looked dirty. The whole building needed a fresh lick of paint and a cleaning. A woman stood at the end of the hallway. She looked as if she were in her fifties, and her back was curved forwards as if she had spent her life doing manual labour. She had a bright-pink satin dress on, which contrasted against her dark skin. Her legs poked out of the dress like matchsticks. She was plunging a mop into a faded green bucket; the water was brown with dirt. When she saw Lisa, she stared at her with a piercing look that sent a shiver down her spine. She continued to mop the floors with the unclean water, as Terrance took Lisa by the hand and led her towards a classroom, introducing her to some of the nuns that ran the institution. She noticed children flitting in and out of different rooms.

She entered a classroom full of eager brown faces looking up at a blackboard. Lisa smiled inwardly. She had not seen a blackboard since her own primary education; white boards and coloured markers had taken over a long time ago. Everything in the class was basic. There were no chairs. Most of the children looked as if they needed a hot bath and some new clothes. They sat on the floor, but they looked more eager to please and willing to learn than most of the privileged kids Lisa had taught back at home.

"Sweet Haven relies on volunteers and donations to survive. The government does not help this orphanage at all," Terrance said as the children all stood to their feet to greet the newcomers. The teacher, Mr Goswami, translated their greetings for Lisa.

"The children eat, sleep, and get schooled in this building," Mr Goswami informed Lisa as he motioned for the children to sit down. There was pin-drop silence amongst them as they busied themselves with the task on the blackboard. "There are sixty children at this orphanage at the moment, and we just cannot afford to take any more. There are so many children whose parents just don't have the money to keep them at home, to feed. There is just not enough room." Lisa could see desolation in his eyes. He was an elderly gentlemen who wore round glasses, and what little hair he had left was grey. Lisa could tell that he wished more children could be housed at the orphanage. He felt her gaze on him and felt he needed to explain his position. "I am a retired maths teacher. I do voluntary work here now."

Despite the unclean feel, Lisa was in awe of the good the orphanage had done with such basic facilities. Terrance had explained that there were hundreds of homeless children in Goa. Their parents could not afford to keep them, mainly because they were illiterate and could not get decent jobs. But they kept reproducing; many did not believe in contraception. The result was that there were too many children per household, and the children suffered. The orphanage was doing a good job preventing innocent children from being sold to prostitution or other forms of exploitation. Lisa recalled earlier in her trip seeing many children sitting by the sides of dirt roads, with nobody watching over them. The way people drove in India, they could be easily killed. She wondered just how many children there were in that situation.

Even though Goa was so westernized, it still had its fair share of Third World problems. It was filled to the brim with tourists, who probably never saw this side amidst the long stretches of beach and old churches. In fact, until Lisa met Terrance, she had been one of these tourists. Suddenly she was angry at the West for taking advantage of these children. When she'd arrived in Dabolim airport, just a week back, a woman had thrust a leaflet into her hand. Lisa had shoved it in the pocket of her jeans and paid no attention to it. Now she recalled pulling out the leaflet the next time she wore those jeans. The pamphlet had a hotline number on it for people to call if they saw any young local children being groomed by tourists. It had chilled Lisa to the bone. She had kept her eyes open after that, but she herself had not witnessed anything untoward. She had assumed that if there were leaflets around it must be a serious problem. The leaflet had gone on to explain that a few Euros or pounds to a family in India would be a small fortune. The parents, often those who sent their children to beg, turned a blind eye when their children returned home with more money than expected. Those who should have been looking after them clearly were not.

Mr Goswami confirmed this. As far as he knew, there were roughly four hundred thousand child prostitutes in India, and at least a hundred paedophiles operated in Goa during the tourist season, despite the age of consent in India being eighteen. Tourists would still approach children on the beach and take them back to their lodgings. Mr Goswami said he had seen it himself, and that is why he was now working for the orphanage, which had saved many of these children. Sweet Haven was a safe place to prevent such atrocities from happening to them. "A place to give these children back their youth in a safe environment," said a blue flyer with a child in a school uniform on the front. It had stood out to Lisa from a notice board in the corridor.

"Lisa is a teacher, too," Terrance pointed out to Mr Goswami. "I will leave you two to talk," he said hurriedly. "I have some papers to sort out with Sister Fatima. It won't take long, Lisa. I'll meet you in the courtyard in ten minutes." Terrance pointed through the classroom door towards the courtyard, and the he left. Lisa spoke to some of the children, using Mr Goswami as a translator. Despite what some of the children had been through, they looked so content with what they had.

As Terrance was talking with one of the nuns, a boy of about six came up to Lisa and started pulling at her pale pink trousers.

"Miss, miss," he called to her. Lisa bent down so her eyes were in line with his. He had a beautiful, cherubic face, she thought. He smiled at her, a toothless grin, and she touched his cheek with the back of her hand.

"I am away," he said in his broken English.

"You are going away?" she asked, trying to understand what he was saying. He nodded but looked shy. It was a silly thought, but Lisa couldn't but help thinking of the movie *Annie*; it had been one her favourites as a child. The girl with the orange, curly hair and the big grin had been saved from the ravages of the orphanage by a rich uncle or grandfather, she couldn't quite remember.

She took the child's hand and squeezed it gently; she didn't want to upset him further. "To a family?" she said brightly, beaming at the child. She pronounced her words fully, "A new family?" A tear rolled down the cheek of the toothless child.

Lisa wiped his single tear away with her finger; she could understand how he must be feeling. The orphanage was his home, what he knew. He had a routine there, but she knew that he would adjust to a new family. He would have so much more opportunity and have the chance to go to school. He would forget the orphanage in no time.

*

As she waited for Terrance, she looked around the barren courtyard. An old tyre was tied to a branch of a large banyan tree. The tree's roots hung down around it, makeshift Tarzan swings for the children. It looked as if it were very well used. A local Indian woman squatting over a woven basket caught Lisa's eye. Her skin was dark from hours of manual labour in the hot Goan sun, and the heels of her feet were cracked. She was picking up piles of leaves from the courtyard and placing them in the basket. The task looked laborious. Lisa framed a picture with her camera. It looked like a scene you would see in a coffee-table book.

Despite the heat and the task at hand, the woman looked relaxed. A brown and yellow sari was draped around her as she went about her work. A thick ugly scar on the woman's back peered out from behind her dupatta. It looked painful. It must have been done by a surgeon without much skill.

"Her name is Gita," a voice said from behind her. It was Terrance. "She has been with the orphanage for many years. You noticed her scar." Lisa blushed, embarrassed by her obvious curiosity. Terrance continued, "Her scar is from a badly botched kidney operation before she joined us. It was in Delhi; she is from there."

"It looks painful," Lisa said, wincing at the sight of it.

"She sold it, you know, for about a thousand dollars. Some rich man owes his life to her, and all she got was a grand. Organ trading is banned in India, you know, but it continues every day," Terrance continued, as if he had to justify her actions. "She has six kids. The prices of basic essentials are increasing daily here—" Lisa stopped Terrance before he could continue, putting her finger to his lips. She understood. He didn't need to say any more.

Marissa de Luna

Lisa was not ignorant; she knew things like this happened. It was different, however, reading about it in a glossy magazine from the comfort of your own living room than actually seeing a victim of such brutality, a violation of human rights. Terrance said something to Gita that Lisa didn't understand, and she turned around. She waved and smiled at Lisa, exposing her gums and the remaining paan-stained teeth. The smile conveyed no bitterness or resentment. She was genuine – and there and then, something changed within Lisa.

She was overwhelmed with what she had seen and heard. It was all too much for her. She didn't feel like celebrating a new year and a potentially new beginning for herself when she would be leaving these people behind. She had awakened something within her. It was a need to make others feel better, to make a difference in the world. She owed this to Terrance. He had shown her a different side to India and a different side to herself.

15

"Thank you, Terrance, for today," Lisa said as they headed towards Calangute beach later that evening.

"Well, after dampening your spirits, which I didn't mean to do, I have a little surprise for you." Terrance had a cheeky grin on his face, and Lisa leant over to kiss him, entwining her fingers in his. They were stuck in traffic, and they crawled at a snail's pace towards the beach. They parked up in one of the few remaining spots left on the road and pushed their way towards the crowds of dressed-up party goers getting ready for the big night. They were on the main strip in Calangute, where Lisa had first eaten with the others at Chi Chi's. It was crowded tonight. Each open-air bar had a different tune playing into the street and had brightly coloured cocktails to lure in passers-by. Scooters and bikes weaved in and out through the crowds, making their way on the dirt-track road towards the beach. Lisa held on to Terrance as they were carried by the crowd of people. She marvelled at the displays of fresh fish; huge lobsters and silver pomfrets looked up at her from chilled glass cabinets. Lanterns and paper stars marked out the little eateries, which were crammed onto the fifty-meter strip. Touts stood outside selling tickets to three-day acid parties at Hill Top and Disco Valley. The atmosphere was electric.

As they reached the edge of the road where the beach began, Terrance instructed Lisa to close her eyes

"What?" she protested. She had made a special effort and was wearing the highest heels she had packed. Her sensible black ballerinas were now a thing of the past; this year was her new beginning. Since her spontaneous decision to come away this Christmas, things had started going right for her. This year her new year's resolution was to stop thinking about every consequence every time she decided to do something. She was going to live a little.

"Go on," Terrance encouraged, kissing her tenderly on her cheek, "or you will spoil the surprise." Lisa took off her shoes and held them in one hand. Terrance took her other, and she closed her eyes and allowed herself to be led by him. She could smell the bergamot and olive wood of his cologne. His hands were warm, and she wanted to be even closer to him; she wanted to feel his strong arms around her. A cool breeze made her skin tingle, and she could hear the waves crashing against the shore, the sound mingled with music and laughter. A few minutes later, they had reached their destination. Apart from the sound of the sea and a dull thud of music in the background, the beach was quiet. Lisa apprehensively opened her eyes, taking in the scene.

"Is this for me?" she asked incredulously.

"Do you see anyone else here?" Terrance asked back, pulling her towards him.

"Oh, Terrance – it's so beautiful!" she said, and her eyes were moist. There was a shack on the only bit of deserted beach in Goa on this busy night. A lone table and two chairs were outside the shack, and two flame torches lit the area. A bottle of wine was cooling in ice on the table.

"Please, sit down," Terrance instructed, pulling out a chair for her. Lisa did as she was told, noting the single red rose that was on her plate. She could not believe the trouble he had taken for her, and despite the romantic thoughts that were running through her mind, she couldn't wait to tell Suzanne. For years she had envied what Suzanne had with Arjun – now *she* had something to be envious of. This holiday seemed like the best thing that had ever happened to her.

A waiter appeared, carrying a seafood starter, a simple knoll of linguine studded with prawns and clams. He opened the bottle and poured them both a glass. It was chilled to perfection for the warm evening and easily slipped down her throat. The waiter retreated back into the shack. It was a cliché that Lisa would have previously laughed at, but now it just seemed right. She was in love with someone who was treating her so well. She had to pinch herself to check if it was real.

"Wow, this must have cost a fortune," Lisa exclaimed. Terrance winked at her but said nothing. Before she knew it, they were opening a second bottle of wine. They had been lost in conversation, and the wine, as usual, had loosened her tongue. She told him in length about her family, how her brother had been travelling around the world and she had never been further than Greece. She told him about her nephew and even admitted that she was a tad jealous of his family life. She disclosed some of her deepest, darkest secrets, things she had never even told Suzanne. The waiter briefly interrupted them to bring out a fillet of fish in a lemon and butter sauce and, finally, a strawberry cheesecake. Then Terrance dismissed him. As the night grew cooler, they moved into the deserted shack. Terrance put a CD in the stereo; it was something familiar and sensual. He wrapped Lisa up in his arms, and she enjoyed the warmth of his skin. They slowly swayed to the music, and he kissed her neck softly, making the hairs on the back of her arms stand on end.

The wine had made her giddy, and she steadied herself on a wooden beam that was holding up the thatched roof. Terrance pulled her towards him and gently lowered her onto her back. She looked up at him and into his eyes. They were a dark brown, almost black, and they gazed back at her full of intensity and passion. She wanted him desperately; she wanted him inside her. Gently, he undid the lace strap that held her dress together, allowing it to fall and expose her body, white against the darkness of his skin. He cupped her breast in his hand and ran his tongue over every inch of her body. He worked his fingers in the warmth of her until she yearned for him. He entered her, pulling her on top of him, and she rocked rhythmically until she felt an explosion within her. A warm sensation washed over her, and she crumbled into his arms. They lay there holding each other, the sweat on their skin slowly evaporating in the cool night air.

When Lisa opened her eyes, the music had stopped. She must have dozed off; she was nestled in the crook of his arm, and her clothes were strewn on the floor. She let her thoughts linger on what had happened that evening, turning over and resting on her elbows to look at Terrance. The beach floor of the shack was still warm and it felt good. She kissed Terrance on his forehead; he looked at her with that intensity that she loved.

"This is crazy, what are we doing? I leave at the end of the week." The carefree attitude Lisa had had at the beginning of the night was slowly disappearing as the effects of the wine wore off.

"I'll tell you what is crazy. We missed the countdown, It's half twelve," he said, glancing at his watch.

"Well, happy New Year!" Lisa said, kissing him.

"Happy New Year," Terrance responded, looking deep into her eyes. "Stay," he added, taking her fingers in his and gently squeezing them.

"I can't. You know that I have responsibilities, commitments. I can't just up and leave, no matter how much I want to."

The reality of the situation was falling into place. Lisa felt a void in the pit of her stomach. She had never felt like this before about anyone. She felt fated to be with Terrance for the rest of her life. Despite only having known him for such a short time, she knew that if he was no longer in her life, she would not be able to breathe. "I love you." The words left her mouth before she had time to stop them.

"I love you, too," he shot back, surprising himself. She smiled, relieved that he had reciprocated, and she lay back down, snuggling against the warmth of his body. She didn't want the moment to end.

"What will we do now? Would you consider England?"

"I don't know, Lisa. Goa is my home. My work is here, and I earn good money here. I don't know; let's not spoil the night, eh? We are meeting the others soon. We can talk about it tomorrow."

Lisa conceded. It bothered her, but she did not want to get into an argument with Terrance today. It was New Year's day, and they had a party to go to.

16

The sun was setting on Lisa's final evening in Goa. It had been the trip of a lifetime, one that she would not forget in a hurry. The thought of going back to her bleak apartment in Oxford with the chill of January in the air made her shudder.

But she was excited about meeting Suzanne and Archana and filling them in on what had happened, as well as proving her mother wrong. She had survived two weeks by herself in a country more than four hours away; no one had tried to drug or kidnap her, and she had even avoided the dreaded "Delhi belly".

More than that, she had left England broken, and now she felt alive again. This was no ordinary holiday romance – she was sure of it. She and Terrance had spoken at length about how they would try to make their relationship work, despite the distance between them. They both knew that it was something too special to just throw away. Lisa was ready to make her way back to Goa in the Easter Holidays, if she was still in love with Terrance and Goa. In that case, she would hand in her notice for the end of the academic year. It was a compromise between the old and new Lisa.

The very thought of a new life ahead of her made her smile, and the excitement shot through her. Terrance had made it clear that he could not leave his father's business, and he had assured her that he had enough contacts in Goa to find Lisa a decent teaching job. He had suggested it would be much more rewarding than teaching the "privileged" back home. She didn't mind the compromise. She was looking for something to drag her away from her dull life, and the orphanage Terrance had shown her was just the ticket. It had captivated her heart, and she really wanted to make a difference, even if it meant being paid a lowly wage to work in a less affluent school. She was determined to do some voluntary work at Sweet Haven.

The real issue for Lisa was her apprehension at what her family would think – well, less what they would *think* and more what they would *say*, her mother in particular. Lisa was sure she would have huge doubts, not only about Terrance, but about moving to India. She could not blame her. It would be understandable even for "the Beast", but she would have to be strong. It was high time that she made her own decisions.

Lisa looked at her souvenirs as she packed them away in her case: the skirts for Suzanne and Archana, a wooden elephant for her mother, and all the other trinkets she had bought. She heard a knock on the door and smiled, instinctively knowing that it was Terrance. He had spent nearly every minute of the last two days with her, and Sonya had increasingly avoided them both. Lisa was grateful to her for introducing them, but despite Terrance's denials, she still had a guilty feeling that she had stolen him away from Sonya and that she was trying to win him back. She answered the door, and he stood there holding out a little red velvet box.

"Open it," Terrance said anxiously as he stepped into the room.

"Wow! Thank you," Lisa said, rising on her tiptoes to kiss him on his lips. She would miss that tingle that she felt ever time their lips touched. She carefully opened the box, and inside she saw an intricately woven silver bracelet. "It's beautiful!" she said. Lisa took Terrance by his arm and led him over to the bed, where he helped her fasten the bracelet. It sparkled against her golden skin. No sooner had he put it on than tears started to well up in her eyes. "I can't believe this is it" she said, holding on to Terrance tightly, knowing that soon she would not be able to hold him again.

"This is *not* it," he said optimistically. "We have the whole evening together, and I am going to drop you to the airport tomorrow. You will be back in less than two months. It's a good job you are a teacher," Terrance said, pushing back her hair and kissing the top of her head.

"I know. It's just such a long way home. I can't believe I have fallen so madly in love in under two weeks. Am I crazy?" she said, smiling at him. He wiped away a tear as it rolled down her cheek. She felt like a lovesick schoolgirl.

"No, you are absolutely amazing, and I love you, and I want you back here as soon as possible. Your flight is the nine o'clock one in the evening, right?"

"The nine o'clock one," Lisa said, not enjoying the thought of having to leave so early. She had grown accustomed to rising at eleven o'clock, at the earliest. "I don't know if dropping me to the airport is a good idea. I can take the courtesy coach from the hotel. I don't want to be blubbing saying goodbye to you. I hate saying goodbye."

"Hey, I want to take you – it's not an option. The more time I can spend with you, the better." He looked into her big brown eyes and kissed her on the nose. "I also have a bit of an ulterior motive," he said, "which I hope you won't mind." He tentatively pushed a strand of her brown hair behind her ear. "I know you won't mind. You know those two little kids you saw running around my house at Christmas?"

"Yes," Lisa responded, wondering where this was going. She vaguely remembered a collection of young children with painted faces causing mischief on Christmas day amidst all his uncles and aunts.

"Well, Shruti and Tariq are flying back unaccompanied. Do you remember I told you that about Aunty Reshma? Well, they are her kids, so I changed their morning flight reservation for your flight. You know how I worry about the kids, and travelling alone can be quite daunting. I know it's safe, but knowing what I know from volunteering at the orphanage, kids being forgotten and left behind, it would make me feel better. Blame Sweet Haven; it kind of does that to you."

Lisa smiled, taking his hand in hers. He was so compassionate, and she was so lucky to have met a man who cared so much. "Don't say another word. I will make sure they get back to England in one piece." She shot him a glance from the corner of her eye. "It would be nice if *you* accompanied me back." She looked at him, falling into his embrace.

As he held her, he said softly, "Immigration, they may cause a problem. You know, a white woman travelling with two Indian children, their English not very good."

Lisa pulled away. "I'm not going to get in any trouble, surely? What would be the difference, if they were travelling unaccompanied to begin with?"

"No, but I know what officials can be like. Just for your piece of mind and my piece of mind, just say that they are extended family, you know, something like that. If they want an address for the children, just give them this one." He placed a piece of paper in her hand with an address scribbled on it. She folded it and put in her bag without giving it a second glance. She didn't need any reassurance; he would never put her in any danger. She trusted him.

He pulled her back towards him and held her tightly, grateful for her willingness to accompany his cousins back. He whispered, "I wish I was coming back with you – you don't know just how much I wish I was." He held her in a tight embrace and kissed her passionately as they both fell into the bed.

*

The next morning, Lisa was on the way to the airport with Terrance and his two cousins. They were quiet, sad to be parting from each other. The sky was grey, and large drops of rain started to hit the windscreen.

"I thought it only ever rained here in the monsoons," she said, looking into the damp atmosphere.

"It normally does. We only very occasionally get a rainstorm out of season," Terrance replied.

"Oh well, it's a good job it's my last day," she tried to sound cheery, but she just wanted to cry. She turned to look at Tariq and his sister in the back seat. "You two are awfully quiet in the back," she said.

They smiled. "No, Leesha, aunty, we fine," they said in unison. Lisa reached over and ruffled Tariq's hair. She could see a slight resemblance to Terrance in his jaw line. Tariq flinched and pulled back, and Lisa scolded herself for doing that; the children were obviously nervous. The boy was playing with a long scar he had just above his knee. Lisa instantaneously touched the faint scar on her elbow. As a child, she once thought she was

Superwoman and thought she could fly from the oak tree in her garden. She had never climbed trees after that, and she had a scar to remind her of her youth.

"They have never been good with flying, and their English is not so good, still. They were in a Konkani speaking school when they lived here. Now look at how it has upset the kids' move." Lisa could see Terrance's love for his cousins in his eyes. She would do everything in her power to make sure they were delivered safely back to their uncle.

"Well, it will be a quiet journey, then," she said, somewhat relieved. The thought of speaking to two chatty children was not appealing at this moment, especially when she knew she was heading back to a classroom of giddy children who had had too many additives over the Christmas holidays. She always noticed the relief in their mothers' eyes as they dropped their kids off at the school gates on the first day back of term. All Lisa wanted now was to be alone with her thoughts of Terrance and their future together.

At the airport, he helped check them all in and made sure they were seated together. Lisa said one final tearful goodbye to Terrance at the immigration desk and guided the children through the barriers. They held on to one another's hands in silence.

On the flight back, the children slept. They were so unlike the group of raucous children she had seen at Christmas. She smiled to herself – how funny children were! One minute you couldn't shut them up, and the next minute butter wouldn't melt.

She had noticed that the blond Scandinavian girl from the hotel was on her flight; they must have been on the same package, she thought. She smiled at her and received a nod in exchange. Lisa had never got around to speaking to her, and now it was too late. Her first, lonely day by the pool seemed longer than only two weeks ago. So much had happened since then. She had really found who she was on this holiday and was beginning to carve out a new life.

Her thoughts shifted to the time she had spent with Terrance. She couldn't believe that she had been the one to say "I love you" first, and she pictured

Suzanne's face as she told her. She would scold her – Lisa could almost hear her voice – "That is the first rule, Lisa Higgins! You never say 'I love you' first!" It brought a smile to her lips. She was bursting to tell Suzanne her news; she was the one person who would truly be happy for her. A sliver of her was excited about going home and getting into her own bed for the first time in two weeks. When Lisa thought of her mother's reaction, however, her smile disappeared. She had tasted what true love was really like, and she didn't want her dream to be shattered and ridiculed by those she cared about the most. It was going to be a battle, but she would win – of that she was sure.

PART II

17

Lisa felt a hand on her shoulder, bringing her back to reality. She looked up with bleary eyes, somewhat detached, as if her soul had left her body months ago. She was an empty shell.

"The verdict is in. We need to go back in there after lunch, for about two." The voice was gentle, but the words pierced Lisa like shards of glass. She rose to her feet and adjusted her suit. At one time, it had been a struggle to fit into. She had last worn it for an Open Day at her school, and on the way home she had unbuttoned her skirt so that she could breathe again. Her mother had picked it out of her wardrobe this morning, carefully running the lint roller over the dark cloth to remove the tiny fibres from the white mohair cardigan that had hung next to it. Margaret had held the skirt open for her and she had stepped in, holding on to her mother to steady herself. She felt like a toddler, a small and frightened one. The suit was no longer as snug as it had once been; it hung loosely over her gaunt frame. She couldn't believe just how much her life had changed. Just eighteen months ago, she had been on her way back from the holiday of a lifetime. The holiday had changed her life. Now she was facing a prison sentence.

Lisa looked at her forlorn parents; the trial had aged them a decade. She turned to leave the courthouse in silence. She didn't need to say anything; they understood she needed her own space. They had been so supportive over the last few months; she couldn't have asked for much more. She would never have gotten this far through the whole ordeal without them. How could she have done this? she thought as she glanced back. They were holding on to each other for support. Her father's silver hair reminded her of their frailty. A guilty verdict would surely crush them. They had been through so much in this last year. She walked over to Regent's Park, a few minutes away from the courthouse. It was a rare spring day in London, when the sun complemented the crisp, cool air. Lisa wanted to feel the freshness that the outside world offered. She wanted to notice everything, but most importantly, she wanted to remember.

Bending to the ground, Lisa plucked a freshly surfaced daffodil and twirled it between her fingers, its yellow vibrancy casting a reflection against her skin. She cast her mind back to how her happy life had ended so abruptly. It was all beginning to blur now; it seemed like a lifetime away. Camille had been right, she thought, the hippy with the heavy French accent nestled in her Anjuna tarot tent. Lisa could almost smell the burning jasmine incense mixed with strong tobacco that had filled the air that day, the grubby and torn blue-and-orange material that housed Camille and her cards. She remembered the warning look Camille had shot her as she had revealed her future. The Reversed Justice card. An injustice would be done to her, and this was it – but just how unjust was it? The revelations at the trial had demonized her. She knew they did not believe that someone could be so naive and ignorant, and she had begun to question herself. As the days passed, the feeling of guilt had grown inside her. What had she done?

*

Her flight back to England had been as she had expected. She had left the children with their uncle at Heathrow arrivals and headed back to Oxford. Suzanne had been ecstatic to hear about her romance in Goa.

"I can't believe it, Lise! Didn't I say you just needed some time away? I am *so* always right – you are positively glowing with that tan, and I am loving your new hippy look! Are those khaki fisherman trousers you have on there?" She turned Lisa around to admire her new carefree look. She really did look so different, as if a weight had been lifted from her shoulders. She seemed confident and, most importantly, happy. Suzanne gave her an approving smile. A sliver of envy ran through her but quickly disappeared.

"He is just amazing, Suze. Look at the photos," she said, throwing her camera over at Suzanne, who was now sitting cross-legged on the sofa in her blue-and-pink striped pyjamas and digging into the box of Indian sweets Lisa had bought her.

"What this?" she said, lifting up a bright yellow-coloured sweet the size of a golf ball. It looked as if it were made of millions of tiny balls all moulded together, with bits of raisin embedded within.

"It's a laddu," Lisa said, showing off her new knowledge. She smiled; it was usually Suzanne who came back with exotic things, telling her about the different types of food she had sampled abroad.

Suzanne repeated the name of the delicious sweet, "Laddu." She liked the sound of its name. She picked up the camera that had landed on the sofa and started scrolling through the hundreds of photos.

Lisa waited patiently for Suzanne to start questioning her. She had always been shy discussing her love life with friends, even Suzanne, but now she was dying to tell her about Terrance. She could not wait any longer, so she plunged straight in, revealing all the little things he had done for her, the romantic evening on New Year's Eve, and the bracelet that she had told herself she would never take off. She felt like a lovesick teenager, and Suzanne let her have her moment, happy that her friend had experienced a good holiday romance. It had lifted her spirits, and she had a better aura about her.

Lisa sat herself on the armchair opposite Suzanne, who was holding her mug of camomile and studying the box of sweets. Suzanne had always had such a sweet tooth. Lisa had known she would like the present the minute she'd found the mithai shop. "I'm going back this Easter," Lisa blurted out sooner than she intended. She stared at Suzanne, waiting to hear and, most importantly, *see* her reaction. She would have to test the waters with her first, before she told her mother.

Suzanne was silent, busy looking into the box of sweets and twirling a white roll with a deep green core the size of her little finger in one hand. She was scrolling through her camera in the other. It was as if she hadn't heard Lisa.

"Well, don't you have anything to say?" Lisa said with a wary tone. The silence was unnerving, her palms were moist and she had started curling her hair in her fingers.

Suzanne didn't even look up; she dismissed the comment with a "humph", still looking through Lisa's endless memory card. "Holiday romance," she said finally, with an air of nonchalance. "Remember what's-his-name from Cyprus?" she looked contemplatively at Lisa and then smiled. "Nikos!" she said triumphantly "Yep, that was his name. He was *lurvely*. My first holiday fling of many. I thought I would go back too, and remember, he never called or anything. I was heartbroken. Wept for days. You remember you were consoling me – all those telephone conversations in the middle of the night telling me that he wasn't worth it, that I'd meet someone else."

Suzanne lifted another sweet to her mouth; it was cream-coloured, in the shape of a diamond, and wrapped in pretty silver paper. "It was a good job he didn't call," Suzanne continued. "When I went back a couple of years ago with Nikki and the girls, the six-pack was no more – it was more of a huge, protruding belly." Suzanne shuddered recollecting the scene. "We ran! The last thing I wanted him to do was recognize me! Ha! Not that he would have. He probably broke a million hearts that summer." She took a bite of the diamond-shaped sweet. "Mmm, the silver paper *is* edible. It's yum."

Lisa was annoyed by this little tale of Suzanne's. She felt as if the one true love experience that she had had was being belittled. "For your information, Suzanne, I am not nineteen; I know the difference between a holiday fling and a proper relationship." But as she said it, she found doubt creeping into her mind, very slowly, like a poison.

All her fears began to materialize right there in front of her. It felt as if she'd just realized the winning lottery ticket that she was holding was a fake. She contemplated stopping the conversation then and letting Suzanne believe that she was not serious, that it was a joke. But over the last two weeks she'd learned that she had to be sure of herself if she was ever going to do what she wanted to do. She was tired of being the person everybody wanted her to be.

She clenched her fists and held them to her sides, plucking up all the courage she could, and spoke: "No, Suze, I am. We are in love," she said with confidence. "I'll be moving there in the summer." The words were out before Lisa could stop herself, and she looked up to face an incredulous look from Suzanne. All of a sudden, Terrance was the only person in the world who understood her, and she wanted to be back in Goa, in the safety of his arms. Lisa didn't know it, but any resistance was going to make her even more determined.

"You've known him for all of two weeks! Why can't he come here? Don't just throw your entire life away, and your career, just for some holiday fling." The words stung Lisa. She didn't want to hear this and couldn't believe her best friend could be so insensitive. She knew that she had approached the conversation in the wrong manner and excused Suzanne's outburst as shock. It was too much too soon, and she knew she would need to be a little more tactful with her mother.

Even though part of her felt that she needed to offer an explanation to Suzanne, part of her wanted to be completely selfish. It was her life – she could do what she wanted with it. Suzanne was in a good relationship, and no doubt she would be moving in with Arjun soon. Suzanne and Lisa would both carry on with their lives, but never would they be so involved with each other as they were now. Things would change, and Lisa would be left alone. Suzanne would not be worried about her then, whilst she was busy getting married and having babies. It was late, and Lisa could feel her eyelids dropping; she was too jet lagged to have this conversation. She would sleep on it.

But Suzanne wasn't going to let Lisa leave without an explanation. She knew her inside and out, and this was not her. That mothering instinct that Lisa always brought out in her had fought its way to the surface, and she was determined to protect her.

Lisa recognized this at once. She saw the determination in Suzanne's eyes, and she knew that when Suzanne was like this, she would have to offer up an explanation. Lisa's tone softened. "Suzanne, you don't understand. I went in need of a change in my life, for myself, and I found that there. I'm happy over there, and I want to live there. Goa is like no other place. I know I haven't travelled much, but something there caught hold of me. I want to go back. I'll carry on teaching there." She added the last sentence to stop Suzanne thinking she was throwing her career away as well. As she spoke, she was now even more certain of her decision, and no one would be able to stop her.

Suzanne did not show any empathy, but she lowered her voice when she spoke. Taking hold of Lisa's hand, she said "Lisa, you don't know him, though. Where will you stay? With him? I though you said he still lives at home. At twenty-eight?" Suzanne's sarcasm was evident and patronizing.

Lisa kept her calm tone, "That's what they do there. People don't leave home the minute they can, like we do here. He is going to get a place by the time I get back." Lisa tried to appeal to her with desolate eyes.

Suzanne could see her friend hurting, but she knew Lisa was making a mistake, and she just had to tell her, make her see sense. Suzanne and Lisa had always been honest with each other, especially Suzanne, who would never hold back on what she felt. She didn't want to hurt Lisa's feelings, but she had to say what was on her mind. If she didn't, and Lisa did go and got hurt in the process, she would never be able to forgive herself. "Oh, Lisa, I know you think you are in love," Suzanne said, trying a softer approach. "You just came out of a bizarre relationship before you left. You have been a bit lonely lately, and I understand, but you have kind of just latched onto the first person who has shown you a bit of affection." She hadn't meant for it to come out quite as harshly as it did. The statement hung there between them, causing almost irreparable damage to their friendship.

"I can't believe you see me like that! A desperate person so needy of love? Well, I could say a few things about you and Arjun that would just rip you to shreds," she said, her voice increasing in pitch. She had surprised herself with the words that leapt from her mouth, but Suzanne's comments had cut her to the bone. Suzanne bore a look of utter shock. Lisa sighed. She didn't have anything on Arjun, and she would never stoop so low as to make something up. She was tired, and she wanted her bed.

"I'm going to sleep, Suze. I can't do this tonight," Lisa said, avoiding Suzanne's glare.

"Tell me, damn you! Lisa, tell me *what* about Arjun and me?" Suzanne looked desperate. She wanted to know now, and she wasn't prepared to wait till morning.

"Nothing, Suze. I just said it, okay, to get you off my back and so you'd know what it felt like. Nothing. You guys are perfect. You must be so happy." Lisa turned, tears welling up in her eyes. She headed upstairs, flinging her black messenger over her shoulder and grabbing her camera from the coffee table. She felt defeated.

"Wait, Lisa," Suzanne said, shaking off the blanket she had pulled over herself to keep warm. She rose from the sofa and reached out to Lisa. They let the hug between them melt their tension.

Suzanne let go of her fears for Lisa. She had to let her make her own mistakes, or she would lose her best friend, and she knew that. "Go and get ready for bed, and I'll make you a cup of tea and bring it up to you. You can tell me all, then."

"Thank you," Lisa said, heading up the stairs. She was relieved. She couldn't fight any more.

As Lisa disappeared out of slight, Suzanne felt a wave of sorrow wash over her. She had already lost her friend to Terrance; she knew that, and it hurt.

18

Lisa woke up the next morning, and in the light of day she began to question her decision. It was unlike her to be so hasty, but then again, she had never really been in love before. Her heart yearned for Terrance as she reread the note he had slipped her at the airport. It was some tangible evidence that he existed and that he loved her and would wait for her.

Grateful for the invention of cyberspace, she pulled her dressing gown around her and padded over to the computer. Her body had still not acclimatized to the cold January weather, after the thirty-degree heat she had become used to. She opened her blue polka dot curtains. It was only six in the morning and still dark outside. Condensation ran down the single-glazed window, catching the yellow of the light that lit up the empty street. How different Oxford was when the students were on vacation. She logged on to Skype, hoping to talk to Terrance. She hovered her mouse over the connection, her fingers trembling with excitement at hearing his voice again. Instinctively she straightened her posture and ran her fingers through her hair, detangling it after her sleep. She reached for her make-up bag and added a touch of blusher to her cheeks; the cold had quickly taken away her tan. She knew in an instant, when she saw Terrance's deep brown eyes staring back at her, that this was for real. No matter what her closest friend had said, nothing would stop her from making that trip out at Easter.

As the days passed, it became a ritual before she left for work each morning that they speak for at least half an hour. Their conversations were centred on their time spent together and how they were just managing to get by without each other. To Lisa, the distance between them was now a minor hiccup in their plan, and she believed that their love was growing stronger rather than weaker.

*

Lisa half smiled to herself now, as she thought of those long conversations they used to have through the night into the early morning. How surreal it all seemed now, over a year later. Sitting on a park bench in the middle of Regent's Park, she allowed the daffodil to fall as she rubbed her hands together, trying to keep warm. She glanced at her watch. In exactly fifty minutes her fate would be revealed.

Staring at the yellow flower on the dewy grass, she remembered the day she had told her mother what she had decided. Her mother had had news for her as well. Maybe she should have stopped her plans then; maybe it was a signal, an omen. But no, she was too wrapped up in her own emotions to even consider that. Laden with souvenirs and gifts, she had knocked on her parents' door. She'd been full of nerves, about to reveal her life plans. However, Lisa didn't know that her parents had some news of their own.

*

"Lisa, how lovely to see you; you are still looking golden," her mother said, embracing her daughter as she pulled open the heavy wooden door that formed the entrance to their family home. Lisa had loved that door; it always reminded her of her childhood; she'd felt safe and secure as long as she was behind that door. Her father relieved her of her heavy bags. Suddenly, she sensed that something was wrong. Her parents seemed to have aged greatly over the Christmas break. Her mother, so bold normally, seemed frail and tired, and her father looked as if he were carrying the weight of the world's problems on his shoulders. But how do you tell your parents that they look older and tired? She thought as she masked her inner thoughts with a smile. She had an inkling that it was apprehension at breaking her news to them that made her see her parents in this way. Her palms were cold and sweaty, and she was fighting the urge to play with her hair, a sure telltale to her mother that something was wrong.

She seated herself in the living room, taking in the floral Laura Ashley wallpaper and the old lemon and pale blue sofas that her mother swore were all the rage. That had been about eighteen years ago, and they still remained. Lisa had never said anything about them, because like the door, they always reminded her of home. A wave of nostalgia washed over her, something she rarely let herself indulge in. She looked at her mother, noticing her high cheekbones. As much as she denied it, she actually looked like her. Family friends had always commented on their similarities, but she had always brushed them aside. Now she wondered why she had been so quick to dismiss these observations. She should have been happy about this. Even now, her mother was beautiful. She recalled, as a child, watching her from the doorway of her room as she applied her blusher and lipstick. She applied her make-up the same way, now. In fact, lately she had seen bits of her mother in herself, in the way she had started to do things, and she secretly liked it. Margaret had soft, brown, wavy hair, with a fleck of grey and an almost perfect complexion. Lisa would be happy to look like her at that age.

She had so many good childhood memories. She could see herself and Paul as clearly as if it were yesterday, playing with My Little Ponies. Apple Blossom and Bow Tie, in their clashing bright colours, had been her favourites. They'd played noughts and crosses on those yellow and blue sofas, being careful not to stain or mark them, in fear of a scolding from their mother. Lisa peered behind the back of the sofa to see if the greasy stain was still visible. It was; she clearly remembered the day her mother had caught her sticking a piece of wax from her cheese on the sofa. They never were allowed to peel their own little cheeses after that.

Lisa poured herself a cup of tea from the white porcelain teapot her mother had placed before her. She held her tongue about her own news as her parents regaled her with stories about Christmas and their new grandson, all the gifts they had received, and the ones that they'd given. Pictures were flashing at Lisa from a digital photo frame that was a new addition to the mantelpiece. Her father was clearly impressed with the gift, which she correctly guessed was from Paul. Lisa felt a slight pang of regret. Although she hadn't felt it much at the time, she had missed Christmas with her family. It was her first one away, and probably the first of many, she thought. She would have to get used to it. Sitting in that living room, she wondered if she had to tell her parents just quite yet about her decision to move to Goa. It would break their hearts, and it was not completely decided yet. She would be going back to Goa for Easter, of that she was certain – supposedly to decide her future, even though she had already made up her mind. She wanted to move out there, where her heart belonged.

Lisa moved uneasily in her seat. She wrung her hands together as she told her parents about Terrance and informed them that she would be going back to meet him again. As the words left her mouth, she braced herself for her mother's reaction. She anticipated her mother pulling out a scrapbook of failed romances of people who had met on holiday. Worse still, Lisa had herself seen a recent article in one of the tabloids, where a Goan man had conned a middle-aged divorcee out of her life savings by promising her the world. It was unbelievable – these stories almost always were – but it was something she knew her mother would pick up on, and she had the sudden urge to run out of the house before the lecture came. But something held her back. Her parents were silent; it was an uneasy silence. Her mother smiled and said something about being glad that she had met someone.

Startled, she looked intently at her parents. It was highly unlike them to agree with her and not to display their unnecessary overprotective streak. She knew that something was wrong. This was a golden opportunity for her mother to shout her down and start criticizing her choice of boyfriend. Through the uncomfortable silence that ensued, Lisa prayed that one of them would speak before she had to again. She was about to justify her decision, a speech she had learnt off by heart, repeating it to herself in the bath last night. Then it finally dawned on her that they had something to tell her, something that until now they had concealed. In an instant, the roles were reversed. Without a single word being exchanged, she became the worried party – and then her mother burst into tears.

*

Margaret was breaking down in front of her and Lisa wasn't quite sure of what to do. Was it what she had said? She hadn't even told them the half of it, she thought. Lisa moved over to where her mother was sitting and put her arm around her, something she had never done before. It didn't feel quite right. She thought back and realized that, from her childhood to now, she had never seen her mother cry. Margaret had always been the strong one.

It was then that her father said just one sentence that sent her head into a spin: "It's cancer, dear." The words ripped through her like a sharp blade, and she felt her whole world crashing down around her. All of a sudden, Terrance didn't matter any more.

The malignant word resounded in her head. She didn't know what to say or do. Would it be okay? She knew friends who had lost relatives and friends to cancer, but she'd never thought it would happen to someone so close to her. Lisa was lost for words. She had too much emotion built up inside her and couldn't find an easy way to express it. She just wanted to cry, but she couldn't. It was her turn to be strong.

"I found a lump in my breast." Her mother had somewhat calmed now, but the words struggled free. A million thoughts were still racing through Lisa's mind. Wasn't that one of the better cancers to have? – if those two words were possible in the same sentence. Wasn't that curable? Couldn't they just remove the breast? She felt helpless at her lack of knowledge. She'd seen countless adverts, and she'd seen pink ribbons being sold everywhere. She'd occasionally dropped a pound in a charity bin for a daffodil, but it hadn't improved her knowledge of the deadly disease. *Why my mother?* she thought, angry now at her own ignorance. *Why not your mother?* a voice inside of her answered her own question.

Margaret continued, "I am scheduled to have it out this coming Friday. You see, they did a biopsy and the tumour is malignant. We were praying that it would not be, but you see, at my age, the chances are ..." her mother trailed off, breaking into a soft sobbing.

In that moment, Lisa just wanted to hold her mother and tell that that it would be okay, as she had done for her when she was young and in bed with some childhood sickness. She recalled her mother tucking her up in bed, calling the school to say that her daughter was unwell, and putting on *The Sound of Music* or *Mary Poppins*. Those old movies always made her feel better; even now she still sometimes watched them when she was feeling unwell. She felt helpless. A movie and a hot bowl of chicken soup would not make her mother feel any better – nothing she could do would. That was the worst feeling, that feeling of helplessness. It caught hold of Lisa and broke her. She vowed to herself that she would research everything about her mother's illness. She would find something to ease her fears.

Lisa felt a pang of unreasonable guilt, for not spending enough time with her mother over the last few years, and for her initial reluctance to visit her today. Suzanne had had to force her to call Margaret and make the visit. Although she might have stressed out Lisa on more than one occasion regarding her single status, and despite the fact that they called her "the Beast", Margaret had always been there for her, and she had always loved her. Lisa couldn't deny that her mother had always had her best interests at heart. She was, after all, her mother, and that love is unconditional. Today she didn't look so much like a beast. She looked so vulnerable.

Lisa didn't know where to begin with her questions. She knew cancer was one of the most evil and ruthless killers, but she hadn't a clue about where it began and ended. A lump was beginning to form in the back of Lisa's throat, and she had to blink back the tears that were rapidly forming in her eyes. Her father, as if reading her mind, explained the gist of the treatment.

"It hasn't spread," he said, placing his arm around Lisa. "They don't think it has, at least. They will know more on Friday when they do the lumpectomy," he said, trying to hold his voice steady.

"What's a lumpectomy? Do they just remove the lump, then, and not the breast?" Lisa enquired, concerned that this would still allow the cancer to attack again.

Her mother took over. "Yes, just the lump and a bit of the healthy tissue that surrounds it. The cancer is only in one part of the breast, so I don't need the whole thing removed. They will probably do some radiation therapy after that. When the wounds heal."

"Oh, will that make you sick?" Lisa asked, remembering that it was often the obliteration of healthy cells along with the malignant cells that caused violent sickness.

"No, that's chemotherapy. I should be fine, Lisa. It's just the shock, that's all," Margaret tried to excuse her outburst. She didn't need to, but Lisa let her; she knew what her mother was like. "Cancer is a horrible diagnosis to receive."

Lisa left her parents' house that day feeling helpless and drained. Archana had once said to her that it was better to be sick yourself rather than to see someone you love fall ill, because there is nothing you can do to take away their suffering. She had dismissed this at the time, but now she knew Archana had been right.

19

The sun shone through the large, arched window, warming up her room to an unbearable temperature. It was a scorching day, temperatures hitting thirty-five degrees, which would have been normal of a typical Goan summer, but it was only January. Sonya stripped down to her underwear and tried to fiddle with the air conditioner. In true Goa fashion, the air conditioner had decided to break on possibly the hottest day ever recorded. Despite the heat, Sonya was smiling. She would be meeting Terrance today. Exactly one week after Lisa had left, Terrance had come back to her.

Sonya was going to take Carl's advice this time and make it harder for him. He couldn't keep doing this to her so publicly. They needed to work out a better arrangement, and he needed to make a decision. It was quite obvious to her just how Terrance was using Lisa, but it wasn't quite so obvious to their friends. Worse still, if her family caught wind of it, they would certainly not approve and might try to prevent her from executing her master plan of marriage.

Sonya walked over to her wardrobe and took out the new outfit she had bought especially for this evening. She'd known it wouldn't be long before he called her, and she'd been right. At least he was taking her out for dinner, she thought, as she held up the short, black dress against her. It had a silver sequinned snake that wrapped around her neck, forming a halter. She wouldn't need much jewellery with this, although Terrance would be sure to give her something. He always did when he wanted to apologize. Sonya had a new take on the whole "Lisa" situation. She was willing to put this episode behind her and start afresh. Time was ticking, and in November she would be another year older. She had to get closer to her goal this year, no matter what.

She admired herself in the mirror. She had recently cut her hair into a short-cropped bob, and the last time she was in Anjuna she had gotten a tattoo, a vine that ran along the front of her foot and around her ankle.

She wanted to show Terrance a different side to her, one that differentiated her from the plain and simple Lisa. According to Carl, her "friend", as he called her recent acquaintance, had gotten into her head and convinced her that a tattoo was sexy. A shiver ran down her spine as she remembered the tattooist piercing her skin, her "friend" holding her hand tightly.

When Sonya had first met Terrance, he had said to her that he loved her spontaneous personality, her "don't-give-a-fuck attitude". That had been nine years ago. She had changed. She had stopped wearing lace leggings and black lipstick, and she'd sobered up, conforming to popular culture and its whims. She'd started following fashion, as opposed to creating it, and she'd begun to worry about what people thought. She wondered if this happened to everyone with age. Her gradual change in personality had not done her any favours, though, except in her parents' eyes. They were relieved that she now looked like all her friends and that she actually fitted in. But now Sonya wanted to revert back to her younger years, when she'd been more carefree. It was what Terrance had first fallen in love with her for. Her new look would remind him of that.

She recalled introducing Terrance and Lisa. He had always liked girls with a little more to them, so when Terrance looked as if he were falling for Lisa, it had surprised Sonya. Had he changed as well? Lisa had probably never set a foot wrong in her life – but he was just using her, *right?* She was a pawn in their little game, and in that case, she had no regrets. Life was too short for that.

But she had a nagging feeling that wouldn't go away. She had heard just yesterday from Teresa that little dreary Lisa might be back during the Easter Holidays. Sonya knew she would have to do something to ensure that Lisa would never set foot in Goa again. *Her time is over,* she said to herself as Terrance pulled up outside her house.

Over dinner she tried to suppress talking about Lisa. She knew what his reaction would be, and she knew she was being unreasonable, but she just couldn't help herself. "Cheating on her already, Terrance? So soon after her departure? She couldn't have been that hot, then." She smiled, happy with her deduction.

Terrance gave Sonya a wry smile. "Sweetheart, this is not cheating. We are two grown adults enjoying each other's company over dinner. Where is the harm in that?"

Sonya took a large sip of her cold white wine and poked around her pasta with her fork. She looked around the restaurant for people that she knew. In Goa there was always a chance of bumping into someone that you didn't want to, someone who would come over to your table to ask you things you didn't want to answer, so they could gossip about you as soon as you were out of earshot. Apart from an elderly couple she recognized from the Coconut Grove, she was all in the clear. It would not get back to Ayesha and Teresa that she had so easily accepted a date with Terrance. That would surely have made their day.

"Okay, T, what's done is done. You publicly humiliated me by going around with her in open view for everyone to see. She has served her purpose. I get it; you did what you had to do. So tell me, why am I now hearing that she will be back around Easter time?" She didn't wish to say her name out loud; the very name irritated her. It was a direct question and lacked the tact that she had initially planned to use, but she was tired of the last two hours of small talk. This was Terrance, after all. She had known him for years; it was no time for pretences.

There was a silence, and for the first time since she'd known him, she could not read him. His body language confused her; his mind was not with her. Sonya looked at him incredulously. Had he actually fallen in love with Lisa? "Not possible," she mumbled to herself. Terrance looked up from his fillet of beef on a bed of wilting salad and directly at her; it unnerved her.

"She is coming back, Sonya. She will be coming to stay with me in her Easter break." He smiled, but there was no malice in it; he said it as if he was merely stating a fact.

Despite the cool breeze from the air conditioning in the restaurant, Sonya started to feel uncomfortably warm. This wouldn't be the first time that Terrance had played hard to get. He wanted her to beg him, to plead with him to take her back.

"You don't understand. I may not be around next time, Terrance. I may have moved on, you know. I am tired of this. I cannot, I just cannot, continue this way." Sonya thought about her recent fling and how happy she had been, but even then she had known that a relationship with someone else would never work. No, she needed Terrance for there to be a wedding. She took another large sip of her wine to relax her, before she continued. It was a game he liked playing, but she had grown so tired of this same old routine. She looked around the restaurant at the deep, red carpets and the gaudy gold-and-black statues. It had once been a Chinese restaurant and had now turned Italian, but the owners had done little to change the Asian theme. She'd never understood why Terrance liked it so much; their food was average. She continued, "Remember, you promised me that we would be married some day. You don't want to marry that girl. She will never understand you the way I do." Sonya looked down at the table, trying to hold back the tears. Why was he doing this to her, she wondered. What was so special about that girl? She looked so damn ordinary.

"You don't understand, Sonya." Terrance looked at her, knowing that he could not afford to lose her, not now, but something *had* changed.

"I thought you were using her," Sonya said, lifting up her glass and glaring at him; she had given up on her food.

He was quiet. He put down his tumbler of whisky and ice, pulled out an envelope from his jacket hanging behind his chair, and slid it across the table to Sonya. "Here, this will put a smile on your face."

Terrance saw the flicker of hesitation in her eyes. "What's wrong now? Don't go all *senti* on me. It's all done." He winked at her and gently touched her hand under the table. She placed her hand on the envelope. As she took it, a shiver ran down her spine as she remembered their first meeting with *that man* in Joel's, over a summer ago. She shook her mind free from that thought and placed the money in her handbag, It just about fit.

"I should have brought a bigger bag," she said. "So that's it – all done?" Sonya said, laying her knife and fork side by side on her plate. She had barely eaten at all, but most of the wine had gone; there was less than a glass left in the bottle.

Terrance smiled at her tenderly. "You need to bear with me, *acha*." He took Sonya's hand and squeezed it for reassurance, but she still looked upset. "That's why," he continued, barely audible, "that's why I need her to come back."

Sonya relaxed for the first time that evening. She wiped away the single tear that was rolling down her cheek and gently took his hand in hers. She allowed herself to enjoy feeling the warmth of his hands, and she knew that he would marry her soon.

That night Sonya didn't sleep much. She was both happy and nervous. Terrance had said he was using Lisa, and there was no doubt in her mind that he wasn't, but she knew, still, what a determined woman was capable of. It was a gamble. If Lisa came back and dug her claws into Terrance, it could spell trouble for her. But she would wait in the wings patiently for Easter to come and go, as long as he stuck to his part of the deal this time and kept it discreet. It would be a testing time for all of them, but afterwards they would be free to continue with their lives. The vibration of her mobile telephone shook her from her thoughts. She looked at the display screen and smiled. It was her backup plan.

20

Suzanne and Arjun were engaged by the end of February, and when the lease for their duplex in St Clements came up in the summer, Suzanne would be moving in with Arjun in Jericho.

She had successfully won over his parents, and they had had a lavish engagement party at the Bear Hotel. Suzanne had worn a beautiful royal-blue *gagra choli* and dazzled with the gold jewellery Arjun's parents had given her as an engagement present. Even Lisa had attempted to pull off a salwar kameez, surprised at just how comfortable the trousers and long tunic were. They had enjoyed a banquet of Indian food, delicious aromas of keema and biryani filling the room, and they had danced well into the evening with the sounds of a tabla and sitar. Lisa no longer worried about being alone in their apartment; she was excited about her next trip to Goa. Terrance had not been in touch as often as when she'd first gotten back, but when he did speak to her, he said all the right things. He had told her that his parents were fully supportive of her moving over if and when she was ready, and she appreciated his concern for her. He had given her time and space and, above all, supported her through a tough time when she'd needed him the most. She knew she could not have coped without him.

Her mother's health had, of course, been a worry. She had gone for a lumpectomy but had then decided to have the whole breast removed, just to be sure. She had reluctantly agreed when the doctor had suggested it, being scared that she would be losing a part of her femininity. The decision had been the right one, though, and although it was early days, she was doing well. Lisa had spent most of her weekends in Leicester doing what she could for her parents, and by the time Easter came round, she really needed a break. There was not much she could do for her mother now, but over the last couple of months they had grown much closer. She'd realized Margaret was just another person, human, with the same emotions. In return, Margaret was being supportive of Lisa going to Goa and only occasionally reminded her to keep her head on her shoulders. Secretly, she was afraid that Lisa would leave them. She was praying that if she did, Terrance would be the right one for her and that he would look after her daughter, but she never said this to Lisa. Those days were over. She would worry about her silently from now on; it was time to let go of the child she most loved.

What did bother Lisa was not knowing whether she would get to see her best friend married. She was saving as hard as she could for her new life away, and this life didn't include jetting halfway across the world on a whim. It was going to be tough saving to go there, because she knew that once she got to Goa her earning potential was slim to none, and she doubted that Terrance would be able to afford flights to England and back. No, once she moved out there, she would not be able to come back often.

Before Lisa had headed out to Goa late in March, Terrance had phoned her with some good news. He had moved out of his parents' house and into his own apartment in Panjim. Lisa would be staying just with him and not his entire family, and she was relieved to hear this. This way, she could really gauge the situation and decide if Goa and Terrance were the right choices to make. She had refused to impose on his family home, and shelling out for a fortnight at the Coconut Grove again would have left her pretty much broke for the next two months.

*

This time Lisa's flight was much more relaxed. The slum dwellings did not impose on her as they had done that first time. She peered into the sea of tin roofs, with their makeshift damp-proofing of bright-blue plastic sheets. When she arrived at Dabolim she effortlessly manoeuvred her wonky-wheeled luggage trolley towards Terrance, who was standing outside the airport, eagerly awaiting her arrival. As soon as she was in his car, she felt as if she were home rather than being on holiday, and as she stepped into their new apartment, she knew she had made the right decision. She couldn't believe that he had done all of this for her.

The apartment was cool and spacious. It didn't have any amazing sea views, as he had once promised, but it was in the heart of the city, and Lisa could easily get about by bus or autorickshaw. It was quite bare, with basic white tiles and an open-plan sitting room and kitchen. The lack of home decorations gave Lisa a chance to put her own stamp on the place; after the two weeks it felt like home. They spent the days lying on the beach and soaking up the sun, and the evenings in beach shacks drinking beer and eating. She saw a different side to Goa, and she was glad that Terrance's other friends were not around so much. Goa seemed much more peaceful this time, with fewer tourists and without the hype of Christmas and New Year's Eve. Terrance had taken some time off work, and the way he was spending provided him with the perfect excuse for not leaving his father's business. She felt more at ease knowing that the money Terrance was earning was enough to support the two of them.

The only real social event that Lisa attended was the wedding of Sanjay and Ayesha. She had been surprised that it had not even been mentioned in December. If Goan weddings were anything like those in England, it would take at least a year to organize.

Terrance had filled her in on the hurried nature of the wedding. "It is so soon for a reason" he had said. "Ayesha is pregnant, and they have decided against 'the *A* word', so yaar, they are getting married."

Lisa had presumed as much, but she hadn't wanted to be the one to ask. "Mmm, I thought as much. How far along is she?"

"Two months."

"She isn't showing; I would have thought she would, as she is so tiny to begin with. I wonder how she will manage with pregnancy. What do her parents say?"

"They don't say," Terrance said, casually pouring himself and Lisa a Kingfisher beer. He continued, "She says she has told them, and they must know, as must the whole of Goa. You don't just decide to get married and then, boom, two months later you are pregnant. Christmas time is the wedding season here, not the height of summer, when everybody is all sweaty."

"If it's common knowledge, then—" Lisa started.

"Then nobody says anything. Everybody just has a good laugh behind closed doors," Terrance added, warning her not to talk about it with anyone.

"But won't people know, when seven months after she is married, she has a baby?"

"Yes, like I said, in seven months time Seema Aunty will say, "Ohhh, my daughter's baby was premature!" he said, mimicking Ayesha's mother in a high-pitched squeal. "And everyone will *coo* and congratulate, all the while laughing with their friends. It is not the first time and not the last time that this will happen, but it saves face, na? And people here will forget; for sure there will be another scandal before long."

Lisa wasn't quite sure if it did save face, knowing full well that everybody knew and everyone was pretending not to know, but it was another quirk of Goan culture that she would just have to adjust to. It was a by-product of this melting pot of East and West, and she would have to adapt whether or not she thought it was hypocritical. At least Goa society had moved on so much that she and Terrance could live together without being married. That was progress.

*

When the day of the wedding arrived, Lisa was thoroughly excited. It was a Hindu wedding, and the only other Hindu function she had been to was Suzanne's engagement party. She was thrilled to be part of the celebration; it would give her a chance to get to socialize with the others in more formal surroundings.

Terrance had taken her shopping to get some suitable Indian attire for the functions she was going to attend. She needed three outfits with jewellery and accessories to match. At first when she'd heard about this, she had been slightly worried. She'd never been good at picking out clothes and generally stuck to subdued colours, but after Suzanne and Arjun's engagement, she knew she would have to pick something brighter. It seemed to be Indian tradition. The colours of their saris vibrantly displayed the rich tapestry of their culture and their welcoming and friendly personalities. She didn't want to dampen the mood in some dark colour.

She chose a stitched pink sari with silver work for the evening reception, which she was looking forward to the most. It looked like a normal sari, but instead of traditionally wrapping the material around her, she just put it on like a skirt. The petite saleswoman had said that this was a "better option" for her. Quite crassly, she said, "If somebody can put it on for you, then okay, fine. But what happens when you need to pee?" She had looked at Lisa for an answer, of which Lisa had none. The saleswoman had made a good point. No one would be helping her to put it back on, and she had no idea how she would hitch the thing up in the first place when she did need the toilet. The evening reception would involve much drinking and dancing.

Teresa was kind enough to give Lisa one of her sister's saris for the mehndi party the day before the wedding. Teresa's sister was a little on the larger side, so she had to take the sari top in slightly. She stood in front of the mirror with the green material in her hand, waiting patiently as Teresa wrapped the length of it around her. She tucked it into a skirt that she had made Lisa put on previously and pinned them together.

"There," Teresa said, admiring her handiwork. Teresa herself looked stunning in a pale light-orange and silver *salwar*. Her make-up was done perfectly and traditionally; she had on dark red lipstick, and a thick lining of *kohl* framed her eyes. She was much taller tonight. She had shown Lisa her shoes – they were at least three inches high, and Lisa wondered just how Teresa would walk on the uneven ground in them.

She thanked Teresa and turned around, looking at her outfit at all angles. Earlier in the week, she had chosen simple silver shoes with a matching handbag that would go with all her outfits. Teresa had explained the mehndi party to Lisa, and she was honoured that Ayesha had included her in these celebrations.

"It's for women only," Teresa said. "There will be a lady that will put henna on your hands and arms," she continued before they left for the party. When they arrived, it was exactly as Lisa had imagined. The party was set in the grounds of Ayesha's house, and a little stage had been created where Ayesha sat with pretty henna designs all over her hands, arms, and feet. Behind Ayesha was a wall of brilliant, bright-orange carnation flowers. The smell drifted through the party. She looked stunning, dressed in gold, and had jewellery dripping from her ears and nose. She was also wearing garlands of white and red flowers. The atmosphere was serene, and the garden was beautifully decorated. The coconut trees shone amidst white and yellow fairy lights, and garlands of bright-orange flowers decorated the tables and chairs.

A young Indian woman approached Lisa with a tube of henna that looked like something she would ice a cake with. "Henna for you?" she asked politely. Lisa agreed, not knowing that the henna would last for at least a month. As the young Indian lady drew the most exquisite patterns on Lisa's hands with the thick, green henna paste, she sang softly a Hindi song.

"It's a beautiful song," Lisa said, trying to make conversation.

The henna artist smiled. "You like it? It's from my favourite movie. There, I have finished. Now, keep this on and wash it just before you go to bed. Then, when you get back to your country, everyone will see that you went to an Indian wedding. Traditionally, the bride is not supposed to do any housework until the mehndi fades completely," she said, winking at Lisa as she moved on to the next guest.

The next day the henna had tattooed Lisa's skin a deep orange, and she was not quite sure that she liked it. It was very pretty in design, though, and it was such a big part of the celebrations that she'd felt she had to. In any case, she had no choice now. It had stained her skin so deeply that no matter how much she washed her skin it would not fade. She had often noticed Indian girls with designs all over their hands and feet and wondered what it was. Now she knew.

The mehndi party was just a prelude to the extravagant wedding ceremony and reception. Lisa tried to get a good view of the wedding, which was again on a makeshift stage. From where she was standing with Terrance at the back of the room, she could just about see Ayesha and Sanjay. The room that they were in was again decorated in garlands of flowers. Sanjay wore white, with a small turban on his head, and Ayesha was weighted down with gold. She wore a traditional red-and-gold sari and sat quietly on the stage with Sanjay. The saleswoman in the shop had been right; the ceremony had taken some time. She was glad she had chosen a gold *gagra choli* for this, a skirt and top easy to manoeuvre in.

Lisa caught glimpses of the happy couple being tied together with a white scarf. "What's that for?" Lisa asked Terrance, who was trying to concentrate on the ceremony. Sonya shot her a look that made her want to sit back down again and blend into the background. She was upset that Sonya was at their table, but then, where else would she be at her best friends' wedding? Lisa was lucky that she was there.

"They are being tied together to symbolize their eternal bond. Here, look, and now they will walk around the fire. Each time they circle the fire it represents a different goal in their lives, like prosperity and liberation," Terrance explained. He was wearing a traditional cream *kurta churidar* with a green border, and pointy brown slippers. It suited him, and Lisa grabbed hold of his hand, wanting everyone to know that they were together. But Terrance withdrew his hand, quickly throwing rice at Sanjay and Ayesha with the rest of the crowd. She could see a smirk on Sonya's face, and it upset her.

The couple then threw what looked like rice into the fire, and Sanjay put a small red dot on Ayesha's head.

"This is how they welcome each other into their respective families," Teresa whispered, realizing that Terrance was too preoccupied with his best friend getting married to explain the ins and outs of the wedding ceremony to his girlfriend.

Lisa was grateful for the running commentary that Teresa had given her, but she was annoyed that Terrance was not more attentive. He had kept her at an arm's length since she had got back from the mehndi party. She couldn't help but think that he had spent that evening with Sonya, as – surprisingly – she had not been there that evening. He had been disinterested when Teresa had dropped her back later that evening, and he had gone straight to bed. It had played on her mind, but she couldn't bring herself to ask him; she didn't want to portray herself as needy and insecure so early on in their relationship. She had driven off a boyfriend before like this, and she was not going to do it again.

The venue they had chosen for their evening reception was perfect. It was set in acres of lush, green gardens, with white cloth draped from trees into the centre of the dance floor providing a canopy for the guests. The evening air was somewhat cooler than it had been during the day, but Lisa was glad of this, as her sari was in a satin material that her skin found it difficult to breathe in. The food and drink were freely flowing, and everyone was in good spirits. The band was playing Hindi music and more popular English tunes, and most of the guests were dancing.

Little lanterns studded the setting, and guests milled in and out of the area. The venue was massive. Lisa had never been to a wedding for over eighty people, and there were at least three hundred here. The guests wore a mix of traditional Indian and Western wear, and their jewellery was exquisite. Lisa now felt that her single-pearl pendant was rather inadequate for the event, but she was glad she had heeded Terrance's advice and worn a traditional sari; she felt as if she slotted right into the party in this attire.

Terrance had grown more attentive once they'd arrived at the evening reception, and now he could not keep his hands off her, a dramatic change from his earlier behaviour. They had danced together to a couple of songs, the warm night seeming even hotter as he embraced her. She could smell the whisky on his breath, and later, in the wee hours of the morning when they'd stumbled back to their apartment, he had made love to her so tenderly that she knew she would spend the rest of her life with him.

The summer in Goa was hot; it was so warm that on some days Lisa felt as though she could not breathe. The wedding had taken up so much of her holiday, but it had made her feel as if she were one of them, included into their group. She had been part of something very special in Ayesha and Sanjay's lives. Lisa's only concern was that Sonya was still lurking around Terrance, making her feel anxious. It was if they had more than friendship between them but Sonya quite coolly had accepted Lisa into their lives this time. Apart from the occasional stare of death she received, there was not so much a mention of her relationship with Terrance. Whenever Lisa did see Sonya, though, she seemed to have a permanent smirk plastered across her face, like a cat that had got the cream, and this unnerved Lisa. At least she reassured herself that she had followed through with one of her New Year's resolutions and made it to the gym most days. She was slightly more toned than the last time, and she needed to be. She needed to compete with Sonya's svelte figure.

21

Walking back from Regent's Park towards the courthouse, Lisa remembered her final day in Goa that Easter – the last time that she would see Terrance – and she felt her heart give way. How could she still have feelings for him after all that had passed since? She laughed out loud now at her own stupidity that day. How could she have let such a heinous crime occur? She no longer felt scared of her imminent sentence. In fact, she felt relieved. She had let these things happen; she had been party to a crime, and it was time to accept her punishment. It would relieve her of her guilt. But when? When had she turned into the kind of person who would turn a blind eye, or worse still, be an accomplice? She had not been so innocent on that final trip back, she thought, as she had tried to lead the jury to believe. In her heart of hearts she had known what was happening, and she had let it be.

*

The day of her departure that April came around quickly. She stood on the balcony of their apartment, watching the workmen in their lunghis climbing up the scaffolding they had erected against the building opposite. It was a dangerous-looking scaffold, made from thick bamboo tied together by rope, and she marvelled at how different Goa was from the nanny state she knew. Terrance had gone to fill up the car before running her to the airport. As she waited for him, her head was filled with lists of items that she wanted to bring over to Goa. There were so many little things, like her moisturizer and the mint and tea tree shower gel that she just couldn't live without. Would she just bring stocks of it over, or would she have to find something more local? She knew that the move would take some adjusting to. Lisa Higgins, who had never really liked much change, would be changing quite a bit.

She saw Terrance pull up as he hooted the horn to signal his arrival. She took one last look around the home they had created. In the two weeks she had been there, she had filled it with terracotta pots for all the plants they had acquired and beautiful silks embroidered with elephants and tigers, which she had found in the market. As she locked the apartment door behind her, she smiled, seeing her apartment key on her tatty leather key ring. It was the key to their home, the key to her future. As she descended the flight of stairs, she noticed another passenger in the car and wondered who it was. She had been under the impression that Terrance had gone to "fill gas", as he put it. As Lisa got into the car, Terrance made the introductions, and all of a sudden Lisa remembered him.

"This is Tariq. You met him on your last trip – you flew back together, remember? I didn't think you would mind escorting him again. You were perfect last time. The kids said it as well, and you said it was no bother." Lisa recalled the boy from the last trip, and she greeted him. He was still very quiet and was now wearing a pair of thick-rimmed glasses. She knew just how mean kids could be and wondered just how long those spectacles would last when he went back to school.

"He came back for the Easter break," Terrance said. "But it is his last trip; he won't be back for a long time now. He just has to get used to life over there." Terrance said something in Konkani to Tariq and winked at him through the rear-view mirror. Lisa recalled his sister and how they had made her feel so welcome on Christmas day. This was a small favour to ask. She asked after the boy's mother, but he just looked down at his shoes.

Lisa took a deep breath; it irked her somewhat that Terrance had sprung this on her at the last minute. They had spent virtually every minute of the last two weeks together, and he had failed to ask her if she would mind? It had not been a problem last time; she had enjoyed being of some use to Terrance and his family, but she would have liked him to ask sooner. She silently debated whether or not to make her feelings known but decided against it. She knew it was her last day, and she would have to let it slide. She didn't want to leave on a bad note. The two weeks had just flown by, and with having to leave Terrance again so soon, she was feeling sick to her stomach. For some reason, the atmosphere was tense in the car. She worried that her annoyance was evident to Terrance; she knew how much he cared for his cousins. "Where is Shruti?" she asked the little boy, turning towards him.

"She did not come this time. She is adapting to life in England much better than he is. She's made some friends and is happy there now – well, happier," Terrance answered for him, looking at the timid boy in the mirror. "Thank you for asking," he said, squeezing Lisa's hand for reassurance. Lisa thought that the girl had done well, then, considering that only a few months ago she had looked so scared, almost frightened – but children were resilient like that. She turned again to the boy.

"You are a brave boy travelling by yourself," she said, trying to encourage him to talk to her. He looked as if he were about to burst into tears, and so she swiftly turned back and said nothing more. She remembered how shy she had been at that age, as well. She could still be shy now.

After a tearful goodbye at the airport, Tariq and Lisa boarded their flight to London via Mumbai. But she was restless on the flight, and she didn't know why. She glanced over at Tariq, who was intently watching a Bollywood movie on the in-flight entertainment system that the air hostess had helped him with. All of a sudden she noticed his leg was unmarked. She could clearly recall the last time she had seen him and how she had noticed a long scar above his knee. Surely it would not have healed so soon, without leaving so much as a faint mark. The boy shifted and covered himself with the airline blanket. Maybe she was looking at the wrong leg, Lisa thought, but now something about the boy made her feel uneasy. He looked slightly smaller than before, but then again, she had hardly been paying attention back then, she'd been so wrapped up with Terrance.

Lisa smiled to herself, relieved as she remembered that, of course, she had his passport and could easily check his name. When she held it in her hand, however, she could not help but feel as if she were betraying Terrance by opening it. He would never try to do something untoward and put her in any kind of danger. Nevertheless, the teacher inside her told her to check, just for her own piece of mind. She flicked open the maroon booklet to the last page. His name was Tariq, and he looked very much like his passport photo – why was she being paranoid? She placed the passport back into her messenger and placated herself, excusing it as nerves from making the final decision to move to Goa.

Nine hours later, they arrived at Heathrow. Queuing up at passport control, Lisa took out the passports, and again that anxious feeling returned to her.

She glanced down at Tariq, who was still in his shorts, despite the freezing weather awaiting them outside the terminal building. She glanced down to his legs once again, hoping that the scar she had seen on the previous trip would be there. Lisa held her breath – there were no scars visible. She looked up and saw an immigration official give her the once-over from behind the desk. His look was not a friendly one. She silently wished she had gotten into the other queue, where the man behind the counter looked more personable.

Her palms grew cold and moist. She clutched onto both the passports tightly, and it suddenly dawned upon her that both Tariq and herself were in the same queue, as they had been last time, for British passport holders. She took a sharp intake of breath, which sent her head into a spin. Terrance had said that they had recently moved to England, so how did they have British passports? As she mulled this over, her stomach churned. Lisa shoved the thought to the back of her mind as she approached the immigration desk and passed over the two passports.

There had been no problems in January. Immigration had been smooth, the passports had been scanned, and she and the two children had walked straight through, so there was no reason for her nervousness now.

"Travelling together, are you?" the stern-looking man in uniform barked at her. His uniform intimidated her, and she shifted uneasily on her feet.

"Er, yes. He is a child from my extended family. He was over in Goa for the Easter holidays." She hesitated before adding, "To see family", remembering what Terrance had told her to say the last time she had done this. She lied easily, moving slightly to the corner of the podium and trying not to sound too nervous, as he scanned Tariq's passport through the machine. He stared at the little boy with his hollow blue eyes.

"Please stay in front of the podium," the officer said. Lisa noticed her hands were still clammy. She put her hand on the boy's shoulder, pulling him towards her to show this official her familiarity. The boy had said nothing to her the whole way there, and she prayed that he would not say anything now. She was desperately trying to think of something funny to say to break the tension. Nothing came to her.

"You all right?" the immigration officer asked the boy. The boy hid behind Lisa.

She smiled, "He's shy."

Lisa knew she had done nothing wrong, but her nervousness had set alarm bells ringing for her. She was not even sure that this was the same child she had met in January. Thinking back, she was not even sure either of the boys she could recall looked like the ones she had seen running around on Christmas day at Terrance's house. Even if this child was illegally entering the country, it had noting to do with her, *surely?* She was an innocent party, she silently argued. She reassured herself again, confident that Terrance would never put her in such a position. He was caring and above board – just look at his work at Sweet Haven! She had jumped to conclusions over a silly scar. Lisa rolled her head, trying to loosen some of the tension built up in her neck and shoulders as they walked towards the baggage carousel. She turned to the boy, "You are Tariq, aren't you?" she asked. The boy looked towards the floor again and said nothing.

As the two of them walked out into the terminal, Lisa recognized the same man that had picked up the children in January, and she walked over to him. He was wearing an off-white shirt, with a white vest visible underneath. The boy looked reluctant to go towards him, but as he did, the man handed him a note scribbled in what looked to Lisa like Konkani. The boy half-heartedly took the man's hand.

"Hi, I'm Lisa. I didn't meet you properly last time. I was in quite a rush to get back, and Tariq's sister seemed to know you." Lisa said this apprehensively, looking at the bulky man. She took in his shabby appearance; she hadn't noticed last time. His large belly hung over his trousers, and his shirt was only half tucked in. Cautious after her scare at immigration, she wanted to make sure Tariq would be in safe hands.

The last time she had escorted the children, there had been a pretty lady in a pink-and-green salwar with him, who had said she was their aunt. The excuse was that Reshma could not drive on the motorway as yet, and so they had come in her place, but Terrance had told her about this and she'd been prepared. He had described her to Lisa, and so she'd been comfortable handing them over. This time their aunt was not present, and although

Hanif was the same man she had previously met, there was something about him that unsettled her.

"Hi, *Leesha*. My wife is *naat* felling well, so she could *naat* make it, I *tink* you were meeting with her *laassht* time, no?" the man said, wiping the remnants of what appeared to be crisps from his thick moustache. He held out his hand to her, which she shook reluctantly. With his other hand, he slipped another piece of paper to the boy. He saw Lisa notice this. "The note I just gave him was from his sister, you know, brotherly-sisterly *tings*," he said, almost out of breath. His Indian accent was heavy.

"Well, I will leave Tariq with you then," Lisa replied, uncertain of what she should actually do with her doubts. With that, she steered her trolley laden with luggage to the lift to the concourse level, to catch the Oxford airline bus. It was then, as the lift doors opened, that she caught a glimpse of the Scandinavian girl from her first trip to Goa in the reflection of the elevator doors. She turned around, but she could not see anyone remotely like the girl she had seen all those months ago by the pool at the Coconut Grove Hotel. She pushed her trolley into the lift. Confused, she squeezed her eyes tightly shut. She was tired and needed some rest. She was worrying about nothing, and she knew it was due to the stress of having to break the news to her friends and, most importantly, her family that she would be leaving England for good. Lisa smiled. She had the rest of her life to sort out over the next two months.

22

After spending a day recovering from jet lag and a considerable amount of time thinking about Tariq, Lisa picked up the phone and called Terrance. Since her flight, she had had a nagging feeling that she had been party to a crime and, worse still, that she had been duped into illegally moving a child over international waters, yet she had no concrete evidence that suggested that this was the case. Immigration hadn't even batted an eyelid. But there was something not right, and she wanted some answers. Had she been involved in the exploitation of defenceless children? Her biggest fear was the thought that Terrance had just been using her. She had woken up in the middle of the night in a cold sweat and with an incredibly guilty feeling that had made her feel sick to the stomach. She needed to know.

Terrance answered on the fifth ring. She could feel butterflies in her stomach, which was twisting and turning. Why was she so nervous about what she was about to ask him?

"Hey, darling. I've been trying to reach you. I was worried you didn't arrive safely, but then my uncle called to thank me for making sure Tariq arrived in one piece, so I guess you must have reached there okay," Terrance said with not so much as a stutter.

"Hey, you," she said, her nerves suddenly subsiding. She felt rather foolish now that she'd heard his voice. She was just being paranoid, and for no reason, but she thought she would make her worry known. "I was questioned by immigration," she attempted, "about Tariq, and I lied, well, kind of like you told me to. I said he was a child of some extended family. I needed to check everything was okay."

"Well, that wasn't a lie," Terrance said, pausing to clear his throat. "You will be family soon." He let the statement hang in the air, and it worked as he had hoped it would. It made her blush, and it made her forget.

"Well, yes, that's what I said," Lisa said, content that he was already thinking long-term, something her previous boyfriends had never given a second thought. So maybe what she had told immigration hadn't been a lie after all; she could sleep easy now. Everything was fine. Lisa's fears dissolved, and the conversation and its tone had lifted her spirits. She was certain about the move, her doubts swallowed by her need for love.

Terrance could feel her excitement and enjoyed hearing it in her voice. He encouraged her to discuss their future, glad that she had stopped with the questions for now. As far as he was aware, immigration in England was a cakewalk if you had all the right documents, which he had ensured the boy had. The country had too many human-rights laws for its own good. He smiled to himself. It was all going to work out well.

*

"Lisa, are you one hundred percent sure this is what you want?" Her mother was quick to ask, but her words were not as harsh as they once would have been. Cancer had changed her, although she had now been given the all-clear by her doctors. Margaret was still adjusting to that missing part of her womanhood. Since then, however, she had taken on a new approach to life. She joked that her wisdom had come too late, in her sixties, to be able to use it, and now she lived with the new motto that risks were there to be taken. She made statements that Lisa could never have imagined leaving the lips of her mother. However, when it came to the happiness of her daughter, she was still slightly sceptical. More than that, she caught herself being slightly selfish – she wanted her daughter close by.

A guilty feeling crept up on Lisa for leaving her mother this way, especially knowing what she had been through over the last couple of months – but she also knew that there was never a right time to up and leave. All she knew was that she had her own life to get on with. After all, this was the happiest she had been in a long time, and she was not willing to let Terrance go; she was only a flight away.

May scurried by, and Lisa was busying herself purchasing bits and pieces for her new life abroad. She had wanted to take so many things with her, including a year's supply of Dairy Milk, as it just didn't taste the same in Goa, but that was just not possible. She would have to pick and choose what she could live without. It would be hard, especially as she wouldn't have the funds to come home for six months when she would have to renew her visa. Paul had promised a visit out there after the monsoons, with Sandra and David in tow, and her parents had come round to the move as well – they were even suggesting celebrating New Year's in the warmth of Goa. It was Suzanne she was really going to miss. She and Arjun were already planning babies and looking for a more spacious house in Summertown. She was scared she would lose her best friend forever.

"Lisa Higgins, I am only a phone call away, and we are going to get that Skype thingy especially so we can chat for hours. It will be like we were next door," Suzanne reassured her.

"I know, but will you come visit before you start having children?" She was tearful now every time she spoke to Suzanne. She couldn't believe it was actually happening. She would be leaving her old life behind in less than two months; after the academic year she would be living in India. She would never have imagined it in a million years.

"You know, Lise," Suzanne said, "when you booked your first holiday out there last December, I thought you were crazy, thought that you would hate it and be back in a matter of days. I underestimated you, and I feel bad for doing that. I should have just supported you, no questions asked. Like a true friend."

"Stop," Lisa said. "You are a true friend, and you are going to make me blub. Saying goodbye is going to be so hard."

"Well, I just want to say, Lise, that I am happy for you now that you have been back and you still feel the same way. I honestly thought, when you got back in January, that you had completely lost the plot. I'm sorry; I should have believed you. You always were the sensible one, still are. I don't know why I thought you hadn't thought it through. But you know, sometimes love just makes us do stupid things. I guess I was just trying to protect you." She paused. "Take me, for instance, a Hindu ceremony – my mum is going to have a fit!"

Lisa smiled; it was a small triumph that Suzanne had admitted that she was wrong. Ever since she'd gotten back from her first trip in January, and they had had that fight, there had been a tension between them. Lisa had always lived in her shadow, and Suzanne had liked it that way. Now that she had accepted that Lisa had her own life and respected her decision, that tension would disappear. They could get back to being good friends again.

Lisa swung into action. With only a few months left before her departure, she was determined to spend as much time she could with her family and friends. Evenings were taken up with family dinners, and they would sit over several bottles of red wine and reminisce about when they were young.

"My little sister, all grown up," Paul had said to her one Saturday evening when they had both returned to Leicester for a family dinner. Margaret was making her famous beef Wellington, which neither of them could ever refuse. Their parents had gone to bed, and Sandra and David had not made the trip. It was the first time in a long while that Paul and Lisa had spent any time together. "I'm going to miss you, you know," he said. "I know we haven't seen much of each other lately, especially since little David came along, but I just wanted to say that I'm proud of you, I really am. It takes guts to do what you are doing, and I never thought you had it in you."

Lisa smiled. Paul had not commented much on the whole Terrance situation. His approval meant a lot to her. He took her hand in his. "I *am*, little sis," he reiterated. "At first I thought you were a little crazy, you know, all those years of repressed rebellion, but I don't think so any more. You have made a decision, your decision, and stuck with it, not letting anyone talk you out of it. Honestly, I didn't think you had it in you. Congratulations," he said, raising his glass of red wine to hers.

Her parents, too, grew accustomed to the idea of her moving away, and to Lisa it seemed that they respected her more for it. In their eyes she was finally old enough to make her own decisions. For the first time in a long while, Lisa wondered what she would do without her friends and family so close at hand, and although she was dying to get back to Terrance in Goa, she secretly wanted something to happen to stop her departure. Maybe it was nerves – or maybe it was a deep-seated notion that something was wrong.

23

Sonya let her phone ring. She could see his name blinking on her phone's display. It was barely two weeks since Lisa had returned to England for the second time, and like clockwork, he'd been incessantly trying to get hold of her. It was a Sunday afternoon, and she and Carl were sitting at a shack on the beach, drinking Limca, trying to sort out their troubled love lives. Carl had finally managed to tell his mother that he would never have a girlfriend, and it had not gone down too well.

"Do you want me to have a heart attack?" she had asked him, waiting for a response, and over the hurt from this response, he could see the pain in his own mother's eyes. He thought about it – and the silence that followed was deadly – for less than a minute. So he lied. Plastering a smile on his face to mask the upset, he'd said it was a joke. His mother had playfully slapped his back, but after that conversation, it was clear what had happened. They could see it in each others eyes, but nothing was said. They knew it would be better that way.

Sonya, on the other hand, had her own problems. Continually drawn to Terrance as if to a magnet, she couldn't help wanting to speak to him, but she knew she could not, not in front of Carl. He wouldn't understand – he didn't know all the details, only what she wanted him to know. He picked up Sonya's phone from the wooden table and started to delete the missed calls from him.

"Sonya, I don't even know why you still have his name in your phone book, yaar," he said, laughing at some of Terrance's messages. Sonya was itching to grab the phone from him. She considered telling him her reasons, but she knew better than that. Carl was too good-natured. They might have been friends, but if he ever knew the extent of what she and Terrance were doing, he would shop her to the police, of that she was almost certain. No, she could not tell him; he had too many morals for her to be able to share the truth with him. She would be patient and wait till Carl left before she spoke to Terrance.

"Sonya, you know it, and I know it. He is the lowest of the low. You cannot get any lower than this. Why? Why does he do this to you? I'll tell you why, yaar." Carl took a sip of the sugary lemon drink before he continued, "It is quite clearly because you go back to him every time, not so much as an argument from you. You are like a puppy chasing after him." Sonya tried to interrupt him, but he stopped her. "You can do better, yaar. There has got to be someone new in Goa at Christmas time, remember?" Carl winked at Sonya in a knowing way.

Sonya knew all too well the answer to that question. "Both you and I know, Carl, that Terrance is my only decent shot at being *accepted* in society."

"Anyway," Carl continued, "he is a *sidey* guy, involved in some dodgy dealings, from what I have heard recently. You don't want to get mixed up in all of that."

"Carl!" Sonya scolded, trying to veer the conversation around. "You know not to believe rumours." Sonya hated rumours – especially if they were partly true! She briefly panicked, hoping their money maker had not been discovered. It would not do them any favours if it got out. Gossips in Goa, they were everywhere – that was one of the main reasons she had asked Terrance to keep Lisa's visit in April low-key. He had failed to do this at Christmas, and it had deeply upset her, so much so that she had nearly called the whole thing off, but this time he had kept to his word. He kept the relationship out of public view. This way, when Sonya did get back together with Terrance, a little bit of her dignity would be saved. That was the most important thing. It had to look right.

She was glad that Terrance kept his part of the deal. He had taken her to more obscure restaurants, telling her he was showing her a different side of Goa. *That's what all the naive tourists want, don't they*, Sonya had thought bitterly. *She will love you even more for it.* Sonya had been right. Lisa enjoyed the intense time she had with Terrance, and as Sonya had feared, she had weaselled her way under his skin. She had even told Teresa that she would be over to live with him soon. Sonya had begun to realize that Terrance might have an ulterior motive and that their master plan might not work in her favour. She had to act fast and do something to prevent this.

Later that night, after Carl had left and Sonya was on her way back home, her phone began to ring again. It was Terrance. Sonya smiled as she steered her car over the Mandovi Bridge. She answered on the second ring. "Your bed must still be warm, surely?" Sonya remarked; her sarcasm was laced with bitterness. She had not spoken to him much whilst Lisa was around. They had only spent one night together on the night of Ayesha's mehndi, and she had made up a tall story to get out of it. On the night, however, Terrance had not seemed his usual self, and she had an inkling he had actually fallen for Lisa.

He ignored her first question; it was a childish jibe he was getting used to.

"I just called to say it's all gone through. It's all done. I will have the money for you this evening. You are at home?" Sonya's heart fell. His tone was serious – he had called for business, not pleasure. She should have acted faster when she'd had that inkling about Lisa. He was about to disconnect, but she wanted him to stay on the line. It would have been better to ask him in person, but she couldn't wait any more. "So, is it true what I hear? She is coming to live here? In *your* apartment?" She added the last question to irritate him; they both knew it was not his. A silence followed.

"I'll see you in an hour, your place. We can go somewhere – dinner, maybe? I'll fill you in there."

Sonya snapped her phone shut. "You were not supposed to fall in love with her, damn you!" she said, and she stepped on the accelerator.

*

Later that evening, Sonya lay in bed, thinking of her one last chance at getting Terrance to put a ring on her finger. It would be a cheap shot, one that could land them all in it, but she was confident it wouldn't. They had covered their backs too well in Goa; it was one benefit of baksheesh. Since December they had had the enemy on their side; it had cost them a small portion of their profits, but it was worth it. Sonya thought about it; she knew she didn't have much of a choice. She had to stop Lisa coming back to Goa, not only for her benefit, but for the benefit of the group as well. They did not want a goody two-shoes sniffing around. Especially after what Terrance had said to her tonight, she was certain that she couldn't wait around to let it happen. There was only one thing left for Sonya to do to ensure her own happiness. She flipped open her mobile and made the call. She would tell Terrance later, and he would understand. He would have to – he had no choice.

*

She poured the remainder of the lavender bath foam into the running bath. She had no more left now, and it was the last bottle she had brought over. She wondered if the new supermarket in Calangute, which was increasingly catering to the tourist market, would be able to get it for her. She rinsed the bottle and placed it high up on the windowsill. A gecko no bigger than her index finger scuttled past her hand and out of sight behind the curtain. It made her shudder. How she hated geckos! As she sunk into the steaming water, her eyes looked out for the little reptile; she could see it now, just in the jamb of the window. Its eyes transfixed on a mosquito close by. She watched it inch its body forward towards the insect, and then, in the blink of an eye, its long pink tongue reached out and wrapped itself around the mosquito, drawing it in. *Dinner*, she thought.

She watched its little almost-translucent body; it was a pale brown beautifully camouflaged on the window frame that had been bleached in the sun. It scurried through the gap where the window had been left ajar; she swiftly stood up and closed the window, trapping it. Its tail fell to the sill, frantically jumping around. It sent a shiver down her spine. Looking through the window, she could see its insides trickling down the sun-bleached wood.

Mia closed her eyes and breathed a sigh of relief. She could enjoy her bath now. She opened the window and slumped back into the foamy hot water. Her phone, propped up by the side of the bath, began to flash. Normally, bath time was a half hour when she was on her own, but she had been waiting for this call. Her lover's name flashed on the screen, and she pressed the green button.

She listened, taking in what was being said and what her instructions were. It was cruel, she knew that, and it was in no way part of the deal that they had agreed to all those months ago. But contracts like this were not something you could argue with. A scapegoat was needed. She considered her options, leaving her lover waiting on the other end of the phone. The combination of the warm water, the smell of lavender, and the cool breeze through the open window calmed her.

Their relationship was less than ideal, but she had fallen hard and was not willing to let this come between them. The bonus would be good, as well; she could travel perhaps one day to see the Taj Mahal and the beauty of Rajasthan. It would mean more creative detail to Simon, but it would justify her need to stay out there for a little longer, and this way she could ensure that no one else was caught.

"Leave it with me," she said decisively as she blew some bubbles off her hand. "I'll take care of it."

24

It was a warm June morning and the sun shone through her windows, telling the world that she had not cleaned them in over six months. Lisa scurried downstairs as she heard the doorbell chime. She was already running late for work. She opened the door, expecting to see Harry in his navy-and-red Royal Mail uniform, but instead she saw the two police officers. At first she was confused, a little startled, even.

"Is everyone okay?" she mumbled. "Has there been an accident?"

"Could we come in, Miss Higgins?" The police officers looked at her with disdain as she moved aside and let them through.

"I was just leaving for work," Lisa managed as the taller one of the two picked up a framed photo of Terrance and her that stood by the television. It was a close-up of their faces. She remembered taking it herself; they'd been at a beach in Palolem on a scorching day, and she had just shared a glass of locally brewed cashew feni with Terrance. They'd both reeked of sour-smelling alcohol, and they were both giddy and in love. She remembered stretching her arm out as far as she could to fit them both in. They looked so happy in that photo, it instantly made her smile.

Then, as if somebody had switched on a light, she knew why the police were there in her living room. The sounds and visions seemed to blur together as Lisa grasped the reality of the situation. Her knees felt week, and she needed to sit down, but she was smart enough to know that she couldn't let these two policemen see the realization in her face. She invited them to sit and immediately took a seat herself. Her mouth was dry; she needed fresh air and water.

Lisa felt a surge of nausea rising up from the pit of her stomach. It was the kind of feeling she had once had when she was seven. One minute she'd been staring up at the huge oak tree at the bottom of the garden and the next she remembered falling off and hitting her nose on the ground. She'd looked around to see who was there, and as she saw her mother running towards her, she'd burst into tears. When she'd seen the blood streaming from her nose, she'd thrown up. That feeling was with her now, but it was accompanied by something much more adult. She knew this could not be made better with a few tissues and a hot bath as it had then. This fall was going to be fatal.

The policemen wanted to take her to the station for questioning. They had made it clear she was not being arrested, but she could tell from the look on their faces that if she refused to go willingly with them that she would be forced to, maybe by arrest.

"There must be some sort of mistake," Lisa said, trying to calm herself. She tried to take in deep breaths to slow her heart, which was beating violently.

"Well, we just need to ask you a couple of questions down at the station," the shorter, tubby policeman said as he jabbed his thumb in the air. Lisa gathered her handbag and cardigan from the sofa; despite the warm weather she felt a sudden coldness. She glanced at the bracelet that Terrance had given her on her first trip to Goa. She noticed now that it had tarnished on the edges. A wave of sickness took hold of her again.

"Well, you can't just take me down to the station for questioning for something you won't tell me about," she said, unsure of what her rights were.

The taller policeman, who she later learnt was PC Ryan, looked at the shorter one. The look seemed to contain a wealth of information. The shorter one spoke. "It's about a recent trip you have taken, to be precise."

"To Goa? Well—" Lisa tried to interrupt. That information hadn't been very precise at all.

"We are not at liberty to discuss this further with you, Miss Higgins. I suggest you come to the station with us now, else we can come back with a detective."

"Well—" Lisa tried again, but she struggled for words.

"We can do this the easy way or the hard way," PC Ryan interrupted her. He grinned at his colleague, as if he had always wanted to use this clichéd phrase and had finally found his opportunity.

Lisa quickly assessed her options. She would not be able to go to work now; she wouldn't be able to concentrate. She pinched her arm, hoping that it was a dream. It wasn't. This was real, and she would have to face up to reality. She had no choice – it was staring her in the face.

"Is it okay if I call work?" Lisa said, trying to take in what was happening. She felt like a prisoner already.

"Go ahead," PC Ryan said. He was seated beside her now, and he did not look friendly at all. The other policeman was still looking around her apartment. He stared intently at the picture of Lisa standing by the elephant at the night bazaar. She called the school, and as she lied about feeling unwell, she turned her back to the police officers. Lying in front of them was hardly going to show her in a favourable light. Her heart was racing. She was scared and confused, and there was no one she could call; no one would understand. Her hands shook violently as she placed the receiver back in its cradle.

Lisa got into a police car for the first time in her life, and she looked up at her building. She could see Gladys and her fluffy white hair peering out from behind her thick navy curtains. Lisa hung her head in shame; Gladys would be the least of her worries.

*

It was two thirty in the afternoon when Lisa returned to her apartment. She wasn't quite sure what to do first. Her head was pounding from all the information she had gathered in the last couple of hours. Just yesterday, everything had been fine, and now her entire world had changed. She felt that all her hopes and dreams of the last year were based on lies. How would she be able to face everyone? People would find out; Oxford was a small place. Her heart ached most of all for her parents. How did you break such news to the people who were closest to you?

She had spent her whole life being sensible and hoping that she would never disappoint her parents and her friends. She had always done things with the hope that they would be proud of her. Now she had truly messed up. The first time she had stepped away from their overprotective shield, she had failed spectacularly.

She tried to compose herself, knowing it would not be long before she was formally charged with something. The interview had been a good indication of what was to come.

At the police station, she had been interrogated for what felt like an eternity, but was actually only three hours. She had eventually signed a statement with her lawyer's recommendation. Well, not *her* lawyer. She didn't have a solicitor; she'd thought it was odd when they asked her to call *her* lawyer. Do most twenty-six-year-olds have their own criminal representation? She was presented with a public defence lawyer, Catherine, a woman of about thirty, who seemed gentle but had a determined look in her eye. She looked professional with her navy pinstripe suit and perfectly manicured nails. Her glasses were rectangular and thick-framed; they suited her. Lisa returned a smile to Catherine, even though she was not in the mood for smiling. She knew that Catherine was possibly the only one who could help her.

Lisa took in the interview room, it was stark white and clean, not at all like those she had seen on television; nevertheless, it was intimidating. There was an alarm strip that ran horizontally around the room. "Press here for assistance" was printed along it in a clinical blue and white. It sent a quick shiver down her spine. Catherine looked at her reassuringly and nodded to Detective Inspector Madden to give them some time alone. When he'd gone, Lisa raised her head and looked directly at Catherine. It would be the second time today that someone would try to explain the situation to Lisa. DI Madden had told Lisa why she had been hauled into the station, and Lisa had not wanted to say much, not knowing, really, where to begin. When she saw Catherine, she felt some hope.

"Basically, Lisa, this is serious." Catherine looked into Lisa's eyes to gauge a reaction. Lisa looked back, but her eyes were glazed over; she was still in shock. "Obviously, you are on record for entering the country on two occasions with young children with, what has now come to light, fake documents."

Lisa's heart fell; she didn't know what to say or do. She recalled the doubt she had felt that day at immigration and that she had done nothing to stop it. She had spoken to Terrance, and she had heard what she wanted to hear, because she wanted to believe him. She wanted the life she had spent the last five months dreaming about.

Catherine had gone on to explain the evidence that they had. It was a case that intelligence had been working on for some time. Several child-trafficking groups were active in Goa, and more and more children were entering the United Kingdom illegally to be exploited.

"The Investigations Bureau had an undercover agent working in Goa at the time that you were there in December, and as far as I am aware, she is still out there working on the case. She infiltrated the group and she gave them your name, but not until you were safely back in England. She has only just given them your details, which was lucky – you would not want to see the inside of an Indian jail, let me tell you," Catherine tried to lighten the mood. She looked at Lisa, trying not to judge her. That was not her job – that would be for a jury to decide.

All of a sudden Lisa knew why she had seen the Scandinavian girl so many times in Goa, and then at Heathrow at Easter. It must have been her; she must have been working undercover. She remembered the girl the first day in Goa, by the pool, exchanging a knowing look to the Indian employee at the Coconut Grove. She now recognized that girl as Sonya. They had set her up; she was almost certain of it.

"I don't have all the details, Lisa. What little information we are getting out of Goa is very sketchy. As far as I am aware, two other people have flown out of India, and they cannot trace them. I don't know exactly who, though. It appears that they were made to take the fall, two small-time crooks from Maharashtra. It is quite possible that they were involved with forgery. The Indian government doesn't want this to be a scandal that will deter tourists from Goa. It is one of their biggest money earners. As far as I am aware, they are not going to follow up the disappearance of these two men."

Lisa berated herself for not contacting the police herself. She had given in to Terrance's excuses too easily. Somewhere in the back of her mind she had known that it was not as it appeared on the surface, but she just hadn't wanted to hear it. As much as she wanted to believe she would, she had not done a thing.

"They are looking to make arrests for forgery, which would not be your biggest worry; we could get you off that one. The work looks specialist, from what I hear, and probably involved the two men that have fled. It's the first charge: child trafficking."

Lisa's head started spinning again. Every time she heard those two words, she crumbled inside. She could never imagine doing something so frightful, so harsh. She worked with children; she was disgusted every time a news story flashed across her television in which children were exploited. Her confusion mounted; she wanted to justify her actions and to plead her innocence, but she knew it would come out all wrong. She needed to digest what Catherine was saying before she explained what had actually happened.

Catherine understood Lisa's empty, sorrowful look. This was the first case she was taking on alone; there always had to be a first. She had worked on teams for defending child traffickers before. Some she hadn't believed, no matter how sincere their stories and the tears that they had shed. At points like these, she wondered if she had taken the right career path. No one was ever really guilty, *right?* It was like an afternoon movie that proved the cliché that truth is stranger than fiction.

The girl who sat before her looked genuinely shocked and disgusted with herself; she exhibited a raw vulnerability. Catherine knew that, even without a prison sentence, what Lisa had done would stay with her for the rest of her life. She would be a prisoner to her own mind, and Catherine wanted to mother her, for reasons she could not define. Lisa looked to be around the same age as she was – she would check the file later – but *she would never have been so naive and foolish, would she?* She walked over to the water cooler and brought Lisa a cold cup of water. How would she break it to her that this could cost her fourteen years in jail? Catherine ran through the Sexual Offences Act, the Identity Cards Bill, and the

Nationality, Immigration and Asylum Act. Lisa barely looked up; she was ashamed, and she didn't understand any of it.

Lisa took a sip of her water and sobbed. "I didn't know," she managed.

"Tell me how it happened, then." Catherine placed her hand on Lisa's to reassure her. All the while, the thought of this young girl being put in jail upset her. Catherine had seen the inside of jails for appeal cases, and it was not something she would wish on Lisa. She was lucky not to have been caught in India. She had heard that some of those jails were filthy and the prisoners treated with hatred. That would have truly been insufferable. Catherine contemplated that the jury might see that Lisa wasn't a criminal, but she knew that the police wanted to make an example of her – and ignorance was never a plausible defence. Catherine took her notepad out of her briefcase, and she started to make notes as Lisa told her story from beginning to end.

"I was in love – stupid, I now realize, but in love," Lisa started sobbing and Catherine passed her some tissues. Lisa told her story, detailing most of the events that had happened. She spoke about Terrance and Sonya, and in particular, she mentioned the orphanage, knowing that Catherine would be able to relay this to the police. As Lisa spoke, Catherine began to believe her. She herself had looked for love for quite a few years before she'd met Dennis. She knew what the pressures were like being in your late twenties and single. These days, it seemed to be socially unacceptable. Catherine hadn't gone that far looking for love, though. Last year she had met Dennis on a police force conference with their law firm, and now they were deeply in love and planning a wedding for next summer. She absent-mindedly played with her engagement ring. It was an incredibly naive thing for Lisa to have done, but there was a chance that a jury would see it the same way. If the police were able to locate the people and places that Lisa had mentioned, they would be able to corroborate her story.

"Before we leave, Lisa, I need you to give me all the contact details, addresses, and telephone numbers of all the places you went to and the people you met on those visits."

Lisa immediately scrolled through her phone book and wrote down Sonya's and Terrance's numbers, as well as all the places she could remember:

the hotel details, and Carl's number; she mentioned Chi Chi, Joel's, and of course, Sweet Haven. Apart from their apartment, she had no real addresses. Terrance had shown her everything in Goa, but even if someone had given her a detailed map of the state, she would have been unable to locate his family home or the orphanage. She could not believe just how blinded she had been.

"Who will look into their details?" she questioned, knowing that if it was the undercover agent, she would be very economical with the truth. She couldn't help but picture the Scandinavian girl as she asked this.

"I will make some enquiries, but we are limited to what we can do from here. We will, of course, pass on the details you have given us to the police, and I assure you that this will be passed on to their agent in Goa. Obviously, any details you can give us will provide leads."

Lisa knew then that it was pointless; if the Scandinavian was in on it, there was no way justice would be served. No, there was no one else to back up her story – she knew that now.

She was given a short break after she had spoken to Catherine, before the detective inspectors returned to the interview room. She noticed a small, inconspicuous camera attached within a small perspex dome to the ceiling of the stark, white room. The detectives sat down and smiled at her before switching on a small recording device.

Three hours later, Lisa was sure that she could not answer any more questions. They had asked a series of inquiries that all seemed to be the same but came from different angles.

"Did you not question who the children were? How did they have British passports? Did you not think that was strange, given that they had supposedly just moved to Britain?"

They looked at her as if she were lying. Lisa knew her answers sounded foolish; she knew they didn't believe her. Worst of all, they brought up the fact that she was a teacher who should have been more responsible, trained to spot signs of abuse and neglect. They questioned her abilities, and she began to doubt herself, knowing that she might never be able to work with children again.

Lisa was itching to get home; she didn't know why. She would have to face reality then. She needed to work out her strategy. *How had she let him get so under her skin?* Despite the potential charges she was facing, some small part of her wanted to believe that he still loved her and that the move would go ahead. Of course, it never could now, but her feelings for Terrance were so strong that she wanted to believe that this was all a misunderstanding, a bad dream that she could wake up from. Deep down, she knew this was just the beginning. She might never get the chance to make her own decisions again, but she wanted *some* part of last year to be real. She wanted something to be worth it.

*

At home, Lisa rested her head on the sofa. There was so much to consider, and there was no one that she felt she could turn to for support. She had been taken in by an exotic man and made a fool of; worse still, she would be facing a jail sentence. There was no one else in this world who could pay for what she had done; she would have to take responsibility for her own actions.

She pulled the telephone onto her lap. She didn't feel like speaking to anybody, but she knew that she had to speak to Terrance. Previously, her heart would have skipped a beat as she dialled his number. Now the only feeling she had was dread. *Child trafficking* – those words resounded in her head; she had not linked these two words together when she had last spoken to Terrance. It was a serious criminal offence, they had told her at least a dozen times. It was punishable by prison, and she would most certainly lose her job in the meantime. She would not be able to afford the rent on her apartment for long. The money she had saved up for Goa would not take her as far here. She would have to move back in with her parents. Her world was beginning to crash down around her.

It would be better if she spoke to him before the police did, she thought. She had failed to tell Catherine and the police that she had spoken to Terrance just a few weeks ago and that he had revealed things to her about what *they* had done. She had hidden that phone call from them, as she knew it would incriminate her if anyone found out. There had to be an explanation for what he had done. But for now, Lisa could not speak; she could not say that she already knew.

Lisa tried all the numbers she had for him. There was no answer at any of them, and then she knew. She knew why he had confessed to her.

25

There is no going back, she thought as she headed back to the courthouse. The idea of a jail sentence scared her – there was no denying that – but her own negligence had already imprisoned her. Not a day went by without her thinking of the fate of those children. Lisa looked up to the sky and made a deal with God. If she was let off, she would do everything in her power to do what she could to help those in need. Although the deal was somewhat false; she knew she would never pass a Criminal Record Bureau check again. Any chance she had of working with the vulnerable was over.

She had committed a crime, and what she had done had been brought to her attention before that fateful June morning, yet she had stayed silent. She was lucky that this had not come out during the long and painful trial. If it had, she knew she would not have had even a sliver of a chance. If she was frank with herself, though, she had known before that final phone call. She had known at the airport. She could have saved that little boy, the last one – but she didn't.

Lisa stood up from the cold bench, treading on the daffodil as she did. She could remember her last telephone conversation with Terrance as if it were yesterday. She could hear his voice.

*

It was Friday, a teacher training day that didn't involve much of her time. She was home by lunch, and after changing her heels and skirt for slippers and a worn-in pair of track-suit bottoms, she fixed herself a cheese and tomato sandwich and a packet of soup and nestled herself in front of the television. She was looking forward to a relaxing weekend of doing absolutely nothing.

She picked up her laptop and opened the Skype connection, calling Terrance. He would be back from the orphanage by now, she thought, and she really wanted to hear the soft lull of his voice. She was feeling particularly tense today, and his voice always calmed her. It would be another long weekend without the comfort of him by her side. She was counting the days now until the summer. She had handed in her notice and was waiting to be with him, but the days seemed to drag, and she knew it was not going to be an easy wait.

She was in luck. Terrance was at home, and they discussed trivial things, like what they had been doing for the last couple of days. Lisa tried to entertain him with stories and funny anecdotes from her class. He gave her all the news about Teresa's new boyfriend and Ayesha's baby bump, keeping his conversation light and airy and trying to disguise the tension he was harbouring. Despite his efforts to keep his emotions in check throughout this charade, he had developed a soft spot towards Lisa. Her vulnerability had awakened something within him, and he was strangely drawn to her. But Sonya had made it clear that he could not mix business with pleasure and that any feelings he did have should be severed. This morning she had dealt her final blow, to make sure that he ended any relationship he was contemplating with Lisa. She had backed him into a corner, and he'd had no escape. He did not want to fight her, even though he knew he could. He knew that he and Sonya were soulmates. No matter who they fooled around with, they always returned to each other, and she was right. If Lisa moved out to Goa, she would never let go, she would cling to him like a child, and he would grow tired of the girl – he usually did. There was a connection between Sonya and him that could not be broken. She knew him like no other, and more than that, he knew that he would not give up his current lifestyle for anything or anyone. But, for once in his life, he felt that he owed their victim an explanation, a heads-up as to what was going to happen. More than that, it would be a strong deterrent to her boarding that plane in August. But he was not truly altruistic; he wanted her to see his side of the story before she jumped to her own conclusions. He wanted to ease what little remained of his conscience.

"Tell me what's wrong," Lisa said, sensitive to the strained tone in his voice. She hoped he was not ill or in some kind of trouble. She wanted to cradle him in her arms and kiss away his fears.

"Why would you think there is something wrong?" he asked, masking his apprehension with a false laugh. There was a long pause, and neither of them spoke. It was an uncomfortable silence, and she could sense a nervousness about him; in someone who was always so confident, it scared her.

"Lisa, I need to talk to you about something very important." He had her attention; she suddenly felt nauseated and light-headed.

"Is it about Tariq and his sister?" Her stomach lurched, and the words just tripped off her tongue. The doubts that had been dancing around in the back of her mind suddenly leapt from her mouth, and the guilty feeling surfacing. Her own words had surprised her. She had dared to ask him the question she had hidden in the recesses of her mind for too long now. Was he going to tell her the unthinkable?

Quickly she thought about backtracking, knowing that she was not ready to hear the truth. In the silence that followed, she thought about changing the subject, but she could not think. Her head was spinning, and her mouth was dry. The moment's silence felt like an eternity, but she was not going to be the one to break it. He knew it was his turn to speak. It was time.

"Lisa, you know I love you, don't you?" he asked, not believing it but knowing that it would soften what he was about to say. He was impressed that Lisa had picked up on Tariq. Clearly he had been a different child; he and Sonya had laughed at her stupidity at the time, although the two boys did bear some resemblance to one another. He had rehearsed this conversation in his head countless times before. Now it was for real, and he was sure that if she loved him as she said she did, she would understand.

Lisa, for the first time in a year, felt her old self return. A sense of rationalization was beginning to wipe away the loved-up haze she had been absorbed in for the last six months. The lovesick teenager she had become since meeting Terrance was starting to walk away.

She didn't want to answer that she did, but she had to reassure him, because she needed to know the truth. "Of course I do," she managed, fearing the worst. She swallowed back the nausea through bleary eyes, hoping that this would turn out to be something hopelessly trivial. She tried to focus on the steam rising out of her mug of soup.

"I hate to do this you over Skype," he said, pausing momentarily "but you deserve to know. You need to know," he said.

"I need to know what?" she asked, wiping her sweaty palms on the arms of the sofa. Tears rolled down her cheeks and onto her Brookes sweatshirt.

"You know how much I care for the children at the orphanage?" The question was rhetorical. "I would go out of my way for those children, to give more desperate children a *home*, a *shelter*." He stressed his words as if he were talking to a child. "You remember Mr Goswami saying that we just do not have enough room for all the orphans in the area? Well, we have been trying to house children elsewhere." And there it was, like a bullet that Lisa had been waiting for. It hit her, piercing through her brain and lodging itself, a dull ache in the core of her mind. Terrance continued, "We aim to give them a better life. Most of them are parentless. Most of them have been left at our doorstep."

"What are you trying to say, Terrance?" Lisa interrupted; she was getting impatient. She needed her darkest suspicions confirmed, spelled out for her.

"Well, Lisa, look at it this way, if we housed all the children in the orphanage, we would be overcrowded. Each child would get less than half a meal of daal and rice, if that. We rely on donations, and they are not huge. It would be a terrible existence. This way, we can look after the children well, the ones that are at the orphanage. Each child will have a better chance at a future. The others will be taken care of as well, just elsewhere."

"What do you mean, *this way* – and where exactly is *elsewhere*? Another orphanage?" She had an inkling of what he was getting at, but for some reason her brain would not accept the truth. She was trying to give him a way out, to take away the guilt that was beginning to suffocate her. She was steering him towards the answer she wanted to hear. Terrance didn't take the bait. He could hear the tension in her voice, that neediness that he had seen in her that first day at Chi Chi's. He continued, determined to tell his story, rallying himself on, knowing that in a few minutes she would know everything. What she chose to do with the information up until she was caught, well, that was up to her. He would stay put until he got word from their contact; after that, he knew what he had to do.

The comforting thought that their contact had assured them protection instilled in him the confidence to continue. He cleared his throat, "Not exactly another institution such as ours. For a small fee, we give the children a home with a family."

Lisa was confused – surely he was making this out to be worse than it was. What he was describing was just the adoption process. "Well, that's what an orphanage is for isn't it? I mean, you give a childless couple children for a fee. That is understandable. Oh, Terrance you had me worried, then. I thought that you were embroiled in something much bigger." Lisa nervously laughed away her fear, skimming over what he was really saying. An old university professor had once said to her that life doesn't let you lie to yourself for very long, and she knew that this is what she was doing, laying a film over reality.

Terrance could have left it at this, lulled her into a false sense of security, but he had a strange desire to make her understand. He also needed her to know the full extent of her involvement, so that she was aware. The next couple of weeks were going to be treacherous for her. Terrance continued, "Well yes, adoption." He took a deep breath; she was making this harder for him than he'd imagined. He decided to explain from the beginning.

"A while ago, I was in a bar. It is known in town that I volunteer for the orphanage. You know what it's like in a small place like Goa. I was with Sonya at the time." Terrance cleared his throat again; it was now or never. "The man who propositioned us for this project said that there was a childless couple abroad, in England, and that they were desperate for a child. The adoption process in England, he said, was 'cumbersome.'"

"There is a reason for that," Lisa said under her breath.

"Well, he made us an offer. You see, Sweet Haven is not a licensed adoption placement agency, so it does not have the facility to obtain No Objection Certificates for couples wishing to adopt. This orphanage is not on the Central Adoption Resources Agency list. In India, any orphanage needs to be recognized and on that list for an adoption to go through. So, because we are not on the list, we do private adoptions." Lisa was silent, but he knew what she was thinking. "So, what do you expect the orphanage to do – let those kids have no future because of some list put together by some government official? What do they know? They are not on the streets of Goa. And the process for that certificate can take months, years even." Lisa was still silent. He wondered if she realized her role in all of this.

He continued, "We got passports for the children, and yes, they were forged, but so well that no machine could tell. I didn't get involved with the forgery part – I can't fake my dad's signature, let alone a passport!" His attempt to lighten the conversation failed, but he could feel the tension between them exasperate. He could see her through the webcams they had set up, her feet up on the sofa, her gaze directed towards the wall. She hadn't looked directly into the camera since he had started telling her his story. He noticed how she winced every time he added a new element to the twisted tale.

"The man we met said that they knew someone, a hippy, I think, from England, who arrived here sometime in the eighties. She employed some Marathi speaking fellows from a village so poor they probably did not even know what they were doing, but their skill was first class. So she had her own little home business. She wanted to make a difference in Goa, this state she had adopted as her own – most probably to feed her ganja habit. So the hippy organized the forgery side of things; all I needed to do was to provide the photographs. The passports, the visas – all that jazz, even the tickets – were sorted by the man we met in Joel's that day. Before you ask, I don't know much about him, we met in public places. He gave us the details and then the money after. We didn't speak much other than that."

Terrance believed that he was doing right by these children; Lisa could sense that. But she wondered whether he was naive or if he knew how sinister it was and was just in it to make a quick buck. Not a second's thought had been given to those children once they stepped off that plane on the other side of the world. A trace of anger started to build up, and her tone changed "You were paid for this, no doubt, and where did that money go? Sweet Haven hardly looks flush! This was not done for the greater good of the children, and *you* are not being altruistic!" She remembered the yellowing walls and the children who'd needed a hot bath and new clothing. It dawned on her then that the children were not the only ones that had been exploited. "I could have been stopped at immigration, Terrance. Did you even stop to think about what would happen to me?

You said you loved me, and all you did was use me. I fell for all your crap. Were you and Sonya having a good laugh at my expense, at my stupidity, this whole time?"

Terrance thought back to when he and Sonya had first concocted the idea to use Lisa to transport the children back to England. Yes, they had been using her from the start – the first time and the second time as well.

*

"She is perfect, Terrance. I will bring her out tonight with us. You will see for yourself." Sonya couldn't conceal the excitement in her voice. She had it all worked out how they could get their hands on that payout. She wondered if this would be the last time, as Terrance had said all those months before. But she was getting used to the luxury lifestyle that this business brought them, so to her it did not make much of a difference. She might not have a ring on her finger, but at least she was working her way towards a life free of dead-end hotel work. She rarely felt guilty for what she was doing; she knew it was better of the children.

"Flirt with her, Terrance; she will be smitten, I guarantee. Don't flirt too much, though," she had squealed down the phone. She had had a tiring day at the spice plantation, listening to the boring spiel on how a banana plant was a grass and not a tree for the millionth time, the boring tourists chirping in with their knowledge of spices and grasses. But today the cash prize was in front of her, in the shape of Lisa. *So simple and naive*, Sonya mused to herself – she would never suspect anything. *Better for us*, thought Sonya. Even the dozy people at immigration would not suspect her. More appealing yet was the fact that she was far too bland to catch Terrance's eye. Yes, that's what she was: *bland*, not spicy, like herself. She smiled, catching Lisa's eye and drawing her in with her butter-wouldn't-melt look. She would regret this thought later, but for now, Sonya was convinced that there wasn't a chance in hell that Terrance would fall for Lisa.

Terrance had met Lisa that night and had quite liked her, solely for the fact that she was going to make him and Sonya very rich. This was a lucrative business world that he had entered into. The work was slow, but the rewards were good. With Lisa they could almost half their lead times and get richer quicker. If this worked out, he could quit working for his father; he was tired of working so hard when his father just wanted to put most of the money back into the business.

"We have to make the business grow, na, son?" his father would say towards pay day every month. "Then only can we spend." Terrance had conflicting views on this, but his father said this was their culture. Terrance did not have a problem with their culture. He respected his culture and loved Goa; after all, it wasn't so "Indian" as the other states. People were so much more liberal in Goa; it was westernized. He played with that word in his mouth. "Westernized" he said out loud; his father clearly didn't know what the Goan culture was about. Terrance wanted to be seen as western. His father's thick southern drawl annoyed him. He had spent enough time with tourists to pick up a less sing-song way of talking, but when he spoke around his son, it brought Terrance down.

He knew that using Lisa was going to be his meal ticket. He would be able to have enough money to do what he wanted, when he wanted. It was true that Sonya was a good judge of character, but he had to see Lisa for himself, feel her naivety before he accepted using her. He could and would turn on the charm; it wouldn't be the first time. According to Sonya, the girl would fall in love with anything, she was so desperate for some affection. Sonya's words made him chuckle. She was not so far from that herself, but Sonya was different from most girls he knew. She had an inner strength that got her through most things, a realism that was absent from any of the girls he had been with, and he loved that about her. Together they would make this happen; he was sure of it.

It had been a success the first time Lisa took the two children across. Terrance and Sonya had been paid what was owed to them and given a bonus for their quick exchange. Together they made a good team; the transaction had gone through very smoothly, without any untoward hiccups. By keeping Lisa in the dark, they did not need to add to the long list of people they had to pay to keep quiet. Something had changed, though, and after the intimate time he had spent with her at Easter, Terrance found a strange attraction to her – so much so that he was not quite sure of using her for the second run. He had all the documentation ready and the child had been prepped, but it was only the night before she was due to leave that he had decided to go ahead with it. They ran a higher risk by using the same person for two runs so close together, but there was little choice. Greed had held Sonya to ransom. He had been unsure, but Sonya had called, reassuring him that the contact they had made in December was finally pulling through for them. They would not be found out, and that was a personal guarantee.

He and Sonya had convinced each other that this was the only way for them to make this kind of money; they believed it was for the "greater good". So the second run happened, and again it ran smoothly. The time and money he had invested in Lisa – the apartment he had had to "borrow" and the expensive meals out – they were paying off, and he was considering letting Lisa in on the deal, making her more permanent for both business and pleasure. After all, she was ready to move out to Goa; she had already handed in her notice.

It had all been going well until three o'clock this morning, when Sonya had called him and told him that their contact was under pressure, and that a name had to be given. It was Lisa's name that would be put forward. It was the only way to save the rest of them.

Terrance sighed when he heard Sonya's elaborate story. He was sure that she had precipitated this event, but strangely, this character trait of hers drew him towards her, this ability of hers to take control and steer her life the way she wanted it to be. It gave her an edge above anyone else. The Lisas of this world could come and go, but there would only be one Sonya. She had done similar things on a much smaller scale, countless times before, when they were growing up. She always got her way; she called it "the survival of the fittest".

*

Remembering Sonya's determinism woke him from his thoughts. "I didn't use you, Lisa. You have to believe me – you have to," Terrance said.

"You didn't love me, Terrance. I may have been a fool then, but do not try to add insult to injury now. Do not lie to me again," Lisa sobbed. She didn't know how much more she could take. She could barely think about what would happen if the police found out. She knew that from this moment on she would be living in fear of losing her freedom and being shamed publicly, and it frightened her.

"Okay, okay," he said, desperate to conclude the call. "Maybe I used you at first, but I fell in love with you. But you have to understand I had already made the deal, and I knew if I told you, you would have done it. You are too kind-hearted to leave a poverty-stricken child, when you could offer it an opportunity, a new home. You know we do this for a good cause, not to line our pockets. I also knew that if I told you it would worry you. You would have been nervous through immigration, and it could have cost you. Believe me, it was better this way."

Lisa sat on the sofa, glaring at the flashing images on television. She was trying to make sense of it all. It had serious implications for her. She worked with children, too. If word of this ever got out, then her career would be over. She needed time to think. Her mind and her heart were pulling her in two different directions. She knew now that it was a stupid idea to move to Goa and live there with a man who had been so callous as to jeopardize her whole future. He had played her, and she knew it. Yet her heart had already started pining over the loss of him. The new life that she had begun dreaming about had disappeared in the blink of an eye. Lisa reflected over the last few months of her life. She had been happier than she had ever been in her life. Goa and Terrance had changed her. She wrestled with an idea. If no harm had come from what she had done, was there really that much of a problem? At least he was telling her now, and he was doing it to help the children, surely. His confession gave him some credibility.

Strangely, she did not feel as guilty as maybe she should have done. A fear dawned on her, as the reality of the situation sunk in. Suzanne's words resonated with her: a "holiday fling" was all it was, but worse than her relationship being a sham, this holiday fling could have severe repercussions. She pressed the receiver to her ear and heard Terrance tell her the truth, for once in their relationship. She no longer had butterflies in her stomach; they had died.

Slowly, questions began to form in her mind. She was finding her old practical self. Pulling the jotter at the side of the phone to her lap, she looked around for a pen. There were some answers that she needed to know, like how badly was she implicated? As she played around with this question in her mind, she realized that she must have knowledge that the children were safe. If her guilt caught up with her, or if – and she prayed this wouldn't happen – the law caught up with her, she would need a defence. Horror stories of abused children came to the forefront of her mind, and she knew she would have to face up to the reality sooner or later. The realization that she had been duped suffocated her, but she was now ready to ensure that it went no further. She had no choice but to save herself.

"How much did each couple pay, then?" She held her mug of soup so tightly that the blood drained from her fingers. If the money was nominal, it would make it seem better, but she knew that it must have been a large amount. People didn't take such risks for nothing; the apartment and the lavish meals out had all been funded by this activity. She didn't know much about transporting children about, but she did know the lengths desperate couples would go to in order to get a child. She prayed that this would be the only reason that a child would be "adopted". At least there was no abduction involved, she thought. It comforted her slightly, but it did not compensate for what she had done.

"They pay a fee; it varies." Terrance did not want to disclose the amount, knowing it would make this sound so much more vulgar than it was. "I love those children at the orphanage. I want to help them. Don't belittle what *we* have done Lisa. *We* have saved children's lives. Okay, they paid us for it, big deal. That kind of money to them is nothing for a child."

The more Terrance tried to convince her otherwise, the more guilt crept into her being. "That kind of money" resounded in her head. They were selling children for money. It was nothing more than that. He was no better than the rich man who had paid Gita for her kidney; no, he was worse! "We"! He had used the term *we* so freely, dragging her down with him. She knew she was in deep, whether she liked it or not.

For a moment, Lisa let her thoughts drift. Would she have taken these children knowingly across international waters? The small child she had met at the orphanage with the tear-stained cheeks? His cherubic face looking up at her infiltrated her thoughts. Would the squalor of the orphanage have convinced her that this was the right thing to do? Would she have allowed a child to stay there if she knew she could offer it a new beginning? She erased these questions from her mind as soon as they appeared; she could not afford the luxury of thinking about what she *would* have done. She had to think of her current situation, whether or not she should inform the police. No, she knew she couldn't. She would have to hope and pray that this would remain in the past. Little did she know that her time of tribulation was just about to begin.

She thought about Shruti and Tariq and the third child, whose name she did not know. She thought of the looks on their faces when they'd arrived at Heathrow. She was a teacher – how had she not noticed how frightened they were? Was she that self absorbed that she hadn't paid attention to the silent cries of these innocent children? She had spent a nine-hour flight with them, and she didn't know. She had further questions that she needed answers to. She began to question Terrance further, "So, apart from the documentation that was faked, you have records of the families that these children went to, right?"

"Well, not really," Terrance said, now not afraid to tell her the truth. The drama that she was creating out of his good intentions reinforced to him that Sonya was the girl for him. She had agreed to sell the children quicker than he had.

His answer was not sufficient for Lisa, though, and anger began to swell up within her. She envisioned the worst reason a child would be sold for. "You are selling these children, and you don't even care where they are going? Surely poverty would be better than selling a child for God-knows-what reasons?"

"No, Lisa, you are not understanding me," Terrance's voice broke her train of thought. His voice carried a defensive tone, trying to justify his actions and make her see the logic behind his madness. "Hanif knows."

"What is there not to understand? You just said you accept money for children, and you don't know where they are going yourself. You entrust that slob with children. For fuck's sake, Terrance, he could be a leader of a paedophile ring!" Lisa was silent, picturing Hanif, his stomach hanging over his dirty trousers. It made her feel sick.

"It's not like that. I check where the children are going. I check that the families that they go to are good families and that they will look after the children. They will be brought up like children should be." He used his knowledge of the Indian private adoptions he had implemented to support his case. "Okay, I will be honest, Lisa, maybe some of the families in India that adopt, in exchange for food, shelter, and a loving home, will give the child more chores maybe than the biological children. But Lisa, they will also put them through school, college, even university. They have a chance to be something better than a servant, better than a labourer. They will have a better chance than in an overcrowded orphanage. You remember the orphanage, what Mr Goswami said. The parents of these children cannot afford to keep them, and they are better off letting them go."

"Okay, maybe you have some control in India, but in England, thousands of miles away, you have no say in what happens. You don't know what you are sending them to. Poverty may be a better alternative. Did you think of that?

"Open your eyes, Lisa; don't be so ignorant. We are helping these children have a much better life." His tone changed; he belittled her by making her feel guilty for her own upbringing. *She* did not know what pain and suffering occurred outside her own little bubble. Because *she* was not living in an undeveloped country, he was making her pay for it. A cloud of ignorance engulfed her when *she* spoke of something she knew so little about. Lisa knew she had been more than privileged her entire life if she compared it to the children she had seen in the orphanage that day.

It worked a dream on Lisa, so in just a few moments she was beginning to see his point of view. He told her that most people in the West were oblivious to it, but she wasn't another ignorant bystander; she had done something to help. This just seemed so drastic to her, though, and with such dire consequences. But this was the Terrance she had met and fallen in love with, someone who was compassionate and did want to make a difference. She should not have undermined him in this way. Terrance loved the children in the orphanage, and he would not do anything to bring harm to them.

"So, why are you telling me all this now?" she said, curious as to why all of a sudden he had found some sense of morality. A part of her wanted to hear that he loved her and had confided in her so that they had no secrets between them.

He said exactly what she needed to hear, "I needed you to know, Lisa. I told you I loved you, and if we are going to take things as seriously as I want to, then you need to know this part of me. I can assure you, though, that I will never do this again." He had thought quickly before answering her. He had not anticipated this question, but it didn't make a difference what he said; she would not have time to board a plane to Goa so soon. She was oblivious to the truth he was concealing, the truth that would chill her to the bone. In less than twenty-four hours the authorities would know. They would be looking through the videotape footage of Lisa arriving at Heathrow airport.

"Why? If, as you say, you believe in it so much, why will you not do it again?" she asked as tears streamed down her face, and she started to sob.

He stuttered, "Well, you know the risks involved. If we were found out, we would not even be able to carry out the adoptions in India. The orphanage would be investigated. The children ... who knows what would happen to the children."

Did he really believe that, or was he just saying it? It was a risk, but if he honestly believed in what he was doing, then why stop? There would be other foreigners that he could persuade to get involved; he could even do it himself, if he was so compassionate.

"So they were three different children, then?" Lisa said, accepting what she had done.

She fought back the tears and muffled her sobs. Terrance waited a few moments before he lied one more time.

"Yes. I'm sorry; I should have told you." He looked at his watch; there was little time left. Within the hour, this ordeal would be over. He would never hear her voice again.

She wiped her face with her sleeve; she did not want to think of the real reason why she was crying. She had had the most amazing six months of her life and had thought she had a new life ahead of her. The thought of giving up her dream was a weight too much to bear. Over the last few months, she had psyched herself considerably and built India up to be something that could turn her monotonous life around. She knew the tears she shed were for Terrance and her new life; even now she believed in Terrance. She had seen for herself the way some children were treated in India and the conditions they were made to live in. She very well knew about the child prostitution that the country suffered. Here was a man trying to help. Maybe he had not gone about it the right way; nevertheless, he had done what he could. He had confessed to her without any real need to, because he wanted her to know everything. Could she hold this against him? Yet, part of Lisa – the old part, the part that always thought with her head, not with her heart – said that this story was just that – a *story*, a tale in a tabloid that she herself would read and laugh at.

So she made a decision; she would find out where the children were and accordingly inform the police. It would be stressful, but she would have to do it before she could believe that she was in the clear, before she could sleep peacefully again. Otherwise, the scared faces of those three innocent children would plague her forever. She remembered the scrap of paper that Terrance had given her the first time she had taken the children to England. She could obtain Hanif's details from Terrance.

"I would like to make sure that the children I took across are okay," Lisa said.

"Lisa, you are thinking too much; you do not have to worry. There will be no harm to them. Hanif will look out for those children. He is responsible for them. I give you my word, Lisa. They have gone to loving, childless couples. This was part of the deal, that we did not bother them once they received the children. You have to believe me. Don't take this any further. It must stop here." His authoritative tone was there to warn her off, but she was not fazed.

"You met them?" She didn't trust Hanif at all; the thought of him now made her toes curl.

"I talked to them over the telephone, looked into their income," he said nonchalantly. "They can support the children. All couples, no single men. The children will have a better life. Did the children make a fuss when you handed them over to Hanif? No? Well then, there is your answer."

"But it's not an answer. They looked scared," Lisa repeated, remembering the initial look of fear in their faces. Now she knew why they looked that way, it was all falling into place.

"Why didn't you tell me at the time?" Terrance was tired of this conversation. He glanced at his watch again; he was due to pick up Sonya twenty minutes ago.

Lisa cleared her throat and replied. The guilt and the loneliness ahead of her stung. "Even afterwards, when I called you after we got through immigration, you laughed at me," she sobbed.

"Lisa, I would never laugh at you." He said the right words, but there was something sinister now in his voice. "If I had told you, you would have been nervous and made it more obvious at immigration," he added. "Here, take this number down," he said as he reeled off a mobile number he claimed was Hanif's. Impatience had got the better of him, and he wanted this conversation to end.

"I would have had the choice, Terrance, of whether I wanted to be party to this scheme of yours."

"You would have done it, Lisa; I know you. You felt so deeply about the children at the orphanage. You would have wanted to do something to help. I was trying to protect you by not telling you."

Lisa wrestled with this thought that he was repeatedly trying to plant in her head. Her life had come crashing down around her, and it was entirely his fault. She looked back up to her webcam, but he was gone. He had terminated their connection.

26

As soon as Lisa had composed herself, she dialled Hanif's number. But since she'd met him at Heathrow, his English had rapidly declined, and his answers were in monosyllables. She tried to discover the whereabouts of the children, but failed, and she couldn't help but think that Terrance had spoken to him already.

It was after two days of persistent calling that Lisa finally got hold of Hanif's wife. She spoke in whispers and denied any knowledge of where the children had gone after they'd picked them up, but eventually she conceded and divulged information about the girl, Shruti. She gave Lisa the name of the school that the girl had been enrolled in. She did not have any information on Tariq and claimed not to know about a third one. Lisa saw this as a glimmer of hope. If the girl was living with a family and having a good life, then maybe what Terrance had said was true, and she could rid herself of the burden of guilt that had taken hold of her. She drove up to the school just as the final bell for the end of the day had rung. She had needed to take the entire day off school herself, feigning a bout of food poisoning. It was the Monday after she had spoken with Terrance, the day she plucked up the courage to make the drive up to Harrow. She stopped at Wembley beforehand, to track down Reshma's address, which Terrance had given her in December the year before.

She had pulled up on a quiet residential street and stepped out of the car. It had started to drizzle. A row of red-brick terraced houses looked back at her. Two Indian women in their salwars and cardigans were talking from their front gardens when they noticed her. They abruptly stopped their conversation and stared at her before scuttling inside out of the rain.

Her heart was beating wildly in fear of what she was about to discover. She heard two boys shouting in the background and felt intimidated. Looking over her shoulder towards where she could hear the voices, she saw that it was just teenagers playing with a football, but they glared at her before they disappeared into one of the terraces.

She walked over to number fifty-four; she could just about make out the number scribbled in Terrance's handwritten note all those months ago. She pressed the doorbell and turned, looking up at the blackening sky. She could just about see the arch of Wembley stadium. The door opened behind her, and she swivelled on her heel to face a frail Indian woman. Her face looked drawn, and Lisa could see her pale brown scalp through her thinning, oiled black hair.

"Can I help you?" she said, looking up at Lisa. Her accent was thick.

Lisa had not really prepared what she was going to say, it had all been a blur after she'd spoken to Terrance on Friday. She had stayed in all weekend, telling her friends she was fighting the flu, but in reality she was just trying to make sense of what she had let herself become involved in.

"I'm looking for Reshma," she said confidently. "And Tariq and Shruti," she added.

The woman looked at her blankly. "I know nobodies of that names," she said

"Are you sure?" Lisa pressed. "Hanif sent me," she tried, but the woman did not alter her expression. She was either good at concealing her reactions, or she genuinely didn't know and Terrance had lied to her yet again; she knew it was most probably the latter. She was no Nancy Drew; she could not investigate this further. She peered above the old lady's head through the door for some kind of clue, but it looked like a perfectly ordinary house, with a mirror, a coat hook, and a small table with a telephone. She had no choice but to walk away.

*

Lisa stood by the gates of the school, hoping that this was not another red herring. She didn't stick out so much as she had done earlier, and she waited patiently with the other parents as the children filtered out of the school in their navy-and-white uniforms. It was an expensive private school. Lisa had googled it the night before, and the fees alone for one term were more than she earned in a semester. The road outside the school confirmed this; it was littered with Range Rovers and Mercedes, making her red Fiesta stick out like a sore thumb.

"Those are my two over there. Look at them messing around, when they know I'm waiting here for them." Lisa glanced over to the two curly ginger-haired children pulling at each other's arms, and she flashed a fake smile at their proud mother. She strained her eyes, glancing around the playground, until she caught a glimpse of black hair and two skinny legs protruding from a navy pinafore.

The child was standing by the four marble steps at the entrance of the school. She looked even more fragile than she had done on the journey she had taken with Lisa in January. Each step that she took seemed like a mammoth effort; she clutched her oversized and overloaded navy-and-turquoise rucksack.

Lisa did well to hide behind the other mothers and fathers waiting impatiently for their children to get to the gates. As Shruti approached, Lisa slipped into her car and watched from a safer distance. The lady who picked her up looked kind, and Shruti seemed to like her. She strapped her into the back of the car, and Lisa gently pulled out after the metallic silver hatchback. Keeping a safe distance, she followed it.

The car pulled into a street littered with million-pound houses, and it stopped outside a white one, whilst the wrought-iron gates opened. A short drive continued up to what looked like a perfect doll's house. There were two large cars parked near the entrance and pretty shrubs that littered each side of the drive. Lisa felt a sense of calm wash over her. These children would have a life they could only dream about. Of course they would. How could she have ever doubted it? For the first time in days, she would sleep peacefully, her faith in Terrance restored.

She would not inform the authorities, not now that she was in too deep. The police would not believe her ignorance now.

*

Lisa recalled the statement she had given the police that day. She recollected all the lies that had tripped off her tongue since she had been arrested, as if it were part of her personality. She had concealed her last conversation with Terrance, because she knew it implicated her further. She knew what she had done before she'd been arrested. When the police had told her what she was being called in for, she had been genuinely shocked – she hadn't faked that. But she knew that it had been distress at being caught.

It was not so easy to lie to interrogators when it was so real, when she could feel the warmth of their breaths laced with coffee on her skin, their all-knowing looks piercing right through her.

*

When the court case started, Lisa's guilt, which had been slow to come, now consumed her. In fact, she had a whole host of feelings running through her and turning her away from food; she was often violently sick. It was as if she were on a drug that was making her ill. For the first time in her life, she understood why people would turn to self-harming, although she knew she had put her family through enough, and she could not bear to hurt them any more.

Catherine had given Lisa the news that the orphanage she had told the police about could not be located. Nor could Sonya, Mr Goswami, or Terrance – but they would keep looking. The apartment she had considered to be her home in Goa was an empty shell, a holiday home traced back to a man from Mumbai who had no connection to any of the people Lisa had mentioned. Investigating Joel's and Chi Chi's had proved fruitless. They had located Carl, but he was unaware of Sonya's whereabouts. She had left the Coconut Grove, and he had not heard from her since. If he knew anything, he was keeping quiet. Their undercover agent based in Goa informed them that the details provided by Lisa could not be verified. Catherine knew this did not look good for her, but the chances of them gleaning any further information from India were slim. Lisa had told Catherine about her suspicions about their so-called undercover agent, but they could not prove anything, and Catherine knew that any search they tried to undertake would prove fruitless and cost them precious time. In the meantime, the lack of verifiable information would mean that the innocent-holiday-victim line would be a hard one to play to a jury. Even

Lisa was beginning to wonder if the happiest moments of her life over the last eighteen months were fictitious.

Finally, Catherine had brought her some good news – all three children had been located and Hanif arrested. Lisa prayed that he would not incriminate her further and reveal that she had been snooping around just weeks before she'd been brought down to the station. Catherine informed her that the children could be sent back and that India was not looking to prosecute her for kidnapping. Lisa was so relieved that the police had found the children. Catherine had warned that the children had been with psychiatrists and seen doctors over the last couple of days and that their stories would be put to the jury. They had not been told under what the circumstances the children had been found, but at least they had been found and they were all alive.

"With any luck, Lisa, the children were put in good homes. There will not be a sense of unknowing, at least, which in my experience can be detrimental to the case." Catherine took a sip of coffee and looked towards Lisa, trying to convey a sense of hope. Lisa caught her gaze; she knew that Catherine had put her heart and soul into her case and worked non-stop to get the information that she needed. She had dark circles under her eyes, which she had attempted to conceal with make-up. This was Catherine's first case, and Lisa knew that she wanted a good result. Catherine continued slowly, wanting Lisa to understand the full impact of what she was saying.

"The prosecution could have played the jury that way, creating fictitious scenarios, playing on their emotional side. At least this way, it's a fact." Catherine smiled; it was a positive, the first bit of good news that they had received since the beginning of the trial. She would go home earlier than normal tonight and open the bottle of burgundy. They both knew that the news would mean: the case would take a better turn. What they didn't realize was that it would be these very children who would more deeply embed the guilt within Lisa – and that it would imprison her for life.

*

It was on the fourth day of the trial that reality hit home for Lisa. It was time for the prosecution to do their bit and have their say. The questions came hard and fast, and with such intensity that it now made the initial interrogation at the police station seem like a breeze. She wondered how she had survived it.

"How did you control the children, Lisa?" The lead prosecutor had the face of Satan. He was tall and carried a look of power, exuding confidence in his dark-grey suit. He gave her an accusatory look that seemed to last for minutes, his bright blue eyes looking through her. It was as if he were trying to see into her soul and make her confess to the crime. She could almost smell his determination on his breath "Did you deceive them through physical – sexual – or violent behaviour? Through instilling fear, and creating distrust and fear of authorities within them?"

That word "objection!" came too late. She heard his question, but despite the preparation and endless questions Catherine had put her through, she didn't know how to answer him. Lisa looked up at the jury. They were ordinary-looking people. She estimated their ages; only two girls looked to be in their twenties. She felt confident in assuming that they weren't parents. She hoped that, by some miracle, they would have some compassion for her. Would they believe her? Could they see themselves being duped the way she had been? Would they be able to get their arguments across when the jury discussed her case to make their final verdict? She had never before questioned the judicial system in England; she had never given it a second thought. It seemed odd now how a handful of people could decide somebody else's fate.

The prosecutor resembling Satan looked towards the jury and addressed them: "As adults, we should protect children. They are particularly vulnerable, and in this instance, maybe they were promised a better future abroad; maybe they were threatened …" He went on at length. Whatever he said, it most definitely incriminated her. She knew she hadn't threatened the children; she had never forced them – but now she was almost certain that Terrance had. She didn't see how the jury would believe her side of the story. Looking back, she could barely believe it herself.

"We will never know these vital facts. The children have been located but are confused. We cannot gain much further information from them at this point; we have only been given limited time with them …" The prosecution let this hang in the air. He looked at his papers on the desk before him and shuffled them before swiftly turning towards the jury to drop his bombshell. He was quiet whilst he scanned the jury, noting the anticipation in their faces; he prolonged the moment, building suspense. With what he was about to say, he knew that he would win. "We can disclose where and how the children were found." The prosecutor gave the jury a grim look. Lisa braced herself; she knew what was coming and a nauseated feeling swamped her. Catherine had briefed her last week as to what was discovered about the children, and it had created a huge problem for her.

In the last few days, the police had located the last boy she had brought back after Easter. He was living in poverty, in the East End of London, probably. It was no worse than his life back home, but he was in a strange country and did not know the language. Furthermore, the British winter hardly compared to Goan temperatures. Lisa broke down as the prosecution showed pictures of his living conditions. The picture showed a bare concrete room, with no paint or carpets; a few rags on the floor made a bed, and a bowl of rice was on the floor as if put out for a dog. A small window let in a sliver of light, so that the dirt and faeces were visible. A few members of the jury let out tiny gasps. "Who would pay for a child, just to leave him like this?" the prosecutor asked the jury. He took pleasure in telling them. "It was an asylum seeker," he said triumphantly, with a dramatic pause, waiting like a leopard ready to pounce on its prey. He wanted the jury to hunger after the answer, to heighten their senses so much that they would be totally horrified by the answer.

"Well, ladies and gentlemen, the answer, the reason for this grand expense on the part of the asylum seeker, was *not* because he and his wife wanted to have a child so desperately, as the defendant 'thought' …" He looked at Lisa and gave her a pitiful look as he trailed his sentence off, allowing the jury to mull over this snippet of information.

"No, the need for a child was more sinister than that. They wanted the child because an asylum seeker with a dependent child gets a huge benefit for remaining within this country for about ten years. Enough time for a lot of things." The prosecutor stood very still in his fancy suit and adjusted his gold cufflinks. He continued, "And think about this. This asylum seeker – let's name him Mr X – this Mr X has obtained this child for reasons I have already mentioned, and as you can see, his living conditions are poor, so he needs more money. What does he do? Rent the boy out for some extra income, servitude to some other family or for acts of a sexual nature? There is no control here. This is the fate of a boy that the defendant 'thought' she was saving!"

Again the objection had come too late; he had painted a picture of the world of child trafficking, and it would stick in the jury's minds. The prosecutor had neatly accomplished what he had set out to do.

Catherine had done her best in forewarning Lisa, but the picture that the prosecution was trying to create for the judge and jury was horrific. Lisa felt almost certain that she didn't have a chance in hell. The jury was going to bring back a guilty verdict, now that they knew this family had cheated the system and that their own hard-earned money was being siphoned off in taxes to pay this family's benefits. It was a personal offence Lisa had committed on *their* pockets. The words that had flown around the courtroom: *servile marriage* and *modern-day slavery* clung to her. She knew she could have saved this child, but she hadn't. She deserved her punishment.

Lisa had done her best to switch off from the questioning when she returned to her parents' house that evening. It was a weekend, and she needed to regain some strength. Instead, she found herself drawn to Internet search engines, researching what she had done. She had spent so many nights on Internet websites exploring information on child trafficking that her mind was overloaded with this information, and she was sickened.

Catherine had told her what a child from third-world countries such as India might cost these days. It was about two thousand pounds. How could Terrance have done this! Was it possible to put a price on a child's life? It was unbearable to think of, but the Internet had proved the prosecution correct. It was all there, facts and figures, and the grim details of what happened to the majority of the children who were found illegally living in England.

She hardly slept that night; she had a sense of foreboding. The first boy had been located living with a family somewhere near Brighton. She instantly remembered Tariq, his scar a glimmer of pink on his brown skin. Catherine had informed her that this was good news. The boy had been enrolled in a school and was settling in well. It proved that Lisa had been easily duped but that the outcome had been for the better. Even if the jury didn't believe that Lisa had not known that she was trafficking children, at least they might think that she was doing it for the good of the children. Catherine knew well enough that this was clutching at straws, but in her opinion, it was worth a shot. It was the only thing left for them to go on. Right now, any piece of evidence in their favour was needed.

*

What Catherine was about to tell Lisa, however, would probably shatter this shred of hope, and Catherine knew just how the prosecution would use it. It was the story of the girl. Lisa had seen this girl with her own eyes, but according to Catherine, the girl found by the police was in a situation very different to what she herself had witnessed. Lisa was certain that she had recognized Shruti at the school gates that day. But Catherine informed her that the girl had been found working as a child prostitute. Lisa had actually thrown up when Catherine had uttered those words, even though she knew the story was false. Yet confessing this would incriminate her further.

The girl the police had located was twelve years old, like Shruti, found through intelligence in a brothel in the East End of London, with a surgically fitted contraceptive in her arm. The girl had timidly told doctors and psychiatrists of her ordeal of being raped continually and being punished for crying. This would be most damaging to Lisa's case. She needed Catherine to know the truth – but how could she tell her that she had found the girl herself, a few weeks before she was even questioned by the police? She was in a no-win situation. She would have to confide in Catherine.

Lisa was thankful that the prosecution had not found this out, even though they had managed to piece together most things. With all the cameras at the airport, it had been easy to locate Lisa arriving at Heathrow both times with the children. Looking at these clips side by side, Lisa could see that the second time she looked uneasy. She had known it at the time, and now looking at the clip, she was surprised she hadn't been caught there and then by the immigration officials. The video footage made her look like a child trafficker. She dared not look back at her parents, Suzanne, and Arjun in the audience.

As Lisa unravelled the truth, Catherine was sympathetic, but she couldn't help but wonder what had been going through Lisa's mind. Why hadn't she alerted the authorities? This would make the case very messy indeed. Catherine herself would now have to investigate this other child and explain how she knew where to find her. Was Lisa correct in thinking that the girl was not Shruti? How much had Lisa known? Catherine felt betrayed by her, but at the same time there was still something about Lisa that made her think that she hadn't committed this crime knowingly. Either way, it was too close now to leave her stranded. It was her first big case, and Catherine was determined to crack it.

Her snooping around would most definitely alert the authorities to the fact that Lisa was not as innocent as she had initially made out, and they would do everything in their power to bring this to the attention of the jury. If she didn't look into it, though, and Lisa was thought to have brought a child into the country to be used as a sex slave, it would cripple the case. There is no way that the jury would let her off for something like that. The prosecution would do everything in their power to bring it out in the courtroom. It could well have been an outcome of Lisa's actions, and they would want to use the case in front of the jury. She had to work fast and have this evidence dismissed before it was heard.

*

Lisa walked over to the bathroom mirror and tried to get ready for her last day in court. She had no more tears left to cry. Looking at her reflection, she took in her appearance, her brown hair scraped back, her forehead littered with lines. She wondered whether she looked like the type of person who would do this. She wondered if people like this looked a certain way, but evil was easy to mask. Terrance certainly did not look evil, and his conscience was clear. He believed what he had done was right, but she knew she would have to find a way to tell him what the police had found out about this girl and make him see the damage that could be done.

*

In Catherine's efforts to validate Lisa's story, she put her neck on the line. She dug up the CCTV footage from Heathrow that had been exhibited as evidence, and she digitally enhanced the images, picking out from the girl the features that were easily identifiable. This was particularly hard, though; she knew that the girl the police had found looked very similar. Catherine had no choice but to visit the house to which Lisa had followed the girl previously. There was a huge risk that the prosecution would find out how Catherine had found this out, but at present, she felt it was worth the risk.

After lengthy discussions with Hanif, who had initially refused to help, she had learned the name of the school where Shruti was enrolled. Of course, she had known this already, but with the information coming from Hanif, she was sure Lisa's prior knowledge could stay hidden. She had even visited the house in Wembley that Lisa had told her about, but that proved to be a dead end. She, along with an interpreter and the police, had thoroughly questioned the couple who lived in the house. They were from Punjab and had been to Goa once. They had stayed at the Coconut Grove on a family holiday, when it was out of season and the prices were considerably lower, the frail lady had stated – she had wanted that written down. They had found nothing, and Catherine could only assume that Terrance or Sonya had stolen their address from the resort.

The second address she had obtained from Hanif's wife proved more of a success; they found that the girl had been exchanged through Hanif. Catherine breathed a sigh of relief. It looked like the girl from the CCTV, but further information would have to be gathered and put together before it could be taken to court. She would be working over the weekend again.

When Catherine approached the family, they were distraught. They had covered their tracks as well as they could, but her persistent questioning broke them down. They were Indian themselves and knew how many children could not be provided for in India. In their eyes, they were saving a child. Why didn't they follow the correct channels of adoption? wondered Catherine. They told her that the system of adopting children was long and drawn out. They had been trying to adopt for years, and it was proving unsuccessful. Shruti had arrived to them in less than six weeks of their first contact with Hanif. If a childless couple wanted children so much, surely they could wait, thought Catherine. Now they would face their own legal battle, as well as the loss of the child they already loved as their own.

Catherine felt their sorrow, but she had more pressing things to think about. Lisa was her priority. How could she prove to a jury that this was the girl that Lisa had brought into the country? It would be difficult. Catherine had only seen pictures of the girl that the police had found, and so far no picture had been provided of the girl that was missing in India. None of the children that Lisa had trafficked had been reported as missing. She would have to rely on the stills from CCTV. It was going to be a struggle. She explained it to the family, but they were reluctant to help. They did not want to incriminate themselves further, nor did they want to lose the child they had come to love. Catherine gauged whether they were the type to run. She would have to make them understand. If they ran before she took it to the prosecution, she would have immense difficulty in convincing a jury that it was the girl Lisa had brought into England.

27

Before Lisa entered the courthouse, she caught a glimpse of a handful of photographers and journalists. She took some comfort in the fact that until now there had been little in the papers about her case. She had already handed in her notice for her job, in order to move to Goa, before she had been arrested, so she'd stuck with it. There was no point retracting it only to be suspended or fired in the coming months. She knew the teaching part of her life was over and she would never be able to teach again. In a small city like Oxford, news travelled fast. Not many people believed she hadn't known what she was doing. They whispered that someone like her, a teacher, couldn't have been so naive.

Lisa looked towards the pavement and scuttled past the reporters.

"What were you thinking at the time, Lisa?" one reporter yelled at her.

"Give us your side of the story," said another, poking a microphone in her face.

She ran past them, grateful for her black ballerina pumps, and went straight to her parents, who were hovering at the entrance of the courtroom. They were silent. Lisa's father squeezed her shoulder. He felt just how much weight had dropped off her in the last few months, and he prayed for a good result. The jury filtered in, and so did the judge. She felt faint. The revelations over the final days were too much for her to bear. Anything that Catherine told her had not stayed in her mind. She drifted in and out of conversations.

*

The last two days had seen the last bit of evidence about the girl that she had actually brought into the country brought to life. She saw the strain on Catherine's face as she questioned Hanif's wife. She saw the shame that filled the woman's eyes as she admitted in her broken English that the girl was housed elsewhere – that the girl Lisa had brought back was not the girl found in the brothel. Lisa silently thanked her for having the courage to testify. The prosecution did not ask who had triggered the search for the counter-evidence. Maybe they had known it was the wrong girl the whole time and had just been using it in the hope that the real girl would never be found. Lisa would not have put it past them, but then again, she couldn't complain. There were thousands of girls just like Shruti out there.

Lisa never did see Shruti again. As Catherine had feared, the family ran, leaving their entire lives behind them. Anticipating this, she had persuaded Hanif's wife, Shilpa, to testify, using guilt as her only tool of persuasion. It was common knowledge in the case that Hanif was responsible for the exchange of the children in England. After Lisa had described him to the police after her arrest, they had caught him at Heathrow, trying to board a flight to Mumbai. Just how many children he had bought and sold was unclear, but it was widely known that his trial was impending. His wife, too, had been arrested, but discovery of the severe domestic violence she suffered at his hands meant that she was not held responsible for her actions.

The outcome was fairly good. It was doubtful whether the jury had believed Shilpa's version of events, but it had created an element of uncertainty in their minds. They could reasonably consider that maybe Lisa *had* brought the child across believing it would have a better life.

Lisa looked down at her bitten fingernails. She knew that even if the result was "not guilty", she would suffer. The pictures of the boy that they had found in a hovel in East London were etched on her mind. The story of the girl in the brothel, even though it was not Shruti, had made her realize just how bad it could have been. She wondered how many children Terrance had illegally moved out of India. She had never asked him that question.

*

"Lisa, I have some news before we go in." It was Catherine, her voice calm and non-committal. Lisa braced herself, her thin frame swaying slightly. "It's good news! India, well, Goa, in fact, is not going to prosecute for kidnapping, the main reason being that these children were never reported missing. And as I said before, their undercover agent still working in Goa is unable to locate the orphanage or Sonya or Terrance, not by the descriptions you have given us. I am sorry, but from what I understand, they have stopped searching." Catherine tried an encouraging smile at Lisa, who looked rather crestfallen; it had all been a set-up. They were all laughing at her now. Nothing she had said could be proven – nothing at all.

Catherine tried to lull Lisa out of her stupor, to make her see the silver lining. She would have to be more literal. "The main news is that you, Lisa, are off the hook – in India, that is. There is only one condition, one that probably will not make the slightest bit of difference to you. You can never enter India again, but like I said, that would be the least of your worries. The two children that have been found will be deported back to India. The authorities will continue to look for Shruti and her adoptive parents." Catherine squeezed Lisa's arm for reassurance and led her towards the courtroom. "Come on, Lisa. Let's hope the result is good!"

Lisa felt mixed emotions. In one breath, she was relieved – she couldn't deny that. There would be no other charges; this trial would be her last one. But the fact was that she had lived a lie for the last year, and that made her want to go back to Goa and find that orphanage, find Terrance and Sonya, and make them apologize for ruining her life. Now she would never be able to do that.

Lisa smiled at Catherine, more for Catherine's benefit than for her own. The fact that she would never again be able to step on Indian soil or visit Goa made her want to cry. It was then that she realized what an attachment she had for the place. Despite what had happened, she wanted to go back. She wanted to make amends, to put right what she had done wrong. As Lisa resumed her seat next to Catherine, she glanced back at her parents sitting immediately behind her. The jury filtered in, bearing blank expressions; from their faces she could not tell what decision they had made.

When the judge handed back the piece of white paper to the juror who just moments ago had passed it to him, Lisa could only hear a jarring in her ears. She placed her hand on the desk in front of her to steady herself; the varnished oak stared up at her, refusing to absorb the moisture from her palm. She felt her father gently squeeze her shoulder, as he had done earlier, reassuring her that they were there for her, no matter what the verdict was. She noted the feel of such affection; it might be the last time she received it so genuinely. She turned around and smiled, catching a glimpse of Suzanne, her belly only slightly showing her pregnancy. Lisa returned towards the jury. She knew that no actions or words would be of any reassurance now. The courtroom was silent. Lisa looked up at the judge. She studied his aged face, one person who had read countless verdicts deciding the fate of so many wrongdoers. As the juror stood up, looked at the white paper in his hand, and started to read from it, she could no longer cope with reality. She fainted.

Lisa opened her hazy eyes; she could see the intricate moulding on the ceiling above her. Lying on the courtroom floor, she could smell the perfume her mother had worn since her childhood. Someone, her mother, was lifting her head up. She turned her gaze towards Margaret, who had stood by her every step of the way. She had not once asked her what she had been thinking of when she had done such a naive and stupid thing. Her mother cradled her and looked at her with moist eyes. She vaguely remembered the verdict and looked to her mother for reassurance. Margaret hugged her, exchanging a knowing look. Lisa did not have to say anything.

"Twenty-one months, darling. It's not so long – a facilitation offence," Margaret said, smiling tenderly at her daughter and trying to be strong. Lisa caught her mother's grip as tightly as she could. This was the last thing Margaret needed; her health was already so fragile. She could see a thin film across her mother's eyes before she closed her own, wanting to dissolve into the courtroom floor.

28

Lisa woke up and pulled the bed sheets further over her, smelling the familiarity of home. She had served her time, refusing any appeals offered to her. She had wanted and needed the punishment. She had so much to put behind her, and she would need to take baby steps to crawl out of this hole she had put herself into. It was her first night back in her own bed, and for the first time in nearly two years, she slept soundly.

She opened her eyes. The white bed linen allowed the sunlight to penetrate. Lisa pulled the bright white sheet back from her face and swept her brown hair away from her face. She smiled. It was over; yet the big sigh of relief that she thought would come never did. She felt empty. Her body and soul felt aged ten times over. Before India, she had lived her life by the book. She had, indeed, been living a life she no longer cared for, a life that she could not go back to. Teaching or anything to do with children would never be a possibility for her. Since the beginning of her sentence, she had promised both Suzanne and her mother that she would look to the future and never look back, and that's what she was planning to do. But she just had one last thing to do.

When she had tried calling before, she had got nothing. His phones had been disconnected, but she wanted to try once more. Nearly two years had passed. She had never felt with anyone else the way she had with him, but what he had done had repulsed her. She wanted him to know the stories she had heard at the trial. She wanted him to accept that what he was doing was wrong and to give her closure. She dialled his number.

*

"I see a new girl making us rich," Sonya whispered to Mia, the stunning blond Scandinavian girl. Mia stayed with her drink behind the huge pillar that propped up the roof of the bar. She was hidden well but had a clear view of Sonya, her lover, who was about to set the wheels in motion for another few lakhs. It had been a difficult couple of years for them, but together they had come out unscathed. No one in India had been found out. She had saved them all, and only poor Lisa had taken the fall for them.

Sonya and Terrance had had to relocate out of Goa for a couple of months, whilst the authorities made like they were actually looking for them. Sonya made a quick exit from the Coconut Grove and severed her ties with Carl. Although he had now moved away, he had gotten increasingly suspicious about where all her money was coming from. She had had no choice but to cut him out of her life – she didn't need a righteous friend like Carl any more. She had Mia, and that was all that mattered. Mia breathed a sign of relief. This was a new chapter in her life, finally out of the clutches of Simon. She was a free agent now, and she, Sonya, and Terrance were able to start their own little enterprise, with herself at the helm. She winked at Sonya, who was making a beeline towards an innocent-looking Indian girl. She took her hand.

"Terrance, I have a friend to introduce you to. Her name is Kelly; she is from Yorkshire, from the UK." Sonya smiled brightly at Kelly. She would be very suitable, indeed. Kelly was one of those Anglo-Indian girls Sonya was becoming more familiar with. Born and bred in England, the only thing that made her Indian was the colour of her skin. At thirty, without a prospective husband in sight and wanting to find who they really were, these young women flocked towards Goa. *Perfect*, Sonya thought as Terrance sauntered over to them and shot Kelly a look that made her melt.

Acknowledgements

I would like say a big thank-you to my parents, who initiated the move to Goa when I was young enough to adopt a new culture. They have continually supported my dream to write. Thanks also go to my sister, Anna, who has encouraged me every step of the way. I am grateful to James, who has supported me despite the hours I have sat glued to a computer in silence, and to Jan, Fee, Subrina, and Neha, who have enthused and motivated me. Together they have encouraged me to pursue my dream of writing my first novel. A huge thank-you to Urmi Kenia for allowing me to use her beautiful photo for the front cover of Goa Traffic. And finally, but most importantly, a big thank-you to Goa and its people, for getting under my skin and inspiring this story. It's a place that I shall always consider my home.